SARA STARTING OVER

DEE ERNST

235
ALEXANDER
STREET

To find more of Dee's books, go to
www.deeernst.com

Comments? Questions? An uncontrollable desire to just chat? You can reach
me at
Dee@deeernst.com

ISBN#9780998033488

❀ Created with Vellum

Also by Dee Ernst

Lucy Checks In

Maggie Finds Her Muse

Stealing Jason Wilde

Am I Zen Yet?

Better Than Your Dreams

A Slight Change of Plan

A Different Kind of Forever

Better Off Without Him

The Mt. Abrams Mysteries

A Mother's Day Murder

A Founders' Day Death

A Killer Halloween

A Deadly New Year

A Malicious Midwinter

A Fatal April Shower

The Eastern Shore Romances

A Safe Place to Land

Building Home

Once again for my mom,
and also for my Aunt Helen —
two remarkable women who helped me learn to love cooking.

SARA STARTING OVER

Chapter One

I was drinking my morning coffee when I read that Marco had gotten married.

The picture showed up in the newsfeed on my phone. Marco getting married was newsworthy. After all, he was quite a celebrity if you were into sports and sports agents. And his bride was *very* newsworthy — tennis phenom Emilia SanTuccio, barely twenty-three and plucked from the obscurity of the Italian Olympic Tennis team five years ago to become the sexiest thing in a tennis skirt to ever hit the clay courts.

There was a mention of the age difference. Thirty years. Yes, that certainly was a difference. The article also mentioned that Marco had been the one to find her in Palermo and guided her spectacular rise to stardom. It went on to mention all her recent wins, named many of Marco's famous clients, and ended with saying the couple would make their new home in New York City.

There was no mention of how Marco left his partner of ten years, chef Sarafina Castellano, with nothing but a shrug and a brief *I'm sorry*. Or how Sarafina, who had been running the much-loved and successful SoHo trattoria, La Cucina, for fifteen years, had to close shop after a small fire mushroomed into a full-scale catastrophe a mere three months before that. And how, once thrown out by the aforementioned Marco, she had crawled back home to her father's house in New Jersey, broke, unemployed and homeless. Or that she was now sitting in a tiny kitchen in a nearly empty rental house down in Virginia, staring at her phone and feeling her heart break all over again.

It's not like Marco was the only man I'd ever loved. I'd been divorced almost ten years when we met. When you're over forty in New York City, you've been around the block. Plenty. And it was not like he was my greatest love. Carl Delaney still held that title. After all, you can only have one first heartbreak, and when you're twenty-one, it's usually monumental.

Besides, I was still a fool enough to think that maybe, just maybe, my greatest love was yet to come.

I stared out my window into the cold February rain. I could barely see the Chesapeake Bay through the fog. The window was cracked open just enough to hear the wind and the far-off barking of Jack Lockhart's dog.

I'd been there for three weeks. I left the house to buy food. I hadn't unpacked the boxes I'd unloaded from my car, except for my clothes. I only knew that it was Jack Lockhart's dog barking because my landlady had remarked on it when she handed over the keys.

I took another look at Marco, smiling and handsome. He looked like he'd just taken his nubile young wife to the same bed we'd shared for ten years. He'd moved on in a big way.

I, on the other hand, hadn't even met Jack Lockhart.

Or his dog.

Of anyone else, for that matter.

Maybe it was time.

There was a knock on my front door that caused me to run from the bathroom in a panic.

Who would knock on my door? No one knew I was here. Not even my family. My weekly phone calls were just to assure my brothers I was still alive. Texts to my friend Maribeth included the view from my back patio...was it possible that she had somehow found a way to pinpoint my position from a tiny scrap of shoreline? I wouldn't put it past her, but it was a stretch.

I peeked through the side window and cracked the door open.

My landlady, Bess Robinson, stood there.

I hadn't seen her since she'd first shown me the house three weeks ago. After a series of phone calls, I arrived at the address a bit early. The house was not impressive: a gray, shingled Cape Cod style house with faded red shutters and a cracked cement walkway. I walked around to the back of the house and stopped, awestruck.

I looked over the Chesapeake Bay. It was by no means a beachfront property: the yard sloped down to meet a bank of scrub pines, then a two-lane road, then a few rows of houses, then another road. But I was high enough that I didn't have to see any of that if I didn't want to. I could look straight out and see nothing but the wide sweep of the water and the pale sky.

I closed my eyes and breathed deeply. I could smell it, too, the salty brine of the bay. And I could hear it above the faint howl of the wind and the barking of a dog.

"Looks good, doesn't it?

I opened my eyes. "It's perfect. And I can almost hear the waves."

The woman came up behind me. "You could hear it a whole lot better if Jack Lockhart's dog wasn't barking its fool head off. I'm Bess Robinson. This is my house. You want to see the inside?"

I followed her, a tall, solidly built African American woman with a tight crop of gray hair and polished nails, through the back door.

The inside of the house was rather dusty and sad.

"I'll give you an allowance at the hardware store in town," she said. "Pick out colors and I'll have the place repainted for you."

"I'll take it," I told her.

"I need to run a credit check and verify your employment."

"I lost my job and haven't found a new one yet. What if I pay you a whole year's rent up front?"

She eyed me with interest. "If you have that kind of money, why aren't you buying someplace?"

"Because I don't want to be tied to anything. I want to know that I can leave if I want." For years, I'd been responsible for my restaurant, organizing the menu, taking care of all the business end of things, nurturing my staff. They were, I knew, some of the best years of my life, but they were also the most exhausting. When a fire had forced La Cucina to close, I spent most of my retirement and savings paying my employees, waiting to reopen. But it never did, and the guilt was crushing. From there, I went back home to be the primary caregiver to my father. That's time I would not have traded for anything in the world, but it drained me so completely that the thought of being responsible for anyone or anything again scared the hell out of me.

She narrowed her eyes. "You a drug dealer?"

I shook my head. "No. I recently got an insurance payment."

She took a minute to look at me closely, as if searching for any outward signs of criminality or depravity, then nodded. "Fine. Where are you living now?"

"The Holiday Inn out on the highway."

She raised eyebrow.

"I've just been driving." For weeks. Since Christmas. Just driving in and out of small towns and cities, trying to find someplace that felt like I could live there. Hills of Andrew, Virginia, hadn't seemed like an obvious choice until I found the rental listing on realtor.com.

"I'll still run a check. And get the paperwork. I'll call if there's a problem, but otherwise...when can you move in?"

"Whenever you tell me I can."

And so I did, the very next day. And that was the last time I'd seen her.

Until today.

Her tall figure radiated waves of disapproval.

"Well," she barked, "can I come in?"

"Of course," I muttered, and opened the door wider.

She took three steps into the living room, stopped, and looked around. Then she walked further into the dining room and stared at the sliding glass doors that opened to the small patio in the back. The dusty vertical blinds were in the same position they had been in my first day. She peered around the corner to the kitchen. "Where's your furniture?" she asked.

I cleared my throat. "Well, I have a bed and a lamp. In the bedroom, that is."

She glared at me. "I gave you a painting allowance. Mike O'Connell says you haven't used it. My nephew Dante does all the painting and repairs on my properties, and he has been waiting. Are you going to spend the rest of your life in a house with dirty walls?"

"No. Of course not." My voice felt rusty, and I cleared my throat again. "I just haven't decided what color I want the rooms to be."

She took a slow look around. The room told a sad story. The windows had the same battered vinyl blinds, there was a pile of unopened boxes in the corner, and my laptop was open on the floor.

Her eyebrows flew together. "What is wrong with you?"

I looked around the living room and saw, maybe for the first time, the clumps of dust in the corners, the smudged walls, the gray tracks of my footprints on the scuffed floors. The front window showed the gray winter sky. The sliding glass doors opened to the wide stretch of water, the view that I'd stared at daily without the feeling of joy and amazement I'd felt when I had first seen it.

I hadn't heard from my family in over a week — Vincent had gotten angry with me during our last phone call and hung up, swearing and yelling. I closed my eyes and felt three days' worth of grit and unwashed skin under my sweatshirt.

And Marco was married.

So, because she asked — and no one else had *ever* asked — I told her. "I lost the restaurant I owned for fifteen years, and my boyfriend dumped me because he met someone young enough to be his daughter. My brothers got all mad at me because I didn't drop everything in my life to take care of my dad, and then when I did go home, he died anyway, and I just read that the boyfriend married the young someone and my life is just awful." I ended on a sob as months' worth of anger and hurt and tears spilled out, all over my unwashed face and down the front of my gray sweatshirt.

"Damn." she muttered. She stared hard for a moment. "Damn, girl, you want a drink or something?"

I sniffed hard and nodded, pointing to the bottle of bourbon that was the only item on my kitchen counter that did not need to be scrubbed down.

She went into the kitchen, opened a few cabinets, and pulled out the only two clean glasses I had left: a champagne flute and a shot glass. She filled the shot glass to the brim, and the flute halfway up the slender bowl. She pushed the shot glass silently across the counter to me. I picked it up and downed it in one gulp.

She sipped delicately. "That's good bourbon," she said. "You haven't been wasting it on pity parties, have you?"

I shook my head. "No. Well, yes. But just the really *big* pity parties."

She nodded to herself and looked around the kitchen. "Sarafina, you haven't been taking very good care of my house," she said wryly.

"No. I guess I haven't. And I'm sorry. I swear I'll get better. And it's Sara. Please."

"Sara? Well, it certainly is easier to remember." She shook her head. "Sitting around this house all day won't get you better."

Her voice was a clipped New Englander's voice, not a soothing southern drawl I'd expected from a woman of color this far south.

"Where are you from, Ms. Robinson?"

She sipped a bit more. "It's Mrs. Robinson, and yes, feel free to sing it if you feel the urge. But Bess is fine. I don't stand on too much ceremony with my tenants." She sipped more bourbon. "Boston. Born and bred. Moved down here fifty years ago for my husband's job. I still sound like Back Bay, don't I?"

I nodded. The bourbon had washed a bit of the choke out of my throat, and my voice felt stronger. "I'm usually not this big of a mess."

She raised her eyebrows. "Well, you have had a boatload of shit to deal with in the past, what? Year? Two?"

I nodded and poured more bourbon. I sipped it this time.

"What killed your Daddy?"

"Pancreatic cancer."

She snorted. "Well, all the taking care of in the world couldn't have helped him. Did your idiot brothers know that?"

I almost smiled. "Yes. They knew that. It didn't change a thing. I'm Italian. I should have gone home the minute he fell ill and stayed with Dad and taken care of him."

"How many brothers?"

"Two."

"And did any of them go home to him?"

I shook my head. "They didn't need to. They lived in the same town we grew up in as kids. They both had houses in the same neighborhood."

"And *you* had to go there and take care of him? What kind of bullshit is that?"

"Italian bullshit."

She finished her bourbon. "Well, I'd get over that, and fast. So, your brothers are stuck in the Dark Ages, your boyfriend is a complete douchebag, and you lost your livelihood. The insurance money...from your dad?"

I nodded.

"I'm sorry about all that, and I can't help you with any of it. But you need a job. I can help you there."

I looked at her. "I don't need a job. I have plenty of money." Which was not quite true. Paying a year's worth of rent had made a substantial dent in my bank account.

She clucked for a few moments. "Money has nothing to do with it. You need a job because you need a reason to get up and get dressed every morning. You need to start meeting new people and start seeing what good there is left out there in the wide world. You want another restaurant?"

I shook my head.

"Good. This town probably couldn't support a new restaurant if it had five Michelin stars. Want to cook for someone else?"

I shook my head again, hoping she wouldn't ask why, because there were no words in the English language to explain how I felt about cooking right now. It had been my life, but that life had been a very long time ago.

"The hardware store usually hires on for the spring, but Mike will probably put the moves on you in the first five minutes, and I don't see you as standing for that." She frowned, thinking. "The library is going to need someone. Molly Packer is finally retiring. The money isn't bad, no heavy lifting, and if the patrons get fresh, you don't have to put up with it."

I finally grinned. "Do you really think I have to worry about anyone getting *fresh*?"

She put her champagne flute in the sink. "You're an attractive, articulate woman with all her teeth and all of her hair, even if it is gray. I bet if you clean yourself up a bit and get out of those baggy clothes, why, you'd be quite a catch around here."

"A catch?"

"Oh yes. Lots of divorced men around here looking for company. Not that there are that many of them worth being caught. The eligible bachelors in this town aren't nearly in demand as they think they are. Well, most of them aren't."

"I don't need a man."

She grinned. "Oh, honey, nobody *needs* a man. But they're nice to keep around, you know. For killing spiders and such."

"Maybe."

She took another look around. "Start with cleaning this kitchen. Then go to town and pick out some paint for these walls. Something that's a proper *color.* I can't stand all those beiges and grays. They suck the life right out of a room." She gave me a hard look. "It's in the lease. You're required to maintain the interior of the property. This," she gestured with her hand, "is not in keeping with the terms of your lease. Then pretty yourself up and go to the library. Rose will want to know she's got a snappy young thing behind the desk. She'll hire you in a heartbeat."

"Snappy young thing? Good heavens, is everyone in this town ancient?"

She drew herself up. "I'm seventy-four. And that's quite a ways from ancient. And get a pet. It is a very comforting feeling to know that there's someone waiting for you to come home."

I opened my mouth to argue, then realized that was the most truthful thing I'd heard in quite a long time.

She closed the door quietly behind her. I stood for a long while, taking an occasional deep breath, before turning to the kitchen to start washing dishes.

Chapter Two

❧

Hills of Andrew didn't really have all that many hills, but apparently, they were all on Main Street. It seemed to me a surprising kind of main street for a small southern town, but I grew up in the suburbs and lived most of my adult life in New York City, so small-town life was something I'd only observed on the Hallmark Channel. The hardware store was a large building, sandwiched between a pizza place and Julie's House of Beauty. When I walked in, an old-fashioned chime announced my entry. The store was empty, but then, it was ten o'clock on a Tuesday morning.

"Hello?" I walked down a few aisles and found the paint section: a display of paint samples, various brushes and rollers, and other items I vaguely recognized as paint related.

I hadn't painted a room since I'd defiantly redone my bedroom hot pink with black trim.

That had been my senior year in high school.

"Need help?"

I jumped, then turned to find a very large, quite good-looking man standing just a little too close behind me.

"Bess Robinson..." I began.

He nodded. "Yep. Been expecting you. Bess called and said I

wasn't to let you buy anything gray or tan." He was fair and rather Slavic-looking, with high cheekbones and bright blue eyes.

I stepped back. "Yes. Well, I'll probably go with, you know, white."

He grinned. His teeth were small and even. "No problem. Take your time. I'm Mike. I'm here for all your home repair needs." He had somehow made what should have been an earnest offer of help slightly... dirty.

The chime sounded again, and a woman entered the store. She was tall and quite lovely, younger than me, probably in her early forties, with a streaked blond braid hanging over one shoulder. Her face was oval, skin pale, and her eyes a deep blue.

"Is Mike bothering you?" she asked, loudly.

I shook my head. "Not yet."

Mike gave her a rather withering look. "Just trying to help," he muttered. "Bess sent her for paint. Just doing my job, Shelia. No need to get all bitchy." He sniffed and hurried away down another aisle.

The woman came closer. "He's a lech, Mike is. Never take him up on his offer to fix your plumbing. I'm Shelia Birch. You're Bess's new tenant? On Bracken Road? I love that little house." Her voice was low and had a musical quality. "What were you thinking? You're a green person. Maybe something like this?" She reached over and pulled out a sample card with six versions of sage green, one almost the exact color I had painted my first bedroom almost forty years ago.

"What do you mean, a green person?"

She pulled another card, frowned, and put it back. "We all have a color. I'm orange. You're green." She smiled. "I'm an artist. Pottery. Color is very important to me." She pulled out a few more cards and arranged them quickly until it looked like she was holding an odd poker hand. "See? This for the living and dining, with this trim. The bedroom would be darker, almost like a forest grove. So peaceful. And that tiny second bedroom? It would make a great office. Something brighter for the bathroom and kitchen, of course, but you can keep the trim color the same throughout. What do you think?"

I stared at her, then at her fanned-out colors. Her hands were callused and rough-looking, with several faded coils of woven string around strong wrists. "How do you know the house?"

"I rented it when I first moved down here. Lived there almost three years, 'til I married Charlie. How do these look?"

"I would have just painted everything white."

"That's boring."

I laughed. "Yes, very boring. But that's what I lived in for ten years. Boring white rooms."

"Why?"

I shrugged. How to explain? I lived in Marco's loft; chic, expensive, and decorated in a simple, minimalist style. Whatever I had saved from the studio I had rented before had remained in storage boxes in my father's garage in Jersey. The same boxes I'd brought down with me but had yet to open.

I had a different home now, but not only did I not have a style of my own to replicate, I also didn't care how it looked. "Long story. And these colors are fine, I guess."

She made a face. "No guessing. I know. I'm always right. About color anyway. The rest of my life is a mess, but I know my work." She walked up to the counter and explained where each color was going. Mike must have known the house as well, because he didn't ask for square footage or any of the other questions I would have thought relevant.

Shelia leaned against the counter. "So, you're...?"

"What? Oh, right. Sorry. Sarafina Castellano. Sara."

"What do you do?"

Good question. Did she want the real answer? That I didn't do anything except stare out at the ocean and wonder what the hell had happened to my life? "I ran a restaurant, but it closed."

"Oh? Where?"

I took another breath. On a tree-lined street in SoHo, right off Broadway, with a multi-paned front window overlooking a cobbled sidewalk. "New York City."

She made a face. "Sorry about that. You going to cook around here?"

I shook my head. "I don't think so."

Mike heaved two gallons of paint on the counter. "A few more to go," he said. "Shelia, are you here for a specific reason?"

She nodded. "More air filters. But wait on Sara here first. God knows I got time."

"So, you're a potter?" I had forgotten small talk. I'd been quite good at it once, schmoozing with patrons and sweet-talking the regulars. That had been a lifetime ago, but something like muscle memory kicked in. "This kind of small town seems like an odd place to set up shop."

She nodded. "It is an odd place. I'm a trust fund baby, believe it or not, but trust funds don't go as far as they used to. When I was done with school, I had to decide if I wanted to stay in Chicago, where money would be tight and I'd probably need a real job, or move someplace else and just do my art. I followed a boy I had a crush on in college to Virginia and found this place, where I can live off my grandmother's money to pay the bills, so here I am."

"And you're married?"

"Not anymore. If you ever come across a handsome bald guy named Charlie Birch, be sure to run like hell in the opposite direction."

Mike put two more paint cans on the counter. "Charlie is a prince of a guy," he said.

"Yes, he is," she said to Mike. When he walked away, she leaned toward me. "But he was a crap husband, and he didn't turn out to be too terrific of a father either. You want me to help you carry these to your car?"

"Yes, thank you." I took two cans, she took the other two, and we went out to where my father's battered Subaru stood parked at the curb. I opened the back hatch, and she bent to look at the plates. "New Jersey?"

"My dad's car." Living in New York City, I'd never needed a car. After Dad died, I kept his rather than sell it and buy a newer one. The car smelled like him: cigarette smoke, spilled coffee, and mulch. He'd been a gardener in the later years of his life, and there had always been a bag of compost or dirt in the back. "Is there more, you think?" I asked her.

She nodded. "Sure. Is Dante still doing the painting? He has all his own brushes and rollers, but you probably have a few more cans."

We went back into the hardware store, and sure enough, the counter was crowded. Mike helped with the second trip, thin-lipped and barely polite. He left Shelia and I standing on the empty sidewalk.

"He doesn't seem to like you," I said.

She shook her head. "He hates me. All of Charlie's friends do. He's also an asshole, but...so, good luck with your painting. I'll see you around, I'm sure."

"What is there to do here?" I asked, thinking that, at some point, I might grow tired of my own company.

"Well, the cafe right there has amazing food for a town this size, and the bar next door has three pool tables and darts every Thursday night. You can drink there, it's safe and friendly. The library is probably the busiest place around. They have free movies and all sorts of programs."

"Bess suggested I look for a job there."

She tilted her head at me. "Well, you would certainly meet a lot of people. And it's probably the right place for someone like you."

I'd opened the car door slowly. "What do you mean?"

She shrugged. "You're an outsider. From the North. And this is a small southern town. Don't think that folks here are going to welcome you with open arms. That only happens in Netflix movies. I've been here almost twenty years, and I'm still that crazy Yankee artist who broke Charlie's heart. But the library, well, there's something to be said for a place that champions the open exchange of information."

"I see."

"Can I give you some advice?"

"Sure." I waited. She seemed to think very carefully about what to say.

"Fix your hair. Get it styled or have some layers put in. And get dressed up when you go over. Appearances count for a whole lot around here. Too much, but that's only my opinion. And cover up that tattoo on your wrist. I know, but Rose is very funny about stuff like that."

I glanced at my wrist. A simple rose in an oval. The logo for La Cucina. "Thanks."

"Sure." She went back into the hardware store. I stared after her. She must have remembered her filters.

I got in the car and drove back home.

I made an appointment on Monday morning at Julie's House of Beauty. One of my go-to home-with-Dad movies had been *Steel Magnolias*, so I thought I knew what to expect, but the inside of Julie's was sleek and bright, with six modern chairs in front of gleaming windows, and not a busty blonde in sight. Julie was tall and built like a fireplug: round and sturdy, with no discernible curves. Her hair was short and an improbable shade of red, and she could have been anywhere from thirty to sixty-five.

She sat me down and ran her short fingers through my hair.

"Keeping the gray?"

"I think so."

"It's pretty. Some gray is just awful. God, your hair is thick. And these waves... do you go all curly when it's short?"

Yes."

"Do you *want* it curly?"

"I want..." God, it had been so long since I'd seriously

15

thought about what I wanted. "I want to step out of the shower, shake my head, and go."

She gathered a fistful and held it off my neck. "We'll need to take off a bunch."

"Fine."

"What about your brows?"

My brows? I frowned and leaned forward, trying to see myself closer in the mirror.

"No. Here." Julie handed me a large round mirror I gripped with both hands.

Holy...

"Ah... what can you do?"

"We're full service here," Julie said briskly, taking back the mirror. "We can wax them. Also, your upper lip."

I didn't ask for the mirror back to confirm. I didn't need to. I came from a long line of mustached women. "Do it."

"Nails?"

I shook my head. "Nope. That's it for today."

Julie kept her tone neutral as she led me to the sink. "So, I haven't seen you before. From around here?"

I leaned my head back and felt the warm water against my scalp. "I just rented a house from Bess Armstrong."

Julie made a noise. Not a pleasant noise. She lathered without further comment, then rinsed. "Bess has a bunch of houses."

"This one is up on Bracken Road." I don't know why I felt compelled to answer, but it just felt rude to stay quiet.

"That's a cute one. Dante been around yet?"

"Not yet."

"Watch him," she said, then wrapped my head in a towel and led me back to the chair.

She combed out my hair and began cutting. Was she really going to take off that much of my hair? Hair that had been growing for months, no, was it really years?

"Why should I watch Dante?"

Snip. "He's an odd bird. Not that there's anything wrong with that, really. There are a whole lotta odd birds here in the Hills. But Dante went over to India and stayed for years and came back with some... interesting ideas."

Did I really want to hear more? Why not? After all, he was going to be in my house. "What kind of ideas?"

"Yoga and stuff. Meditation."

I gripped the arms of the chair. Yoga and meditation made a person an odd bird? What kind of town was this, anyway?

"I went to a yoga class three times a week back in New York," I told her. In a downtown loft, where Chloe led us all through a long, soothing session that began at six in the morning. It kept me focused when my restaurant had been roaring and I had been on my feet for fourteen hours a day, six days a week. And it kept me sane when I had nothing else to do for weeks, waiting for the restaurant to reopen. Nothing to do but get out of bed, listen to the news, and try to imagine my life without La Cucina every day.

Julia stopped cutting and met my eyes in the mirror. "Really?"

"Yes. I guess that makes me an odd bird, too."

She nodded slowly at me in the mirror. "Yes, I guess it does. He has a studio down by the beach, so he gets a lot of summer people. They seem to like that yoga stuff. You can ask him about it if you like."

She finished cutting in silence, then poured a dab of something into her hand, ran her fingers through my hair, and began to scrunch up my curls.

"You want me to dry it?"

"No. Thank you."

She took off the bib and I stood, bending over and shaking my head, hard. I stood up and looked in the mirror. "It's perfect."

Julie looked smug. "Of course it is. I know hair, and yours is a dream. Sure you don't want color? You'd look years younger."

I didn't want to look younger. The younger me had been a

very different person than who I'd become, and I didn't want the reminder. I shook my head.

Waxing my brows and upper lip took another ten minutes. Then I was done, and I walked out into the brisk air, head high, curls dancing.

The next morning, I put on a simple linen dress, my favorite Ralph Lauren blazer, gold earrings, and drove over to the library for my first job interview since my internship, at age twenty-three, with Salvatore Callisto of Genoa, Naples and East 43rd Street, New York City, New York.

Hills of Andrew had a library to be proud of. Tall and imposing in brick, it had a wide staircase leading up to impressive double doors and obligatory stone lions standing guard on either side. The cornerstone read 1954.

Inside was cool with the low murmur of voices, and the hint of my favorite smell in the world, right after garlic and oregano: the smell of books. Slightly earthy, musty, ripe. Books had been so much a part of my life for so long, I felt like I was stepping back into my mother's womb.

I approached the main desk, a respectable oak counter with pamphlets crowding the scarred surface. A dark-skinned woman with graying hair and bright yellow glasses peered at me from behind a computer monitor.

"May I help you?"

"I'm here to see Rose Shipman?" I had filled out the online application just the previous Friday and had received an immediate email suggesting a time for an interview.

The woman behind the desk looked me up and down carefully before jerking her head. "Follow me, please."

We walked past wide wooden tables, surprisingly crowded for the middle of the day in the middle of the week. Several people were at the computers and there were the obvious students.

"Looks busy," I said.

The woman nodded. "It's the wi-fi. We have many regulars." Her southern accent was obvious. "People here read. And watch movies. But not many people have lots of expendable income, so..."

We turned at a row of bookcases, and went through a wooden door with the sign, 'Staff Only Please.'

The door opened to a wide, windowless space with a few desks and doors along the back wall.

"Rose," the woman called.

A head popped out of the end office. "Sarafina? Hello. Please, come on through."

Rose Shipman was younger than I expected for a Library Director, but then, I was getting used to the idea that my expectations were very New York centric, and that Virginia was practically another world. She was very thin and dressed entirely in black, with messy dark hair pulled into a topknot, and watery blue eyes.

I sat across from her at her desk and she stared at her computer screen.

"Well, you ran a restaurant in New York, so I know you have organizational skills and people skills. You'll be a real asset at our pot-luck suppers." She sat back and looked at me. "Tell me about what you're doing now, and why you think you'd be a good fit for us."

I tugged at the sleeve of my blazer, making sure my tattoo was out of sight. What on earth could I tell her about what I was doing now? I watched cooking videos on YouTube. I was re-reading all my childhood favorites. I had just finished *Wind In The Willows*. Again. And why would I be a good fit for the library? I had a hard time imagining fitting in anywhere.

"I've, ah, been going through some personal issues." That sounded uncomfortable, but the truth usually was. "Family things. So, I've been taking some time to just regroup. And I need to start over on a, ah, different trajectory. Career-wise. I don't have the energy to go back into the food service industry and ..."

And what? I wanted a job that I could leave at the door when I left for the day. I didn't want responsibility. I didn't want to have anyone looking to me for anything other than an eight-hour shift. And if I woke up one morning and decided I didn't like Hills of Andrew anymore, I wanted to be able to leave that job without the numbing, heart-wrenching guilt I'd felt the last time I left a job.

But I also wanted to be somewhere that made me feel safe and happy, and books had always done that for me. Reading in the small bedroom in my grandmother's apartment had been almost as good as following her around in her kitchen, stirring, watching, carefully adding pinches of salt to her simmering pots.

I leaned forward. "Look. My head is not in a very good place right now. It hasn't been for months. Books have always soothed me. I know a lot about them. I read practically everything, so I can talk to people about all sorts of book. I want a job that I can enjoy but leave behind at the end of the day. I like people. I haven't been around them much lately, but..."

I was foundering, I could feel it. Rose Shipman's face was smooth and blank.

I sat back and closed my eyes, took a long breath, and reached deep down for the inner bitch, the one who hadn't backed away from crappy waitstaff, unreliable suppliers, or moody line cooks.

"I would be a great fit for you because I'm a fast learner, I'm hardworking, and I'm good at problem-solving. I'm computer literate. I believe in great customer service, and I play well with others. I also have a keen interest in books, which I imagine would be a plus in a library. I just paid a year's worth of rent on a house, so I'm here for the long haul." That wasn't true, but I didn't want to tell her I'd have no more problem leaving this job as I'd have leaving a house with a year's rent paid on it. "I need to put down new roots, and Hills of Andrew seems to be a good place to do that," I finished, and thought I sounded sincere.

Rose sniffed. "Well." She leaned back in her chair and narrowed her eyes. "The only concern I have is who I'm hiring — the person who started this conversation, or the person who ended it."

"Fair enough. Maybe I could volunteer for a week or two? Just shelve books. That way, you can see who's coming through the door in the morning and make a more informed decision."

She smiled. "I'm a big believer in giving someone a chance. You won't have to volunteer. And liking books is a big plus around here. Believe it or not, we have people working here who haven't cracked a book since they left school." She looked back at the computer screen. "Can I check your references?"

"Absolutely."

"The position is full-time. There is a sixty-day probationary period, after which you would become a county employee with full benefits. We can only pay three dollars over minimum wage to start. We are severely underfunded, but so are most libraries. You'll be expected to work one night a week, and a half-day Saturday once a month. Is that okay?"

Relief surged through me. I had the job. I wouldn't run out of money, which meant if I did leave, it would be on my own accord, not because I didn't have any other choice. When I drove away from New Jersey, I had felt that way, that there were no other options, that there was nothing left for me except pain and anger, and I had no choice but to leave that behind.

"When can I start?"

She stood. "I'll check your references. And if everything looks good, you can start next Monday." She held out her hand. "I'll call."

I stood and shook her hand warmly. "Thank you. I won't disappoint."

She tilted her head. "I hope not."

I gave myself a quick turn around the library before I left.

The second floor had a hushed reference section and a bank of small study rooms. Downstairs was the children's section, and two rather large meeting rooms. It looked to be a bustling and productive place. I took a deep breath and told myself that I could be happy working here.

I could be happy working.

I could be happy.

Maybe.

Chapter Three

Y ou know how, when you're a little kid, you think that everyone's life is just like yours?

I grew up in a two-bedroom apartment in a four-family house in the Italian section of a bustling New Jersey city. I wore a uniform and walked to my Catholic school. I went to Mass every Sunday morning, then had dinner at my grandmother's, whose apartment was across the hall from ours. Food and family spilled out of her eat-in kitchen into the living room and, in good weather, to the front stoop. After we'd eaten, my cousins and I ran out into the tree-lined street and played stickball, jumped rope, and drew hopscotch boards with stubs of white chalk. We were always busy playing, shouting, running up and down the street under the watchful eye of one or more relatives, perched on the stoop, smoking cigarettes and gossiping.

"Did you hear what Joey said to her?"

"Frannie is never going to stand for something like that."

"But what can she do?"

"We all know he hits her.'

"And the kids."

"We could call —"

"NO!"

My aunts threw their hands in the air and sipped wine from jam jars, their voices rising and lowering, depending how close we kids were to them. We all heard everything they said, of course, but we didn't talk about it, my cousins and me. It never occurred to me I could talk about family problems. In our house, everything was fine, despite blackened eyes in church, quiet sobs from Aunt Fran's upstairs apartment, or my father drawing Uncle Joe aside for quick conversations.

Later, when Aunt Fran lay dying, she clutched my hand with both of hers and whispered, "I hope I don't go to hell. I don't want to see Joe ever again."

The revolutionary fervor of the sixties and early seventies made little an impact on the lives of my mother or her three sisters. They were of a generation born and bred to be good wives and mothers, to cook and clean and turn a blind eye to whatever their husbands might be doing. But, watching it all unfold and carefully taking notes, I never wanted that life for myself.

I remember a time when I had the small back bedroom to myself. When I was four, my brother Vincent was born. We both moved into the bigger bedroom, which had barely held my parents' double bed. Now, it was crowded with my single bed, an elaborate crib and a changing table. A year later my second brother, Dominick, arrived. There was no room for a second crib, and things reached a critical point.

My father insisted we move. My mother wept and pleaded and wrung her hands, so I simply slept across the hallway in my Nonna's back bedroom. Every night at bedtime my mother would give me my bath and send me across the hall where my grandmother tucked me into my own bed and let me read for fifteen minutes before she sang me to sleep in Italian. I woke early, trotted back across the hall for breakfast, and went on with my day.

All my toys and clothes were crammed into the cupboard in the bedroom my brothers shared, and I spent all my waking hours in the noisy confusion that was my parent's home. At Nonna's though, she let me help her cook. And there were my books. On rainy afternoons or snow-filled days home from school, we would putter around her tiny kitchen, and then I could sneak away and read.

My grandmother never learned to read or write in English, but she knew how important it was and would feed my habit with tattered picture books from the church bin or creased and faded Nancy Drew books from the used bookstore down the street. Because of Nancy Drew, who camped out in the country with her best friends, George and Bess, I wanted to camp in the country too.

I had carefully prepared my case. I'd been a Girl Scout for two years, had applied for and won, with the help of my Scout leader, a campership that would pay all my fees. All I had to do was find a way into the wilds of Sparta, New Jersey.

My parents were, of course, dumbfounded.

"You want to camp?" my mother asked. "Sleep *outside?*"

"No. There are tents. I'd sleep in a tent."

Vinnie snickered. "You'll have to pee in the woods."

"No. There are outhouses. And showers."

"Outhouses?" my mother gasped.

"I'll learn to cook around a campfire. There's a lake."

"You'll drown," she wept.

"I'll learn to swim."

"What about bears?" Dominick asked.

"There are no bears," I said with confidence. At least, the brochure I'd been reading endlessly for weeks hadn't mentioned any bears.

"What kind of people will be watching you?" Mom asked, finally getting practical.

"Grow-ups, Mom. It's their job to watch us. And it's Girl Scouts."

My father cleared his throat. "We'll ask Father Tim."

And so it was that an aging Irish priest, after hearing my

mother's lengthy arguments against, and my own plaintive pleading for, decided that my immortal soul would not be endangered by going away to camp. My father borrowed a car and drove me into what looked like another world, filled with mountains, taller trees than I'd ever seen before, and roads so dusty and rutted my mother clutched her purse and began a rosary as we bumped along.

I was only there for two weeks, but my whole life changed.

I learned what grass smelled like. Not the grass that grew in the city parks, or between the tall buildings around City Hall. This was real grass, sweet and cool beneath my feet, that you could lay down on in the middle of a field and no one would tell you to move along. I heard night noises that were not cars rumbling by, or sirens in the distance. Water did not have to be lukewarm and smelling strongly of chlorine, like the neighborhood pool, or an icy blast, like the ocean. Lake water was cool and soothing, and you could lie back and literally float the afternoon away. I learned that if you wanted to eat spaghetti, you didn't have to cook the gravy all morning long, carefully stirring and adding red wine if it got too thick. And no one there called it gravy. At camp, people called it sauce, and you could pour it right from a jar and eat it in just fifteen minutes.

More importantly, I learned what it felt like to have people respect what I had to say. Here, if I gave my opinion, no one looked over my head, clucking their tongue and muttering about what a fresh girl I was. The girls in my cabin didn't worry about going to hell for disobeying their parents. They didn't watch their brothers get attention and love simply because they were boys. They weren't afraid of school because there were schools where the teachers were not nuns, and every digression was not scribbled down for a later talk with your parents and Sister Mary Catherine.

I learned to swim, paddle a canoe, and start a fire with one match and a few dried branches.

I also learned that my life was narrow and closed off from a world that I sometimes glimpsed on the television, but never actually believed.

Hard lessons all.

"What do you mean, you don't watch *Little House on the Prairie?*" Maribeth Howard asked. "Everyone watches."

I fell in love with Maribeth because she had very long, straight, blonde hair that she braided herself every morning. My own hair was in a short pixie cut, which was the only way, my mother claimed, to tame all my curls. I envied her long hair and pale skin and her exalted position as the only child.

"We can only watch one show on television a day," I explained. "And my brothers get to pick." We were gathering firewood, a boring but useful exercise that let us talk without a counselor hanging on every word.

"You mean, every time? They get to pick *every single time?* How does that even happen? That's not fair!" Maribeth always spoke in a hurry, and no matter what she said, her sentences ended with an exclamation point

"Well," I said, parroting my mother, "there are two of them."

"So what?" She said, indignant. "That only means that every third time, it should be your turn. After all, that would only be fair. Right? Fair!"

Of course, she was right. I had never heard anything so logical before in my life. "Right."

"You only have one TV?" she asked.

I nodded and picked up a straggly-looking branch. "Yes. How many do you have?"

"Three," she said, catapulting her into a sphere of wealth and privilege I had previously only accorded the woman who sat behind us in church and wore a fur coat in the winter.

"Where are they?" I asked. Where indeed? After all, there were only four rooms in our whole apartment, not counting the bathroom.

"One in the living room, one in my parents' room, and one in the den."

I frowned. "What den?" I asked, picturing somewhere outside the house where bears slept during the winter.

"It's in the basement. It's where we have a TV and a couch and a ping-pong table."

My brain exploded. The basement in my building had a furnace, the old coal bin, shelves full of Nonna's canned tomatoes and everything that could not comfortably fit into a four-room apartment: Christmas decorations, off-season clothes, beach chairs, books, Dad's old desk, more books, Mom's vanity with the big, round mirror and a single lightbulb dangling from a frayed cord.

"Golly," I breathed.

"It's a big house," Maribeth explained. "Do you live in an apartment? I want to live in an apartment when I grow up. In a city, so I can get on a bus anytime I want and go shopping or to the movies. I'm going to have a job and a roommate and go down to the shore every summer."

I was confused. In an apartment, the landlord turned the heat on and off on a whim and yelled when something wore out like it was *your* fault. I took a bus everywhere, and it was no fun at all. I hated the crowds and the jostling, the smells of the exhaust. And my family spent weekends down the shore, and I hated that too: the sand in my underwear, the sunburnt skin, the constant minding of my brothers when I wanted to wade out into the waves. And someone wanted that life?

"I want to live in a house," I declared. "All by myself. With a huge kitchen and no neighbors. And no roommate. I never want to live with anyone ever again."

"What about your husband?" Maribeth asked. "You have to get married and have babies."

Did I? I thought about Aunt Celeste, my mother's youngest sister, who never married and sold cosmetics at Bamberger's. She seemed happy. She certainly never complained about her husband drinking too much, her kids being disrespectful, or how her mother-in-law hated her cooking.

"I'm not getting married," I announced. "I don't have to if I don't want to."

Maribeth nodded. Her spindly arms were full of branches. "But what if you fall in love? After all, you can't control love and it happens. To everybody. All the time!"

She had a point. I was certain, by that time, that if I could just find my way to California, John Travolta would want to marry me right away. For him, I'd make an exception. But otherwise...

"We have enough wood," I announced. Maribeth nodded and turned back toward the campsite. Here, everyone looked to me as a leader. They took my suggestions and let me make decisions. When was the last time I'd decided *anything* back home? Here, people thought I was smart and could do things. At home, I was told to sit and be quiet.

I never wanted to go back home, and that evening I explained to my camp counselor that my parents were the worst people on earth, they hated me because I was a girl, and would never let me do *anything*. I suggested she tell my parents I'd been eaten by a bobcat when they came to get me on Sunday. Then, I could go home with her instead.

Of course, she argued with me. My parents loved me, she said. They probably let me do all sorts of things—after all, they let me come to camp, didn't they? I tried to explain about Father Tim and his place in this story, but she wasn't having it. I felt my hopes sink like a meatball in pasta water when she told me that, even though she may *seem* old, she was still living with her parents, so going home with her was not an option.

I was surprised how happy I was to see Mom and Dad when they did arrive. I had missed them, after all. Maybe they had missed me, too, so much that they would let me grow my hair out, stop wearing a uniform to school, and let me watch *Little House on the Prairie*.

Any expectations were dashed when, upon arriving home, I was reprimanded in the following days for not folding my clothes back into the suitcase (but Mom, they're dirty) failing to wash behind my ears, and, finally, daring to suggest we not watch the baseball game on Channel 9.

"I want to watch *Little House on the Prairie* instead," I said, boldly getting up off the sofa and changing the station. "I've read all the books." And I had. Multiple times. "Now I want to watch the TV show." I sat down, calm and feeling perfectly justified in my actions.

My brothers stared, dumbfounded.

"We're gonna watch the game," Dom said.

"You've watched every game every night all summer," I argued. "It's my turn to watch what *I* want."

"Sarafina," my mother chided gently, "you're outvoted. There are two of them."

I pointed to Vinnie. "What did you watch *every* night the week before I left for camp?" I asked.

"The game," he said promptly.

I looked at Dom. "The week after that?"

"The game."

I looked at my mother. "There. They each had a turn. Now it's *my* turn. We're watching *Little House*."

Th uproar was deafening, but I sat, arms folded, chin high, safe and smug with my logic.

"Sarafina," my mother began, "the boys —"

I jumped up and set my hands on my hips. "Why do we always have to watch what they want? Why do we only buy vanilla ice cream, because that's what *they* like? What about chocolate, huh? When I want to play Clue with my friends, I can't, because what if the *boys* want to play, too? If I have to share everything with them, how come they never have to share with me?" I was on a roll. "Why don't they have to set the table? When I was six, *I* had to set the table, but I *still* have to do it *and* dry the dishes and *they* get to go outside and play. When am I going to get to go outside and play? When is it going to be *my turn?* "

My mother's eyes grew big, and my father came in from the kitchen where he'd been sitting, reading the evening paper over a glass of Chianti.

"You love them more than me just because they're boys, and you hate me!" By then, I was yelling. No, screaming, for all the hurts and injustices that I had endured in my short but undeniably miserable life.

"Sarafina," my father said quietly.

Usually, the sound of his voice was enough to send me cowering into a corner, but I felt tears of anger instead of fear. "It's not fair," I wailed. "It's never been fair. Just because I'm a *girl.*"

My mother threw up her hands. "It's that Woman's Liberation. I bet she heard that in that camp. I told you, Frankie, camp was a bad idea. God only knows what else she's thinking." She rose and stood over me. My mother, on the tallest day of her life, didn't top five feet even, but she towered over me then. "What else did they tell you there?"

"That I mattered," I shot back. "That what I said was important. That I could make decisions and think for myself."

She covered her eyes with her hands and sank back into her chair, muttering.

My father pushed his glasses on to the top of his head and looked at me, an expression on his face I'd not seen before. I fought my sobbing down to a series of hiccups and sniffles, waiting for the axe to fall.

"Maria," he said at last, "we're moving."

My mother dropped her hands from her face.

"No."

"Yes," my father said. "She is right. She should matter. But she's never going to be able to do that in this tiny apartment, with those nuns looming over her, and every woman she meets

31

worrying about what to make for dinner instead of what's happening out in the rest of the world."

"Frank," Mom whispered.

"We're getting that house we saw last spring. We'll need to buy a car, but we can afford it. Sarafina is smart as a whip, and if we stay here, she'll waste away to nothing."

My brothers, shocked into silence by my father's pronouncement, exchanged worried looks. Any thought of their unquestioned power being usurped was cause for worry, but I knew what they were all thinking: we were finally going to buy our own car.

That's how we ended up moving to the suburbs.

That is when everything changed.

And those changes still reverberated through my tiny rental in Hills of Andrew.

Chapter Four

❦

Maribeth Howard did not like FaceTime, but she had insisted on it ever since my father died.

"I need to see you," she said. "You're too good a liar. But if I can see your face, I can tell if you're all right or not."

So, I FaceTimed her from the back patio of the house, huddled in a plastic chair I found in the detached garage, wrapped in a blanket against the wind.

"I thought Virginia was warm," she began. She was one of the few people who I had told where I'd moved to. "You look like you're bundled up against a blizzard."

I shook my head. "No. It's the bay. It's been kicking up all day, and the wind is fierce."

"Wait. Is it still hurricane season down there?"

"No, Maribeth, this is not a hurricane. This is winter. How are you?"

She had propped up her phone and was sitting in her living room. I recognized the leather chair she was sitting in. I'd sat there myself many times. Felix, her cat, was curled up on her lap. He was her third Felix, as she insisted there was no other name suitable for a cat.

"I'm fine. Well, no. Brian just got laid off, which means he'll be moving back home. And I just had his room redecorated from the last time."

Brian was her son, who, at thirty-one, had still not decided on what he wanted to do when he grew up. "What was he doing?"

"Insurance. I think. I've lost track. You got your hair cut? Thank God. You were looking like one of those crazy gray-haired ladies on Facebook who are always talking about how to start your second act in life."

"Maribeth, I *am* one of those crazy ladies. I *am* starting my second act."

"Fine. But that's no reason to let yourself go. Did you buy a couch yet?"

"You know, you never cared about my furniture before you met Leo." Leo was her partner of almost ten years, a tiny energizer bunny of a man, a popular interior designer who, tired of paying rent on an expensive downtown showroom for years, decided to post decorating videos on YouTube and, more recently, TikTok. Almost overnight he became a major influencer, suddenly fielding offers and endorsement opportunities from design houses all over the world.

"Hmm...," Maribeth said. "That sounds like a no."

"You're right. No couch. But the place is getting painted. And I got a job. I think, anyway. At the local library."

She sat up so suddenly that Felix slid off her lap. "Oh, Sara, that's great! You and books? That's almost as good as you and food."

I managed a smile. "There will never be anything as good as me and food."

"That's true. But since you and food have apparently parted company forever... unless you've started cooking?"

The question sounded casual enough, but she and I both knew that the reason I had cooked nothing more than scrambled eggs or boiled hot dogs in months was a complicated one.

"I bought a box of pasta."

She closed her eyes briefly. "You *bought* pasta?"

"I may even cook it someday."

"I see." She folded her hands in her lap. "I read about Marco. Such a prick! How are you dealing with that?"

"It's not like I didn't know it was coming. After all, he told me she was the love of his life."

She made a noise. "God, I hate men."

"I know. Except Leo, of course. How is he?"

She broke into a smile. "He's just lovely, thanks. In Scotland this week on a buying trip. He'll come home with lots of wooly things and, I hope, good whiskey. He'll be back by the weekend and we're going to plan our spring trip. Maybe we could come down and see you?"

Something caught in my throat. To see Maribeth again, to be in the same room with that toothy smile and boisterous laugh, to pour her glass after glass of wine and watch as her eyes grew bigger and brighter...

"I don't know. That would be wonderful, of course, but why would you come down here? You could go to Paris or Istanbul or back to Egypt. There's nothing to see in Hills of Andrew."

"There's you," she said. "And Leo is a history buff. You know that. We could tour Civil War things. Battlefields and such."

"Well, it would certainly give me an incentive to buy a couch. And a dining room table, since I know how important it is to your personal happiness that I have furniture."

"If you have furniture, it's not so easy to cut and run." She stopped and I could see, even across the miles, the change in her face. "I'm sorry, Sara. I shouldn't have said that."

"It's okay, Maribeth. That's exactly what I did."

She was silent, and twisting her hands together, and I knew she was, in that moment, desperate for a glass of wine to ease her into the next conversation.

I saved her the effort. "Listen, I'm getting cold, and I can barely see you in the dark."

"Next time, call me from inside, so you won't have any excuses to hang up when the conversation gets uncomfortable."

The silence drew out. "I will," I said at last. "I love you."

"I know, honey. I love you too. A lot of people love you. Look at Carla."

Carla was Carla Marissa, my niece, my brother Vincent's oldest and my favorite. I know you weren't supposed to have a favorite, but she was, of all my nieces and nephews, the one in whom I saw the most of myself. She had been born an artist. I had loved cooking as a child, as she had loved her crayons and tempura paint, creating something of the heart and soul from practically nothing. My grandmother had nurtured me along and had always been my champion. Carla hadn't had that, despite her obvious talent and love of art. Although I had always admired and encouraged her work, she'd chased her dream almost completely alone.

"I miss her," I mumbled.

"And I know she misses you. Don't look at the assholes in your life and think they're the only ones who count!"

"Okay. I'll give that a try." I switched off the phone. The wind had really picked up, the whitecaps churning in the ocean below.

I waited a long time in the cold and dark before going back inside.

Dante Robinson stood in my doorway, wearing paint-spattered jeans and a tight gray t-shirt, slouching just a bit with a bucket full of brushes in one hand and a ladder in the other.

"I'm Dante. I'm here to do the painting. Unless this is a bad time." He was tall, over six feet with broad shoulders and narrow hips and strong looking, beautifully shaped hands. His hair was in long corn rows that fell half-way down his back. His face was all hard angles and chiseled features, and his eyes a clear, brilliant green. He smiled briefly, teeth flashing against his dark skin.

"I'm Sara." I stopped. I hadn't been around too many attractive men in the past few years. This guy was hot. As in, if I were ten years younger, and without all the baggage of those ten years weighing me down, I would have made a play for him right then and there, but like so many other things in my life, my libido had quietly shrunk away nothing but a faint tug of memory. I stepped back and watched as he walked into the living room, looking around.

"Man, this place looks like shit. Where's your furniture?"

"I don't have any yet."

He looked at me. "Oh. Waiting for me to paint first?"

Oh, thank God. "Yes. Exactly."

He set down his brushes and leaned the ladder against the wall, then squatted down beside the line of paint cans. Mike had put a smear of each color on the lid, and Dante nodded as he looked at each one.

"I bet Shelia had something to do with all this," he chuckled.

"Yes. How did you know?"

"Because that woman is a genius with color, and these are really nice."

I closed the door. "How do you know I'm not a genius with color?"

He stood up and smiled again. "You don't even have furniture, so I'm thinking that decorating is not high up on your list of priorities. And color... well..."

"You know Shelia?"

"Everybody knows Shelia." He nodded toward the closed front door. "I have to get my stuff."

"Oh. Right." I opened the door and watched him walk back outside to a plain white van parked on the street. He walked in long strides, the muscles playing across his back under the tight t-shirt, his butt outlined in those jeans.

I took a long, very deep breath. I hadn't thought about sex in a long time. Why should I have? My father had been dying, I'd been fighting with my family and the man I loved dumped me. I was over fifty and depressed and menopausal. I felt a slight twinge. If this beautiful young man couldn't elicit even a slight reaction, what hope was there for me of ever connecting, even casually, with a man again?

He came back in and began spreading drop cloths on the floor, and it occurred to me that standing there just watching him work might prove uncomfortable. The email had arrived that morning telling me I had gotten the job at the library, but that was days away. I could sit on the back patio, but it was cold and damp and I'd probably get pneumonia if I stayed out there for any length of time. But where else could I go?

"Ah, Dante? As you pointed out, I need furniture. Any suggestions?"

He stopped working and turned, one hand on hip, obviously thinking. "You a Pottery Barn kind of person?"

Now *I* had to think. "I don't think so."

He raised an eyebrow. "You don't think so? You don't *know*?"

"To be honest, this is my first place in a long time. Before this I lived with my dad, and before that at my boyfriend's place, and before that a one-room studio with a pull-down bed. When it comes to home furnishings, I'm really out of practice as far as what I know."

He nodded slowly. "Ah. Well, if you head down Route 35, there's a whole bunch of antique shops. You can find cool stuff for cheap. There's the mall, of course. That's where you'll find Pottery Barn. And a bunch of other places. If you're into cooking, there's even a Williams Sonoma."

My heart gave a jump. Williams Sonoma? Copper pots and Staub casseroles. Whisks and wooden spoons and Wusthof knives and tongs...

"Thanks. I think I'll do the antique thing."

Good. I had a plan. I had something to do today besides Stardew Valley and old music videos. Maybe I could find a place on the road to eat. It would be good to eat something besides scrambled eggs and salad, which had been my diet for weeks.

"Okay then. I'll see you later."

He nodded again. "Happy shopping."

Right. All I had to do was turn around and get my keys and purse and walk out into the world and shop.

Easy.

Or not.

The first place I stopped was The Antique Mall, which looked like an airplane hangar and was filled with booths from different vendors. The person behind the desk barely looked up as I walked in. The place was empty. Ninety minutes later, I had two small tables, a milk can, and a massive china cabinet that would hold the entire set of Blue Willow dishes I'd also bought. There was also a set of cut crystal glasses that almost sparkled in the dim light. Delivery for the china cabinet was extra, but I didn't care.

Buying the furniture had given me a hit of feeling I hadn't had in a while: power. This was all mine. I hadn't had to ask for anyone's opinion. The choices were mine and mine alone to make. I loaded the tables and two boxes of tableware into the car and went further down the highway.

The second place was a barn that still smelled faintly of former inhabitants. The owner was a sweet older lady who was happy to show me every single item in the place. Two chairs fit in the back of the Subaru, and she recommended the barbecue place right down the highway for lunch.

BBQ Hut was jumping. The gravel lot was full, and I had to pull around to the back of the building to park. As I got out, I immediately started salivating: the smell of roasted meat filled the air, spicy and robust.

Inside, there were a few rows of booths and narrow tables running down the middle of the place. I stood at the counter and gazed up at the menu. There were only six items available in a variety of combinations. I went with brisket, fries and a birch beer. The girl behind the counter was young and perky. She took my money, gave me a number and told me someone would bring it over.

I sat at the only single table that was empty. Professional curiosity kicked in. The place was very clean but plain. A few pictures on the wall wouldn't hurt, I thought. Maybe a few plants? The windows were wide and let in bright sunshine. Hanging ivy, I decided. And curtains? No. Shutters across the bottom of the windows would give an illusion of privacy, although the diners sitting in the booths did not seem to care that anyone driving by could see them. There was a low murmur of conversation, but everyone seemed busy eating. Happily eating.

I looked at the offered condiments bunched in the middle of the linoleum table. Four different hot sauces. Ketchup. Three mustards. Salt and pepper. There was barely room for a plate and silverware.

A mug of birch beer was set down in front of me, along with a stack of napkins and cutlery. The mug was chilled, the silverware sturdy and of good quality.

That was one of my superpowers. Distinguishing good cutlery from bad. You should see me with knives.

"You want that brisket on a roll or white bread?" the girl asked me.

I looked up. "I'm not from around here. What would a local pick?"

"White bread," she said.

"Then white bread. Please."

I pulled out my phone and scrolled. A text from Carla, my niece, lamenting the season end of her favorite British mystery series. I texted her back a few suggestions to fill the time until the next season got underway. British Crime drama had become a staple of my television viewing during Dad's sickness, along with old movie musicals and sappy southern melodramas.

Anything that would take me away from New Jersey, if only for an hour or two.

"You're not from around here?" A red plastic tray appeared on the table. White bread sandwiched a mound of steaming brisket, lightly sauced, with a pile of shoestring fries piled on the side. It all smelled like heaven.

I glanced up. The man standing beside me was tall and thin, probably close to my age, with sparse gray hair pulled back in a ponytail and wearing a stained apron.

"Nope. New Jersey. I'm not a big barbecue expert, but this smells amazing."

The man nodded. "Yeah, we're pretty authentic. Smoke our own meat right out back. All local produce, too."

He was a man who knew his job and was proud of his work. Food people were like that. There was something that crept into their voices, like a mother bragging about her children.

"And the white bread is preferred because..."

"We make that ourselves, too. Soaks up the sauce real good."

"Those aren't pre-cut potatoes."

"Nope. Hand cut."

I picked up one golden-brown fry and took a bite. "Perfect."

"How do you know?" He was smiling. "You a critic?"

"Not a critic. But I know." I jabbed some meat with a fork. With him standing over my shoulder, I wasn't going to try to pick up the sandwich and eat with my hands. It would just get too messy.

"This brisket is also perfect."

He grinned. "You're right. You do know." He narrowed his eyes. "Are you staying around here?"

"Yes. Hills of Andrew. Just moved in. Bracken Road."

His eyes widened. "Into Bess's place? I'm your neighbor. Harry Lockhart. I live with my big brother, Jack."

My mouth was full of brisket. I chewed and swallowed and smiled up at him. "Hello neighbor. I'm Sara Castellano."

"Well, welcome." He leaned down. "You need both hands for that. No point in being polite at the cost of enjoying your food." He straightened and waved at someone in a booth as he backed away.

I didn't watch him walk back to the kitchen. I was too busy eating. And he was right — I needed both hands. I picked up the sandwich. The bread was just firm enough to hold shape, but caught and held all that sauce, all that didn't drip down my fingers, that is. I licked the side of my hand then took a bite and chewed. Then another bite. Then, another fry.

I tried to remember the last time I had enjoyed a meal so much. Some foods are called comfort foods because they bring back a memory. We all have them: mother's meatloaf, the favorite sandwich in your lunchbox, your neighbor's fresh-baked cookies. Some foods are comfort foods because they fill all your senses and make you think that, if everyone could have this same feeling, the world would be a better place.

That was brisket and fries in a spare roadside cafe. I left thinking that yes, I could conquer the world.

Which is why, on the way back to Hills of Andrew, I stopped back at the Antique Mall, bought three copper pots in varying sizes, nesting mixing bowls, a cast iron frying pan and a vintage Corning casserole dish.

Dante's truck was still parked in front of the house when I got back. The front door stood open and as I turned off the ignition, he emerged, carrying the ladder.

"You can leave it in the house," I called to him.

He stopped. "You sure?"

I slammed the car door. "It's not like it will be in the way of anything."

He turned and went back into the house. I followed.

The living room was done. All my boxes were in the middle of the room and covered with a blue plastic tarp. The walls were a soft, sage-y green, with creamy trim and a white ceiling. The dining room was also painted in the same colors. I walked in further. The kitchen ceiling was done, and the trim, but the walls were still a grubby tan.

"This all looks just lovely," I told him. "But how did you know which colors went where?"

He shrugged. "I didn't have your cell number, so I just called Shelia. She came down and told me what went where."

I felt a momentary twinge at the thought of Shelia in my house, with the sad walls and dirty floors. But I had cleaned the kitchen and bathroom, and besides, did I really care what she thought?

"That was nice of her."

"She's a nice person. I saw there was some stuff in the back of your car. Need help?"

"Please."

We carried in the two chairs and small tables, and I let him bring in the boxes of dishes and cookware on his own, while I moved my chairs and tables from one side of my empty living room to the other.

Dante stood watching me, his hands on his hips. "Well, now you can have company."

"Yes. I guess I can." I stopped abruptly and realized that something else needed to follow. "Would you like a drink? I have wine."

He glanced toward the door, then shrugged. "Not a big wine drinker."

Relief flooded me.

"But my aunt mentioned she had some fine bourbon here the other day," he said.

I heard the uncertainty in his voice, and that changed my mind. It would never do to be rude. That was one of my mother's lessons. "Bourbon it is."

His eyes lit up. "Thanks. Do you care which chair I sit in?"

I laughed. The sound was odd in my ears, but it felt good. "Take your pick. I'll be right back."

I dug two crystal tumblers out of one of the boxes he had set on the counter and washed them quickly. I filled a plastic bowl with ice and grabbed the bourbon off the shelf. I arranged everything on my mother's aluminum tray, which had a scene of a vaguely Asian-looking bridge and a few willow trees etched into the dull surface, and went back in.

He had moved the larger of the chairs, a wingback in a faded chintz, to the front window and sat, looking out. I put everything on the table next to him, dragged the second chair over, and poured. We sat in silence, looking out into the rapidly darkening evening.

"No lamp, I suppose?" he asked.

"Ah, no."

"Candle?"

"Nope."

"Mood music?"

I laughed again. "I didn't realize this was a seduction. Sorry."

"Oh, well." He sighed. "At least the bourbon is good."

It was good, smooth going down. "You have a yoga studio?"

He grinned. "You can call it that. *I* call it that, so I can write off a house on the beach as a business expense. Believe it or not, yoga is not such a welcome topic here in Hills of Andrew. I think most people think I'm performing satanic rituals down there."

"Seriously?"

He nodded. "Yes. I studied in India for a couple of years, came back here determined to spread the good word among my people. Unfortunately, my people didn't want to dabble their toes in what could easily be the devil's work." He took a long sip of bourbon. "I was talked about for months, and every church in the county preached against me."

"Oh, come on. This is the twenty-first century, for God's sake."

He shook his head. "Not down here. Even the enlightened white folks were wary. I get by, doing four or five classes a week. More during the summer season. I make most of my money painting and doing carpentry. Aunt Bess paid for my trip out to India, but she insisted that, before I went, I learn a few practical skills. She is, without a doubt, the smartest woman I've ever known."

My glass was empty. I rattled the ice. "More?"

He looked down into his glass, drank off the bit that was left, and held it out. "This is very good."

I poured a bit more. "Yes. I packed four bottles when I left Jersey because I wasn't sure I could find it wherever I landed."

"You packed four bottles of bourbon, but no lamp?"

"I was pretty sure I could find a lamp anywhere. There is one in the bedroom. I can bring it out here in a second."

He shook his head. "No. That's fine. I like the dark. Anyways, I gotta go after this." He flashed a smile. "Hot dinner date."

"And where, exactly, does one go for a hot dinner date in Hills of Andrew?"

"My place."

"Ah."

We sat in silence. I tried to imagine what I would do on a hot dinner date with Dante Robinson, and there was nothing. I felt a flood of anger and sadness.

"So, you're from New Jersey? Must be like living on another planet down here."

"I don't know. I always thought that people were pretty much the same, no matter where you went."

He made a noise. "I can tell you right now that is not true. This..." He stopped and swirled the bourbon in the glass, the ice making faint clicks as it hit the sides. "Did you grow up in a small town?"

"Probably around sixty thousand people. Is that a small town? I don't even know."

He made another noise. "Hills of Andrew is probably less than five thousand. That includes lots of the folks outside the town limits proper. I'm talking *small*. You'll find things and people are different here. Then, of course, there's the whole *South* thing."

"You mean race?"

"Yep. Be careful what you say, and to whom, until you get to know folks better."

I almost mentioned how Julia had called him odd, but he'd just given me a very astute piece of advice and thought I should take it. "How do you know I'm not a racist?"

He drained his glass. "Because I'm sitting here with you, alone, drinking this most excellent bourbon. But now I must go. I'll see you early tomorrow." He stood. "I'll be painting the bedroom, so if there's anything you want to store away…"

I stood with him. "Nope. Just cover everything up."

He nodded. I walked him to the door and watched as he got in his truck and drove away.

Chapter Five

❦

D ante arrived early the next day while I was still
drinking coffee, sitting in the wing chair. He set down
his bucket of brushes and looked around.

"This looks good. Everything in the bedroom ready?"

I nodded. "Yes. I even emptied out the closet." Not that
there was much there. I had only packed three suitcases of
clothes, and most of them were now in plastic bins under
the bed.

Maybe I should buy a dresser.

He squatted down by the rows of paint cans. "What goes
where?

"The darker green goes in the two bedrooms. And the third
color for the kitchen and bathroom."

He nodded and stood up. "Got it. I have extra white. I'll do
the inside of the closet with that. You need to be able to see your
clothes." He flashed a grin. "Nothing upstairs?"

I shook my head. "I can't even imagine what I would do with
that space."

He shrugged. "Well, whatever. Buying more furniture today?"

"Yes," I said. I hadn't planned on it, but where else could I
go? I looked down at my coffee mug where I had set it down on

47

the floor, the faint aroma filling the air. Manners kicked in again. "Coffee?"

"Sure. Thanks."

I had not emptied my boxes of Blue Willow, but I had a few stray mugs that I'd been carrying from one place to another for most of my adult life. They all had the letter "S" on them, in different fonts and colors. "How do you take it?" I called.

"Just sugar."

Back in the living room, he was looking out the window. "Shelia's coming up the walk."

I opened the door as she stepped up onto the stoop.

"Welcome. Come on in. Coffee?" Why not? It looked like I was having a bit of a morning get-together, whether I wanted to or not.

She looked surprised. "What? Yes, please. I hope you don't mind me just coming by, but yesterday Dante needed some help."

I waved her in. "No problem. We just cleared up the wall color issue. How do you take your coffee?"

"Just black, please. Great chair. I love me some chintz."

"Me too." I went back to the kitchen for another mug. Thank God for Keurig, I thought. I brought out the mug and sugar and set them on the little table.

"You're going to need a nice, big table in the dining room," Shelia said. "For all your dinner parties."

A lump rose in my throat. "I'm not a big dinner party person."

She raised an eyebrow. "Really? I would have thought you'd love to cook, having a restaurant and all."

I gulped down coffee. "I'm not doing a lot of cooking these days. And besides, I really don't know anybody yet."

Dante grinned. "You know us. And we are delightful company."

I looked at them both. Had she been his hot date?

"Maybe I'll find one today," I said. "But I was mostly going to get cleaning stuff. I really need to get this place into shape or Bess will be really pissed off."

"And trust me," Dante said seriously, "you do not want that."

Shelia walked into the dining room. "There's a whole lotta room in here."

I followed her. "There won't be after tomorrow. I'm having a china cabinet delivered, and it's huge."

"Cool. And that view is just great. I would sit and stare out for hours when I lived here."

That was pretty much all I'd been doing for the past few days. "Yes."

She raised the mug. "Good coffee."

"Thanks. And thank you for all your advice. My rooms look amazing, so much better than plain white."

"When I was in college, we had a red living room in my first apartment, and we all fought like hell. When we moved, the same group of people got along just fine. Color is important. It makes a vast difference in how you live in your space."

The lump was gone from my throat. She was a nice person. And I had just bought a casserole dish. Why couldn't I have a dinner party? "As soon as I get a table, I'll let you know. "

"Ah, you'll also need chairs."

I smiled. "Yes, I guess so."

"You've been to Brewster's?"

I shook my head. "Nope."

She turned to Dante and made a tsk-tsk noise. "You didn't tell her about Brewster's? Epic fail, Dante."

He made an exaggerated sigh. "I'll try to do better."

"Google it. Brewster's in Hardeeville. Lots of consignment stuff. Unless you're a Pottery Barn kinda person, because the mall —"

"I'm not," I said. "I'll check it out."

Dante disappeared into the bedroom, and I heard furniture being pushed across the hardwood floors. Lucky for him, there wasn't much.

"Thanks for the coffee," she said, walking through the empty dining room and setting the mug on the kitchen counter. "If you've got extra time today, stop by my studio. It's right off the main drag, on Oberland Street. Can't miss it, it's the barn behind the house."

"I'll try to come by," I said automatically, then realized I meant it.

After she left, I poked my head in the bedroom. Dante was taking off the single closet door. I turned and left, closing the front door behind me.

Shelia's studio was indeed a barn, gambrel roof and all. It was down a long gravel drive, sitting in the middle of a brown, quiet field. It seemed to be a million miles from nowhere, even though the driveway was, in fact, barely three minutes from the center of town.

There was a large kiln off to the side protected by a low roof, and that's where I found her, carefully loading in clay pieces.

"Looks high-tech," I said. It stood as tall as me, chrome glistening in the shadows.

She stepped away from the kiln, sweat glistening on her face despite the cool air. "Yes, it is. I considered a wood fired kiln, but it would have required twenty-four-hour monitoring, and I just don't have the time for that. How was your shopping?"

"Good. Brewster's was fabulous." And it was. Dining room table? Check — a long, narrow table of scrubbed pine. Chairs? Check — eight matching bentwood chairs, cafe-style.

I'd been on a roll, buoyed by the fact that I now had a job and could afford more than the necessities. I also purchased a set of watercolors by some local artist, matted and framed. Another watercolor, a seascape that captured the colors out my sliding glass doors as I looked down to the bay. Two bookcases that would reach almost to the ceiling and would fit on either side of the front picture window. They were badly in need of repainting, but it would give me something to do over the weekend. Three lamps. And a dresser of some dark wood that would more than hold my scant wardrobe. I had realized I'd been smiling all the way back to Hills of Andrew, imagining how it all would look in the newly painted rooms.

"I still need a couch," I told her as I followed her through the wide double door leading into the barn. "I may have to break down and order something online. Wow, this place is huge!"

And it was. If there had been any stalls for animals, someone had removed them to make one vast room, three stories high, with wide windows and a bank of skylights that flooded the place with light. One wall was all shelves, filled with objects in a panorama of color.

I moved closer to the shelves. There were bowls, mugs, platters, plates, vases...

"You made all these?" I asked, then shook my head. "Stupid question. I guess I just thought..."

She came up behind me, fanning her face with a rag. "I know. It's a whole lotta stuff. But then, I've been here for a long time, and this is my job. This is all on my website. That's where most of my sales come from. And I do shows. You need to have a lot of product for shows. I do about forty juried shows a year."

"Juried?"

She shrugged. "A juried show is for serious artists. You don't find your average church basement craft show stuff there. Your work must be deemed 'worthy'. I hate that it's so friggin' elitist, not to mention expensive, but at least the people who show up don't try to bargain with you. They don't mind paying eighty dollars for a sugar and cream set."

I pointed at a shallow oval tray, beautifully glazed in a swirl of vibrant blue and pale green, shot through with lines of metallic bronze. "That would be perfect for my dining room. It matches my wall color and my Blue Willow dishes."

She came up behind me. "Take it as a housewarming gift."

I shook my head. "No, thank you. This is your work. And I won't mind paying."

"One hundred and ten dollars."

"Sold. But I want to look some more. Do you mind?"

She shook her head. "Feel free. Some people spend hours just looking."

I didn't spend hours, but I could have. Her work was a perfect combination of simple shapes and beautiful glazing, colors that should have not looked good together but flowed into each other seamlessly.

"You're very good" I told her. "How long have you been doing this?"

She took my credit card. "I just experimented with pottery during school. I didn't take it up seriously until about twelve years ago. I spent the summer in Japan the year before my son was born and I studied with a very respected artist there, learned his techniques. That's why I wanted a wood-fired kiln." She handed back my card.

I took my platter, carefully wrapped in newspaper. "As soon as I get my China cabinet, this will have the perfect place to live. I'll call you. You can come over and see."

"Sounds good. I can bring wine."

I smiled. "And I can drink it." I paused. "Do you know Dante well?"

Something flickered across her face. "I've known him for over ten years, I guess. When he was sixteen, he broke into Charlie's gas station and stole some money. Charlie cut a deal and had him work it off instead of going to juvie, so he spent some time at our house doing chores and stuff. My son is crazy about him. He's turned into a good man."

I took the chance. "A sexy man."

She grinned. "Oh, yes. He is that. He's, how can I put this... omnisexual? Is that a thing?"

That threw me. "What?"

She shrugged. "He is just a very sexual person. Men, women..." She gave me a look. "Why?"

"No reason," I said. "It's just that, well..."

Her grin broadened. "Yeah. I know."

I shook my head. "No. Really. There's no reason at all." A smile tugged at my lip. "But he is sexy."

At that moment, a young boy burst through the double door- way. "Mom, listen, Taylor is having —" He drew up short when he saw me. "Excuse me," he mumbled, his face turning red. He looked to be at the most serious of adolescent ages, barely a teen.

How polite, I thought. "No problem. I was just going."

He looked at his feet and visibly gulped. "I'm Cody," he mumbled.

I glanced at Shelia. She watched him carefully, a tight smile on her face. "Good job Cody. What else?"

He looked up. "Pleased to meet you." He was obviously painfully shy and worked hard to make eye contact.

"I'm Sara. I'll be working at the library, and I might see you there."

Something flickered in his eyes, and he almost smiled. "I go to the library a lot," he said, words tumbling out in a rush. "They have the coolest science books there, and Ms. Rose lets me sit in the grown-up section for as long as I want, so long as I don't make any noise. And there are these really neat fossils and arrowheads in the display cases downstairs. Have you seen them? I have arrowheads, too. They're real hard to find, and —"

"Cody," Shelia said gently.

He turned red again, his gaze once again dropping to the ground.

"Thanks for the tip," I told him. "I'll check out those display cases. Maybe you can explain a few things to me if you happen to be there when I am."

That almost smile returned. "Okay."

I smiled back. "Yes. Well, Shelia, thanks again for all your advice. I may need more help when I start painting all that furniture I just bought."

"My phone number is on my card. Just send me a picture of whatever and I'll be more than glad to offer an opinion. Chalk paint?"

I nodded. "Yes. Fifty YouTube videos have made me an expert."

She laughed. "Truthfully, that's the fastest and cheapest way to learn. It's easy. And remember, you can always start over if you mess up."

"That's good to know." I looked at Cody. "It was a pleasure meeting you, Cody."

He nodded, glancing up at his mother and almost smiling again.

I walked out to the car. The sun was going down and the wind had picked up. The afternoon was suddenly cold and dismal. I'd be going home to an empty house to eat scrambled eggs alone. At least I'd have a table soon, so I could sit down and eat like a normal person instead of standing at a counter, hunched over my plate.

Maybe I was finally looking forward to being a normal person again.

My little house was painted, and I had spent an entire day cleaning the wooden floors with Murphy's oil soap. The kitchen was spotless, and all the furniture I'd bought earlier in the week had been delivered. I had a half dozen large jars of chalk paint and enough brushes and rags to refinish my purchases three times over.

I took a picture of every piece: the china cabinet, the bookcases, the dresser and one of the tiny side tables. Then I took a picture of all my chalk paint jars and sent them all to Shelia with a single word:

HELP!

When the doorbell rang, I was half expecting Shelia, coming to the rescue. Instead, there stood an older man of South Asian descent, smiling broadly. He was very handsome in the traditional Indian sense: black hair and brows, bright dark eyes, high cheekbones and a square jaw. He was holding a pet carrier in each hand.

"Hello. I am Dr. Rajani and I'm here with your kittens. And thank you so much. It is good of you to want two of them. The shelter is having a very hard time right now. These two were very much at risk."

I took a step back. "My kittens? What kittens?"

His smile cracked. "You did not want kittens?"

"I don't know if I want kittens or not. Why would I want kittens?"

His shoulders slumped, and he lowered both carriers to the ground. "She did it again," he said, half to himself. He looked up at me, his beautiful dark eyes two pools of misery. "She did it again, and I believed her. I always believe her. I feel like Charlie Brown. You know Charlie Brown? And every time Lucy promises to hold the football for him? And every time she pulls it away at the last minute? That is me. I am Charlie Brown. And she always pulls the football."

"Who is *she?*" I was trying not to laugh. The man was obviously embarrassed and feeling angry. But Charlie Brown? And *kittens?*

"Bess Robinson. She told me you wanted to have kittens. She does this all the time, sends me to people's houses with animals from the shelter and I am always turned away like the fool that I am." He shook his head and stooped to pick up the carriers. "I am very sorry."

"No. Wait." I looked down at the pet carriers. "What did you mean, at risk?"

His face was impassive. "They were going to be sent to the county shelter, but they would only keep them for thirty days before, you know. Anyway, there are always too many kittens in the spring. We try to find as many homes as we can, but it is hard." He shrugged. "I am sorry I disturbed you."

"What would happen after thirty days? Would they be put to sleep?" I felt a sudden rush of horror as a tiny gray paw snaked out the front of the carrier. I took a breath.

I'd never had a pet. My mother would not allow it. After she died, life was too hard to complicate it further with added responsibility. As an adult, working twelve-to-fourteen-hour days did not leave room for any type of pet. But now I was alone and, as Bess Robinson had said, it was good to have someone — or something — waiting for you to get home. "Come in, Dr. Rajani. And tell me all about these kittens."

His face lit up. "These are very good little girls. They are sisters, and have been fixed, so no babies, yes?" He carried the two carriers into the living room. If he noticed the cluster of furniture in the middle of the room surrounded by jars of paint, he didn't let it show. "Also, they are caught up with their shots, although you will need to bring them back to me in eight weeks for a check-up. I have a litter box in my car and a bag of cat food. Would you like to meet them?"

He handed me the first one, black with two white front paws and a white nose, and she squirmed out of my hands and clawed her way up my arm, settling on my shoulder, where her tiny sharp claws dug into my skin as she settled in.

"She likes you," he crowed. "Look at that. She is very friendly, that one. Her sister is shy. Here."

He reached into the other carrier and pulled out a pale gray bundle and thrust it into my arms. The kitten immediately curled into a ball; its nose pressed against the bend of my elbow. Her sister, on my shoulder, let out faint mew.

"Tell me how to take care of them," I said.

"Clean water all of the time. Feed them twice a day, in the morning and at night. You can leave the food in the bowl all day if you like dry food, that is, but refresh it for them. Clean the litter box every few days. Cats are very neat. Very clean."

I could feel the breath of the one kitten on my shoulder, warm on my ear. The second kitten burrowed further into my arm.

"They need toys," he went on. "Kittens like to play and will find all sorts of things to knock about, so it is best to give them toys. Do not let them outside, please. There are many outside cats here in Hills of Andrew and much disease. You do not want these two to get sick."

I stroked the back of the gray kitten. Her fur was like silk against my fingertips. "What are their names?"

He made a face. "The shelter named them. Gladys is the black one. The gray one is Fluff. I do not think they are very good names, but they probably ran out of good names a long time ago."

I smiled. "You're right. Those aren't very good names. I'll have to think of better ones."

He clapped his hands together. "So, you will take these two sisters?"

The one on my shoulder shifted, claws moving against my skin. "I've never had a pet. I'm not sure this would work for me. Can I, you know, foster them? For a few weeks until maybe you can find them another home?"

He nodded. "Of course. Some people find they do not like pets. I would not like for you to feel obligated. And I can perhaps find another home for them."

I looked down at the gray kitten. "I have a job. They don't need for me to be home all the time, do they?"

He shook his head. "No. But make no mistake. These kittens will form an attachment. I know many cats that greet their owners every day when they come home, just as dogs do. Cats can be very affectionate."

I took a breath. "Bring in your litter box. We'll give this a shot."

"Oh, thank you. That is very kind. Not everyone would accept such a surprise." He went out the door and returned moments later with a covered litter box and a shopping bag. "Where should I put these?"

I walked to the small room off the kitchen. It had probably been a back porch once but had been closed up. It now functioned as a mudroom, and it was where the washer and dryer sat, and an old-fashioned slop sink. I pointed to the space beneath the sink.

"The litter box can go there," I said. I carefully let down the gray kitten as the black one jumped off my shoulder, skittered on the floor, and ran behind a pair of my shoes, piled by the door.

The shopping bag was emptied of a small bag of cat food, and a bag of cat litter went up on the shelf over the dryer, and the two small bowls fit against the wall. He tossed three tiny stuffed mice into the corner. "They will be happy here," he said. He looked at me and added swiftly. "Even if it is only for a short time."

We walked back into the living room, and he looked around, interested now. "You will be painting? I would keep them in that room while you work, or you will have cat-paw prints all over your very nice floors."

"I'll do that."

"And here is my card. Please call if you have any questions."

"Okay. Thank you. But don't I owe you money for the kittens? I mean, don't shelters usually charge something?"

He nodded. "Yes. But Bess Robinson paid their fees."

The black kitten came tearing into the living room, skittered to a stop at my feet, then turned and ran into the hallway toward the bedroom. Her little paws made a faint thump-thump against the floor.

Dr. Rajani grinned. "They will be endlessly entertaining. Better than the Internet. But do not put anything fragile or of value where they can reach. Cat videos are very accurate. They will knock things over and break as much as they can if you let them."

I smiled as she raced back in. "Socks."

"What?" He looked at her. "Yes. She looks like she is wearing socks. That is a good cat name. What about her sister? She needs a matching name."

"Shoes."

He laughed. "That is very good. Shoes and Socks. I think maybe you will become cat person." He walked to the door. "I will tell Bess Robinson. She will be happy."

"I'll tell her myself. I need to thank her." I said and closed the door behind him.

My phone pinged. Shelia replied to my text.

Linen White in LR Gray in DR Dresser black Need help? Cody at his dads tonight

Did I need help? Probably. Did I want Shelia to come over?

I always need help. After dinner?

C U then. I'll bring wine

Perfect

I thought about wine and cheese. Maybe fig jam. Was there a store in twenty miles of Hills of Andrew that had fig jam? And stone wheat crackers?

Socks raced into the living room. Shoes followed, and they chased each other for a few minutes as I stood, the smile on my face grow bigger, until I finally laughed out loud.

It was the simple things, I realized, that I was finally looking forward to enjoying again. Wine and cheese. An easy conversation.

Shoes and Socks.

Chalk painting was not exactly as easy as it appeared on YouTube videos. For one thing, all those smiling women never seemed to get paint anywhere but where they wanted it to go, whereas I got paint on the furniture, sure, but also on my fingers, palms, arms, jeans, shoes, floor...I could hear the two kittens racing around in the small back bedroom and was grateful for Dr. Rajani's advice. I was sure if they were anywhere near my bottles of paint, the consequences would be mind-boggling.

Shelia came by as I was halfway through the second book-case. She looked carefully at my progress and managed not to burst out laughing. I admired her restraint.

"I'm sure that, with more experience, you'll get much better," she said as she poured white wine. I had respectable crystal wine glasses now, delicate and sparkling in the lamplight. "And you should probably do this during the day. The light here is, ah, well..." she trailed off and looked around. "It's looking so much better in here," she said. "These bookcases are perfect. And that cabinet? That's a whole lot of storage."

Unless I went on a major buying spree, it was probably more storage than I'd ever need. I didn't see that happening. I had eight place settings of my Blue Willow dishes and could not imagine any occasion where there would be more than eight people around my table, especially since I owned exactly eight chairs.

"I'll fill in with books," I said. "I always seem to find myself buying books." I would buy any number of books that looked even vaguely interesting. I was a sucker for mysteries and thrillers. After reading, I generally gave them away or donated them, simply because I'd never really had the room to keep many of them. My childhood favorites had taken up half the space in the Subaru, packed in cardboard boxes that were still stacked in my bedroom.

She settled into the wing chair and watched as I finished painting. "Then the library is going to be a good fit. They have book sales two or three times a year. I always end up spending too much money on books for Cody. He loves science stuff. And math books. What twelve-year-old boy wants math books?"

"A prodigy?" I suggested.

She made a snorting kind of noise. "I hope so, though I don't know where he gets it from. I need a calculator to add up more than three numbers, and his father, well, he's a mechanic." She frowned. "Although that requires a special kind of logic, doesn't it?"

I looked up from the bottom shelf of the bookcase. "Absolutely. Engines are complicated and delicate beasts."

She sighed. "I always thought Charlie had something of a brain, but just chose not to use it most of the time."

I laughed. "How long were you married?"

"Five years. You ever married?"

I stood, trying to ignore the ache in my knees. I was not old enough to have knee problems, was I? "Yes. It didn't last. I also had a long-time partner, but that ended a few years ago."

"Kids?"

I shook my head. "No. But I have nieces and nephews to spoil, especially Carla. She's the oldest of them all, my goddaughter, and I love her to pieces.

Shelia nodded. "Yeah, there's always that *one* kid."

"She's an artist," I said. "She could be a great one, maybe. Unfortunately, her father refuses to encourage her because he says he doesn't want to support a starving artist for the rest of her life."

Shelia laughed. "Well, he has a point there. I had a day job for years until I got where I am today. It's a tough road."

I went into the bedroom and brought out a drawing my niece, Carla, had done years ago. Shelia gawked at it. "My goodness," she whispered.

"She was eight when she did it," I told her.

She reached out and took the small, framed picture from my hands. "Eight?"

"It was our first trip to the Metropolitan Museum of Art. We went with my friend, Maribeth. Most eight-year-olds, when they had a chance to explore New York for the first time, might have wanted FAO Schwartz, or a carriage ride in Central Park, but she already knew what she wanted to do with her life. She wanted to be an artist. So, we went to the museum."

Carla had stopped in front of every painting, looking carefully before moving to the next. Maribeth and I exchanged smiles over her serious expression. Then in front of John Singer Sargent's masterpiece, Madam X. she froze, her mouth open.

"Can I draw her?" she asked in an awed whisper.

I'd shrugged. Why not? I'd seen other people drawing other works of art, although none had been eight years old. She sat on the bench before the painting, pulled a pad of plain white paper and pencil out of her My Little Pony backpack, and began to draw.

Maribeth pushed me away. "I have a membership. I'm here all the time," she'd said. "Go. Look some more. I'll stay with her."

I smiled at the memory. "There ended up being about ten people who stood around and watched her. She was so intent on her sketching she didn't even notice until one of them applauded her. Poor Carla, she was so embarrassed. She'd thought she had done something wrong."

We'd gone back to my apartment and then out for pizza, then she'd slept over before I took the bus with her back to New Jersey the next day. But I'd asked her for the drawing and framed it first chance I'd gotten, carefully taking it with me every time I moved.

"Goodness," Shelia said again. "Why are you hiding this? It should be under a spotlight."

I propped the small, framed sketch on the center shelf of the china cabinet. Carla had only drawn the figure of the woman. There was no attempt at a background, and the figure was just from the waist up. But with careful pencil strokes she had captured the velvety folds of the black dress, the quiet expression, the pink of the ear, the gold chain against pearl of skin. It was extraordinary.

I looked back to survey the cluttered mess in the living room. "I think I'm done here." I carefully screwed the lids back on the paint jars and carried them and the brushes into the kitchen, put them next to the sink, and then filled my glass with wine. After opening the door in the small bedroom, I went into the living room and sat down.

"Wait," I said softly.

She frowned. "Wait? For what?"

I heard a soft thump-thump, and Socks came careening into the dimly lit room, racing around the chairs and sped off into the kitchen.

Shelia grinned. "Oh, a kitten! I bet Bess is responsible for her. Him?"

"Her. And her sister." Sure enough, Shoes poked a cautious head around the corner, then scampered in and followed Socks into the kitchen. "Dr. Rajani dropped them off this afternoon. I was completely unaware, and they're only here on a trial basis, but for now they're quite fun."

"Dev Rajani?" she repeated, her voice a bit shrill. "Here?"

I looked at her. "Yes. He dropped off the kittens and all their necessary add-ons: litter box, food, a ridiculous number of toys. Why?"

She took a long sip. "No reason. Just, that is, I happen to think he's a very nice man. We have a dog who has a few problems, and he's just lovely." Her cheeks reddened slightly as she spoke.

I half smiled, remembering the vet's strong face, beautiful dark eyes, thick black hair. "He's also rather attractive."

She narrowed her eyes. "That's the second time you've mentioned that a man is attractive. First Dante, and now Dev."

I chuckled. "I'm not in the market. At all. You?"

She looked thoughtful. "To be honest, I don't need a man for anything anymore. I guess growing older had taught me a few things I wish I'd known in my twenties. I'm very happy with my life. I love what I do, and I make good money. Cody and I have issues, but every parent and child have issues. I like this town and I have a few good friends, a whole lot of social acquaintances I can call on if I ever feel lonely, which isn't often."

"But *Dev?*"

She made a face. "He's under my skin, I guess. A nagging little itch I can't quite scratch. Five years ago, I would have already made a fool of myself over him. I still might. Turning forty was very good for me."

"Wait until you turn fifty," I told her. "Then things really come together."

She looked at me thoughtfully. "Is this your second act thing?"

I nodded slowly. "Yes. I suppose it is."

"And you're not cooking, which I'm guessing was your passion before. Are you bringing nothing with you this time around?"

I thought about my brothers, angry and still blaming me for everything that had torn us apart over the past few years. I thought about Carla, my beloved niece, who I could do nothing for other than smile in encouragement as she tried to find a place for what she loved. I thought about the responsibility I had felt for my employees. That guilt had stripped me of my only financial safely net, leaving me with the same guilt and a need to never again bear the weight of anyone's burdens other than my own.

"Most of what I'm bringing I wish I could leave behind," I said. "More wine?"

She held out her glass. "Always."

I poured, thinking that I had found my first social acquaintance I could call on if I ever felt lonely.

Chapter Six

I sent Maribeth pictures of my painted bookcases.
Becoming an expert at home improvement. Who knew?
She texted back the next morning.
OMG! Next you'll be quilting! Or saving cats!
So, I sent her another picture, this one of Shoes and Socks, curled up on my pillow.
Too late. Meet Shoes and Socks
There was a very long pause, then
Excuse me while I pick up my jaw from the floor
My new life. But I AM getting a couch
Well thank God for that at least
I loved that woman.

My new couch was arriving from Pottery Barn on Thursday, sometime between noon and three in the afternoon. As much as I'd pooh-poohed the idea of Pottery Barn, like it was some huge capitalist money trap, the truth was their furniture was well-built and quite nice. The vague Thursday delivery meant I'd have to step away from my brand-new job, but Rose didn't even blink when I asked her that first morning.

"You need a couch. Of course, you can take off. You'll just be following Molly around your first week, anyway."

Molly Packer was obviously past the generally accepted retirement age, but she was chatty and energetic. Her snow-white hair was in a short pixie cut, her thin body in a long, flowing boho dress in primary colors. Her voice was low and measured as she explained everything that she did, why she did it, and why it was important.

I had made the mistake of thinking that working in a library would be about standing behind the desk and having lengthy discussions with patrons about books. I was wrong. I spent the first morning getting a crash course on all the computers and their various appendages: the printers, the scanner, the copy machines, the digital camera available for lending, the iPads and Kindle. The items, Molly explained, were available to patrons who were in no financial position to buy such things themselves.

"Maybe it's different up where you come from," she said, "but there's lots of folks here who will never in their lives own a laptop. In a digital world, it's hard to be poor. We have folks in here all the time who still have a landline and get their news from the local paper."

I had never even considered the possibility, but I saw it in front of me now. Older people came in who did not understand what, exactly, Wi-Fi was, but knew they needed it to pay their bills, sign-up for Medicare or renew their prescriptions.

And yes, I learned to check out books.

I walked into the tiny house after that first day with my head spinning, only to catch Shoes and Socks curled up on the third shelf of one of the living room bookcases, sandwiched between my battered copy of Winnie-the-Pooh and a vanilla-thyme candle.

"Hey," I whispered. "Did you miss me?"

Shoes opened one eye and yawned, showing a tiny pink tongue, then snuggled back into her sister.

I sat at my new table, my blue and white china in front of me, and stared at my dinner: scrambled eggs, sliced tomatoes and Ritz crackers. I was hungry, but more than that, my brain was still buzzing, ramped up from a day of new things to learn, a new place to be and new faces to examine. I pushed my plate away. This had been my standard meal for weeks, but tonight, it was not enough.

I went into my kitchen. It had been scrubbed; the shelves lined with pretty contact paper; my meager pantry supplies lined up in just two cabinets.

I pulled out the dried pasta, scooped a bunch of garlic out of the wicker basket on top of the fridge, and found a tomato and an onion. I filled my biggest pot with water and set it to boil. I looked around for what had always been on my counter: fresh herbs, cracked black pepper, sea salt, two or three finely honed knives.

I could forget about the herbs and spices, but my knives, not so much.

I went back to my bedroom, found one of the boxes still stashed under my bed, and pulled out my knives, carefully stored in their worn leather roll. The weight of the knives was heavy in my hand. I carried them back to the kitchen and carefully unrolled them.

I had not seen or touched my knives since La Cucina closed its doors that dreadful day after the fire. I drew out my paring knife, the most used, my favorite knife, and held in my hand, feeling the wood warm against my skin. Then I drew out another slightly larger knife and chopped the tomato, pushing aside all the seeds, and smashing the pulp with the heel of my hand. Then I diced the onion and smashed and diced the garlic as well. The water for the pasta had begun to boil, and I tossed in a handful of dried linguini, shook in some salt and stirred with the one wooden spoon I had in the drawer. I once had a wide crock full of wooden spoons, wooden spatulas, and wooden forks of various sizes and shapes.

I heated the cast iron skillet and drizzled a bit of olive oil on the bottom. I used to have olive oil imported from a small town in northern Italy, bought just for my kitchen. I waited for it to smoke before adding the onions. I stirred until they became slightly translucent, then added the garlic and tomato. By then, the pasta was cooked, and I scooped it out and placed it into the strainer in the sink, letting it drain before adding it to that cast iron pan as well. More salt. A small shake of pepper. There was a sizzle, and a thin stream rose in the air, filling the air with an almost heavenly scent. A bit of pasta water to loosen everything up, then I slowly poured everything into my Blue Willow serving bowl.

I needed Parmigiana-Reggiano cheese, brittle and salty, grated over the top. I needed freshly baked bread, rubbed with garlic and drizzled with oil, then toasted on the grill. I needed a glass of red wine, dry and smelling faintly of oak.

I twirled the pasta around my fork and lifted it to my mouth, eyes closed.

The scent of the garlic hit my nose first, then the cheese, and finally, the steam from the hot pasta. I felt my stomach twist and I dropped the fork.

I felt nauseous, then a bile rose in my throat. I stared down at the bowl and fought the urge to vomit.

I picked up the bowl and dumped the contents into the garbage can. I dropped the bowl into the sink. I backed away from the kitchen and ran outside, taking deep gulps of the cool, evening air, trying to calm my pounding heart.

I needed a warm, crowded kitchen, my mother sipping wine from a jam jar. I needed Nonna, nodding and smiling as she scrubbed her favorite pan clean in a small, porcelain sink. I needed my father, reading the newspaper, crinkling the brittle paper as he read.

I went to bed without eating a thing.

Molly and I were behind the main desk, her organizing books that patrons had requested. We had pulled the books from a print-out earlier in the morning. Now, the computer spit out a narrow piece of paper with the last name, and it was fastened around the book with a rubber band, the name on the spine. The process was so simple I could have been bored out of my mind, but Molly's running commentary kept me more than amused.

"Martha Bishop is reading her way through every true crime book she can get her hands on. If I was Devlin Bishop, her husband, I'd be worried sick."

"Here's another romance for Sarah-Lynn. That poor girl. Married to a man who probably has never brought her a flower bouquet or a box of candy the whole of their fifteen-year marriage. Can't even imagine what their sex life is like."

"Marion Cole? She's in here every other day. I'll point her out. She's hard to miss. She has resting Popeye face."

"Molly," I whispered, fighting back a laugh. "Do you really think it's appropriate for you to share your, ah, personal observations about the patrons?"

She looked up at me. "You didn't strike me as being one of those politically correct types," she said slyly. "Being from New York and all."

"New Jersey," I corrected automatically. I had lived and worked in New York City most of my adult life, but once a Jersey girl...

She sniffed. "Same difference."

Not at all, but I wasn't about to argue. "You're right. I'm not all that politically correct."

She snatched the paper as it slid out of the small printer and wrapped it around a book. "You might get in trouble for that. Just sayin'."

"Do you?" I asked. "Get in trouble?"

She shook her head. "Nope. But I was born and raised here. I taught at the elementary school for thirty years, retired, then started working here. I knew most folks when they were still wiping snot from their nose. I get away with all kinds of shit."

The black woman with the brightly colored glasses who I had

first spoken to when I came for my interview, Jennie Lee March, snorted with laughter.

"She does too," she said. Jennie Lee had been working beside us, not saying much, mostly just nodding at Molly's comments. "Everybody loves Molly. Everybody is afraid not to love her. Molly knows things," she added mysteriously.

I looked at Molly. "Will you share?" I asked her.

She shook her head. "Then I'd have to kill you," she said, and she stopped smiling, so I just ducked my head and reached for another rubber band.

"Why retire now?" I asked.

"Because I've been all over this country, but I've never seen a blessed thing." She looked up and shrugged. "You'd think during all those summers off as a teacher I'd have done traveling, and I did, but I was always *doing* something. I spent summers building houses in Appalachia, running kids' programs in inner cities. I once rebuilt a library that had flooded. Spent three months hammering wooden bookshelves and cataloging books. But I've never seen the Pacific Ocean, and I want to before I'm too old to get out there and do it."

"Do you have a plan?" I asked.

"Not really. I'm going to clear out my house of junk, get down to the bare minimum so when I get back here, I can live my life more simply. I'm going to sell all I can so I can get a new car and start driving."

"What about your family?"

She shook her head. "Only child. Never married. I was in love for years with Helen Mitchell, over Fort Dresher way, but never did anything about it. I'm telling you, sometimes living in a small town just sucks. And by the time we were brave enough to maybe act on how we felt about each other, well, we ran outta time. She died. Now I'm about to embark on my great adventure and I'm alone." She shook her finger at me. "Don't wait for the right time. Ever. The right time is now."

She looked past me, and her eyes lit up. "Jack? Hey darling,

good to see you. Do we have something here for you? Sara, do
we have a book on hold for Jack Lockhart?

Jack Lockhart? My neighbor with the barking dog? I saw his
name wrapped around a thick volume on climate change,
grabbed it off the cart and turned around.

Jack Lockhart did not look at all like his brother. He wasn't
tall and thin. He didn't have gray hair pulled back in a ponytail.
He was short, probably not much taller than me, and he had
broad shoulders and a narrow waist, well-built for a man in his,
what, late fifties? Maybe sixty? I had figured Harry to be my age
at least, and he called Jack his 'big' brother. Jack's hair was thick
and dark, going to gray at the temples, and longish at the neck.
He had bright blue eyes behind horn-rimmed glasses, and a
clean, strong face, all smooth skin and a square jaw. A very well-
fitted t-shirt was tucked into jeans, a wide belt around his waist.

"Here it is," I said. I went up to the counter and held out the
book.

"Ah," he said. He was staring at me. "You're new here." He
looked back at Molly, his eyes questioning.

"She just started, so you behave, hear me?" Molly said.

He turned his eyes back to my face and ignored the book in
my hand. He didn't speak.

"She's also your new neighbor," Molly said.

Confusion passed over his face. He opened his mouth, closed
it again, looked at Molly, then shifted his stare back to me.

Poor guy, what could be wrong with him? The silence became
awkward. I spoke slowly. "I moved into Bess Robinson's place," I
explained. "I'm Sara Castellano."

He swallowed hard. "Sara? My brother, my brother Harry?
He said you stopped by his place, but he didn't say, I mean,
pleased to meet you."

He stuck out his hand, and I put down his book to take it.
His hand was warm and dry in mine, and he kept the pressure
for a few moments before letting go. "He thought you were a
critic. Although why a food critic would stop by his little place is

beyond comprehension. I mean, Hills of Andrew? Hardly a culinary destination, right?"

"His little place had some great food," I said, dropping my hand. He kept staring, and I felt a rise of heat on my cheeks. Why was he staring? And how did I escape? Should I just turn my back and find something that had to be done immediately in the back office? Drop to the floor in a pretend faint?

In the nick of time, Molly cleared her throat. "Hey, Jack, you want this book or what?"

He stepped back and seemed to shake himself out of a trance. "Yes. Thanks, Molly." He picked up the book and gazed at it as though it had dropped down from another planet. His cheeks flushed. "So, is this the person who will ostensibly take your place? Not that it would ever be an actual possibility."

Molly had a grin on her face. "Why, thank you for that, Jack, and as a matter of fact, she is. I think she'll be a great addition to our little community. Aren't you lucky, living right down the street and all?"

He fumbled in his wallet and pulled out his card, handing it to her across the desk. Jennie Lee, busy with another patron, kept glancing over. Molly slowly scanned the card, making a very elaborate show of checking out the book.

I busied myself with a stack of books, looking at him from beneath my lashes. His hands, as he put his card back into his wallet, had long slender fingers and no callouses. His brother's hands had been rough and scarred, and I knew all about that. My own hands looked like I'd been a rock climber in a previous life, with hardened blisters, remains of countless burns that never quite faded, scars from more sliced fingers than I could remember. Jack obviously didn't help his brother at the restaurant.

"Do you help Harry at his place?" I asked. The least I could do was be polite.

He cleared his throat. "I help on the business side. Bills, payroll, that sort of stuff. I used to be an accountant."

He took the book from Molly and held it against his chest. Was he leaving? No, not yet...

"Used to?" I asked, curious. "What do you do now?"

"Jack here owns our local theater," Molly said brightly. "It had been closed for years and Jack here had a real project getting it into shape, but they're back up and running now. Isn't that right, Jack?"

"Yes. We have a full schedule. Do you like live theater, Ms. Castellano?" He was looking everywhere now but at me.

"It's Sara. And yes, I love theater. I lived in New York City for years and saw just about everything that opened."

His eyes finally met mine and he grinned. "That's a lot of theater."

I grinned back. "Yes, it was. Some of it was even good."

He laughed. It came from deep in his chest, and for a rather small man, it reached up to the ceiling and bounced around the shelves.

"Shh," Molly admonished. "And go. We need to work."

He nodded his head. "Right. Well, it was a pleasure meeting you, Sara."

He backed up, then turned and bolted out the large double doors.

I went back to checking in the books.

Molly chuckled. "That was pretty impressive."

"What was?"

"The fact that Jack talked to you. He's usually, well, shy," Molly said.

Jennie Lee snorted. "He's more than just *shy*."

"Yeah," Molly sighed. "He's the nicest guy in the world if he knows you. But getting there can take a while."

"So why does that matter?" I asked.

Jennie Lee giggled. "Honey, are you blind? In Jack's world, this was like that scene from *The Godfather*."

Molly nodded. "Exactly."

I was even more confused. "What scene?"

Jennie Lee sighed. "When Michael went to Italy, and he saw what's-her-name and married her? Thunderbolt. He was hit with a thunderbolt." She made a clucking sound. "We all saw it. Don't you even try to look all innocent over there."

I looked at her, then back at Molly. "Excuse me? You call what just happened a *thunderbolt?*" I shook my head. "You two are crazy."

Molly shook her head. "Sara, how long has it been since you dated anyone?"

I didn't have to think about that one too long. "Twelve years. But I think I'd recognize the signs."

Jennie Lee tut-tutted. "I think you totally *missed* the sign. Now, since it was Jack, I can understand the confusion, but trust us on this one."

I stared at the closed door where Jack Lockhart had left the library. "Really?"

Molly looked at Jennie Lee and they both laughed.

I decided to go for a walk after dinner.

And why not? After all, it was almost sixty degrees, and what was a bit of rain? A wave of fog coming in off the water? Or a blast of almost-cold air right behind that fog? If I wanted to walk around my neighborhood, then, by God, I was going to walk.

Maybe I'd get barked at by a dog.

I was, if nothing else, curious about Jack Lockhart. And I was curious about the fact that I was, well, curious, as that had not happened to me in quite a while.

I walked out three times, driven back inside to add another layer of clothing to protect against the sudden turn of the weather, but I was finally ready. I walked out to the end of my driveway, squinted into the growing darkness, and stopped.

Which direction had that damn barking come from, anyway?

Bracken Road was a narrow two-lane paved road with no shoulder to speak of and scrub grasses growing right to the edge where the worn pavement met sand. It was not a necessarily pedestrian-friendly situation, not even in the best of conditions. In this weather, a driver didn't have a chance in hell of seeing someone walking along the road.

I stood at the end of my graveled drive and listened. The wind blew so loudly I doubted I could hear a dog barking unless it was barking while humping my leg.

I looked up and down Bracken Road, mentally tossed a coin, and walked north.

The houses on Bracken Road were mostly small cape cod houses, ranches, or the occasional two-story colonial. Most were on the side of the road that overlooked the bay. The opposite side of the road sloped up and away. A scant hundred yards from my driveway, on the opposite side of the street, was a tall, imposing Victorian home, three stories high, with a wrap-around porch, turrets, gingerbread, and a tall, white picket fence around the yard.

In the yard was a medium-sized dog, brown and nondescript, who stared at me as I came closer to the house, ears perked and alert, tail barely wagging.

"Hey," I said softly, and reached a hand through the fence.

The dog suddenly lunged forward, barking wildly, and I snatched my hand back just as snarling jaws snapped at my fingertips.

"Hey," I said again, in a much different tone.

The dog stood on his hind legs up against the fence, barking in a most unwelcoming manner. This dog was not, I instantly decided, of the warm and fuzzy sort. Any vision of Jack and I walking, the dog frolicking happily between us, vanished. Not that I was actively imaging Jack and I doing *anything* together.

"Rags," a voice called loudly. "Radagast, come here."

The dog immediately stopped barking and tore back toward the house. I looked up and saw Jack Lockhart coming down the steps of the porch, peering at me through the fog.

As he recognized me, his face froze. Was that a look of

panic? "Hello. Sara, hi, what are you doing here? Not that it's bad or anything. I mean, of course you can be here."

He was fumbling for words again. Was that all part of this so-called thunderbolt effect? Or was there something else going on?

"Hello," I called. "I didn't mean to upset your dog. I was just walking, and..."

He came up to the fence and leaned against the gate. "Just walking. Well, that's fine. Of course, it is raining." He looked at me and I swear he forced himself to smile.

"It wasn't when I started."

"Would you like to come in?" He seemed under control now, his voice even and pleasant, his hand on the gate latch.

"Oh, no. I don't want to impose. Besides, I wouldn't want your dog to have another tantrum."

Jack blinked. "He was not having a tantrum. He was protecting his territory."

I felt suddenly defensive. "I told you. I was just walking by."

A bit of a smile flickered across his face. "No, you had to have done something more than that. He doesn't just bark if you're not somehow in his space. Did you put your hand on the fence?"

I nodded. "I was trying to be friendly."

He shook his head. "Rags doesn't do friendly when he's on one side of the fence, and you're on the other."

"Obviously," I said. I was beginning to feel very wet and a little cold and not so friendly myself. "Has he ever bit anyone?"

Jack looked shocked. "Rags? Never. He's not a vicious dog."

"Could have fooled me," I muttered, now feeling embarrassed and wondering why I had bothered to take this stupid walk in the first place.

"He's not vicious," Jack said again, more slowly this time, rain now falling steadily, his hair soaked and plastered to his head. "Radagast just doesn't want people coming into his yard uninvited."

"Who?"

"Radagast." Jack Lockhart did not sound as nearly as polite as he'd been seconds ago.

"The dog's name is Radagast? Is that Swedish for savage beast?"

He straightened, no longer leaning against the gate in a relaxed and welcoming fashion. "He's named for the wizard in *The Lord of the Rings.*" The rain clouded his glasses. He took them off, shook the water away, and put them back on.

"There was no wizard named Radagast in *Lord of the Rings,*" I shot back. "I've read the books."

"Yes, there was. He was mentioned first in *The Hobbit.* Then, during the Council of Elrond. And *The Silmarillion.*"

Okay then. He was a full-out geek with a crazed dog who obviously had a bit of social anxiety around the edges. Staring at him, I wanted to hit myself over the head because I felt an almost uncontrollable urge to reach out and brush back a strand of wet hair that had fallen across his forehead.

"Nice talking to you," I said at last, then turned and walked away as quickly as I could in the now-pouring rain, the water squelching out of my shoes, cold rivulets running down the back of my neck.

I got home, peeled off my clothes, took a hot shower, put on clean sweats and burrowed under my blankets, staring at my phone. After a few minutes, I felt a tugging at my feet and saw Socks climbing onto the bed, little nails digging into the faded quilt. She found a suitable spot right at my ankle. A few minutes later, Shoes made an appearance, settling in on the other side of my feet.

Imprisoned, I scrolled through my phone, Googled Radagast, then found my downloaded copy of *The Hobbit* and began reading on the tiny screen until the cramps in my legs forced me to stretch. I reached over to plug in the phone and settled further under the covers. The kittens rearranged themselves accordingly, and we were soon all asleep.

. . .

The next day was sunny, all the rain and chill and fog gone. A perfect day for having a couch delivered. I arranged my few chairs and tables in the living room three different times before deciding on the perfect spot for the couch to go. I had the picture for over the couch ready to hang, a side table and lamp standing by. Maybe I could get a rug. I sat, scrolling, while the kittens careened around the room, then found a *washable* rug. So far, the litter box had proved one hundred percent successful, but there was always the possibility of spilled wine, coffee...

I watched as Shoes launched herself from the top of the armchair into the bookcase, crashing into a brass candlestick.

The possibilities were endless. I clicked the 'BUY' button.

When the knock came, I was delighted at the promptness of Pottery Barn and opened the door with a cheerful smile.

Which quickly froze on my face.

Jack Lockhart stood on my front stoop, a book in one hand, a leash holding Radagast in the other.

"What are you doing here?" I blurted.

"I brought this by the library, but they said you were home today," he said, abruptly. He thrust the book at me. "I thought you might want to read this."

I took the book from his hand. *The Silmarillion.* "Oh." Well, now I felt a little silly. "Thank you," I said faintly.

There was an awkward pause, and I weighed the idea of inviting him in. I heard a telltale thump-thump behind me.

Radagast had been sitting quietly, ears perked, when he heard the thump-thump as well. His ears flattened, and he sprang forward, knocking into me as he lunged at Socks, the leash slipping through Jack's fingers.

"Rags," he yelled, but Rags did not appear to have heard. He galloped through my living room after Socks, who leapt up onto the dining room table. Rags could not make the jump but managed to put his front paws on the top of the table and barked his damn fool head off.

Jack brushed past me, grabbed hold of the leash, and called

the dog's name again, much louder, and jerked hard on the leash. Rags backed away from the table and sat at Jack's side, looking up with the face of a complete innocent.

Socks, on the other hand, was in the middle of the table, tiny back arched, hissing madly. Just when I thought the situation was under control, Shoes, possibly incensed by the treatment of her sister, leapt from nowhere onto the dog's back, tiny nails digging in. Rags, understandably, yelped and jumped up, turning his head to try to see what could have inflicted such sudden and acute pinpricks of pain.

Shoes leapt back to the floor and tore off, Rags in pursuit, once again the leash slipping through Jack's hands. I heard them gallop into the bedroom and I stared at Jack, who looked completely dumbstruck.

"What the...?" he whispered, then took off in the direction of the barking.

I was right behind him. Shoes made the jump from floor to bed to dresser top. Rags had hopped onto the bed and stopped short, obviously trying to judge if he could make the last leap, when Jack once again grabbed the leash and pulled him back.

Rags, dragged off the bed, sat once again at Jack's feet.

Shoes hissed from the safety of the dresser, looking very proud of herself.

"You have cats," Jack finally said.

"Two. I'm guessing Radagast is not a fan?"

Jack, breathing a bit heavily, nodded. "His mortal enemies. Worse than squirrels"

I raised an eyebrow. "That bad?"

He nodded. "Yes." He looked over at my kitten, now calmly licking her front paw. "Very agile. What's his name?"

"Her name. Shoes."

He raised an eyebrow. "Shoes?"

"Yes." I was still holding the book, and now I hugged it to my chest. "And her sister is Socks. They are both, I believe, mentioned in *The Hobbit* and the first two books of *the Lord of the Rings.*"

He blinked. "Actually, hobbits have no need for shoes *or* socks, as they have very tough and hairy feet."

"True. But I think Aragorn wears them. Socks, at least."

"Ah." Jack nodded. "I know Aragorn wore *boots*, so that may be true." I could hear the laughter bubbling right beneath the surface of his voice.

I held up the book. "I'll check as I'm reading this, to see if there are any references."

He grinned. "Yes. You do that. "He shifted on his feet, looked again at the kitten on the dresser, then at me. He seemed to have made up his mind about something. "Would you like to come by for a drink tonight? There are going to be some people at the house. It's a birthday thing. Nothing fancy, but you could meet a few of the Hills' finest."

I took a beat. He was inviting me to a party. "Finest what?" I asked, stalling for time.

"Since you're new in town, and a neighbor, you should prob-ably meet some people. I'm not really good at that. Meeting people, I mean, but I happen to know a wide assortment, many of them screwballs and eccentrics. After all, I run a theater."

So, this was *not* a date. Good. It was a party. There would be no pressure for me to charm or entertain him, and the truth was I wanted to meet more people. I had never been a solitary person and being alone for the past weeks had not done my psyche any good.

"Sounds like my kind of crowd. What time?"

"After eight."

"I'll be there."

He looked over at Shoes. "Are you one of those cat moms who insists on bringing your darlings everywhere?"

I shook my head. "I'm not really a cat mom. More like a cat appointed guardian. I've had them less than a week so I don't see myself going in that direction." I looked at Rags. "I assume the Radagast will be there?"

"Yes but restrained." He breathed an audible sigh. "Excellent. See you tonight."

I walked him out, my eyes following him and Radagast down the road, still clutching the book to my chest, until a white delivery truck swung into my driveway.

Oh, right.

My couch was here.

I did not own many clothes.

There were several reasons for that, the main one being I wore chef's whites for most of my adult life. I had clothes for yoga, clothes for Very Important Events (which I once had a genuine use for) and then clothes for doing chores outside of the house: jeans and t-shirts, khaki pants and polo shirts, and an assortment of simple linen dresses. The library dress code just specified no jeans, so I had enough to wear until all the clothes I had ordered online arrived.

But a birthday party? At the private home of a man who had, apparently, been struck by a thunderbolt? Unless, of course, his sole mission in life was to spread the word of Tolkien.

I was leaning toward possible interest, and I was surprised to find myself intrigued by the idea. That meant I wanted to cobble out a sexy but not-to-suggestive outfit suitable for making a great impression without trying to appear to be working at it, and at the same time introducing myself to more of the people in the neighborhood in a relaxed social setting.

I hadn't been in a relaxed social setting since I'd left Manhattan, as most of my spare time in the past year had been spent caring for my father and fighting with my brothers. I knew my small talk skills could carry me through most of the night, and I had always felt, if not comfortable, at least not intimidated by a roomful of strangers. Still, there was apprehension.

That's how I ended up with most of my clothes spread across the bed, singing "People in the Neighborhood" from Sesame Street at four in the afternoon, nursing a bit of bourbon. I drank in small sips because I remembered that showing up for drinks when already drunk was generally frowned upon.

Shoes and Socks, delighted at all the new things on the bed to jump on, crawl under, roll in and generally play around with, were having a great time. I, on the other hand, was stressed.

So I FaceTimed Maribeth.

"Hey, so I got invited to someone's birthday party tonight. I probably won't know anyone, but the person who invited me runs a theater, was an accountant, and named his dog after an obscure Tolkien wizard."

"Who's Tolkien?" She was in her kitchen, and I could see into her vast pantry.

"Lord of the Rings."

"Where the schoolboys on the island killed each other?"

"No. That was *Lord of the Flies*. This was... never mind. But you know my clothes, so what should I wear?"

"The theater and accounting crowds are very adversarial, outfit-wise."

I sighed. "I know. That's why I'm calling you." I arranged khaki pants and a loose boho shirt on the bed. "What do you think?"

"Epic fail. Is that a kitten? You still have a cat?"

"Yes. I have two."

"The shirt is fine. Do you have leggings?"

I dug through the yoga pile. "How's this? Are you cooking tonight?"

"Seriously? When do I cook? I'm having something brought in. Thursdays are the new Saturdays here, and people from work are coming over. No one socializes on the weekend anymore. The good thing about Thursday nights is that everyone has to work the next day, so by nine, they all leave. The leggings are out, unless you have thigh-high black boots."

"Please. You know I've never owned thigh-high *any* boots in my whole life. Wouldn't ballet flats work?"

"Maybe. Don't you have another tunic? What about the thing with all that paisley?"

I found the tunic and replaced the shirt. "You hate the paisley."

"I know, but theater people won't. Hmmm... you still wear earrings? Those jet dangling things?"

"Yes. And I have the matching necklace." These were two of my most treasured items, genuine Victorian pieces of jewelry that Marco had bought for my birthday one year.

"The necklace would show off your cleavage. I think this is a keeper. So, who is this man?"

"I told you. He's an ex-accountant who runs a theater. His brother has a barbecue restaurant, a little dive of a place that has fabulous food. He's a neighbor."

"And he's welcoming you to the neighborhood? Is he also the welcome wagon?"

"No. He came into the library, and we chatted. Then I met his dog, and he met the cats, and he invited me to a birthday party."

"That sounds like a very abbreviated version of a much longer story. You can tell me when we come down to visit."

I stared into the phone. "Really?"

"Yes. In April. Is that too soon?"

I shook my head. "No. That will give me some time to put together the guest room."

"You have a guest room? We were thinking a local Hilton."

I snorted. "There is no local Hilton. Or Marriot. Or a Four Seasons resort. You can stay with me."

"Do you have room service and a spa?"

I laughed. "I have a kitchen and a fantastic shower."

"We'll take it. I have to go put food in bowls. Have a good time tonight."

"I'll try."

"There is no try. There is only do." She flashed a smile. "See, I can geek out when I want to."

"Yes, you can," I laughed, and clicked off the phone.

I showered, dressed, and even put on some make-up. Then I sat on my new couch, head back against the pillows, and decided it belonged on the opposite wall after all.

But I would move it tomorrow. Tonight, I had a party to go to.

Chapter Seven

The front gate was open as I approached the house. It was a much different night than the previous one: warm, with a gentle breeze coming in from the bay. Cars parked in a long drive on the other side of the house, and more cars pulled up onto the sand and scrub grass, partially blocking the road.

This was more of a to-do than I imagined. This must be some popular birthday boy. Or girl.

As I went toward the house, there was no barking, and the front door was ajar. I walked up the few steps. There were a few people sitting in wicker chairs on the porch, and they barely glanced my way.

So much for curiosity for the new girl.

The door opened to a rather grand foyer, two stories high, with an elaborate chandelier and arched doorways leading off to the left and right. I followed the loudest buzz of conversation to a large living room, two long couches on either side of a marble fireplace, several comfy-looking chairs scattered around the room, and lots of people: sitting, standing, talking, drinking, and all smiling. It was a happy room, and I felt myself relax.

Here, I realized, what I wore didn't matter. There were men

in jeans and scuffed work boots, women in simple shifts and one older woman in a long dress of brilliantly colored silk, suitable for an opening night or gala. As she turned, I recognized her as Molly Parker, a pale orchid tucked behind one ear. Her face lit up as she saw me, and she hurried over.

"Jack said he invited you! I'm so glad you came. Let me introduce you to everyone. Do you need a drink first? Some people do."

"That would be lovely," I said, grateful for a familiar face.

She slipped her arm through mine and led me from the living room, through a dining room with elaborate Chippendale furniture and massive breakfront, to the kitchen, not at all renovated to 21st century chic, and very comfortable.

A long narrow island ran the length of the room, lined with bottles, glasses, buckets of ice, and various pitchers. Harry stood at one end, dressed in a gray t-shirt and faded cargo pants, his hair over his shoulder. When he saw me, he grinned.

"You're here. Excellent. Jack said you were coming. And Molly has you. That's a good thing. What can I get for you? I can pour you straight from the bottle, or maybe a cocktail?" He yelled over his shoulder. "Jack? You're needed." He turned to me again. "Well?"

"Bourbon, if you have it," I said.

Jack came from another room, and behind him was a woman, taller and younger than he, and very beautiful, with blonde hair in a straight, asymmetrical cut, thick and perfectly arched brows, and startling blue eyes.

Jack's face lit up. "You made it?"

I nodded. "Of course. I'm only down the street after all."

"This is Sandra, our birthday girl," Jack said, looking back at the blond who snaked her arm across his shoulder. "Sandy, meet Sara. New library person and my down-the-street neighbor."

She waggled a few manicured fingers at me. "Pleased to meet-cha," she said. The arm slinked down over Jack's shoulder, the hand resting on his chest.

He shrugged off her arm. "Sandra," he said, "is our star player. She's an excellent actress and, more importantly, an excellent benefactor of the arts."

She made a face. "You make it sound like I bought my way in."

Harry shook a silver shaker, the ice clattering loudly, then poured into a short, crystal glass. He then reached into a small bowl, pulled out a slice of orange, dropped it in, and held it up. "My version of an Old Fashioned," he said.

"Garnish and everything?" I walked closer and took the glass. "Very high-class party you've got here."

Jack grinned. "I told you. Only the finest. My brother is a master mixologist. Molly, do you need another?"

"Of course."

Harry looked up. "Vodka martini. Twist?"

Molly nodded. "And happy birthday, Sandra. What are you now, thirty-seven?"

Sandra made a face. "Thirty-nine. One more year and I may as well roll over and die."

I was surprised. She looked at least five years younger, but I supposed, as an actress, it was part of her job to look good. "Yes. Happy Birthday. And forty isn't so bad." I sipped the drink. It was excellent.

She looked at me with measuring eyes. I stared back. Sure, I wasn't beautiful or glamourous. I wasn't bone thin. After all, food had been my life for decades, and that came at a cost. But I knew I looked good: thick, healthy hair, even if it was gray, clear smooth skin, a gift from my mother, and cleavage for days, also from my mother. I raised my glass to her and took another sip. "Even fifty has its perks."

She made a face. "I can't imagine what fifty could have to offer."

I leaned forward and dropped my voice. "After fifty, you stop caring about what other people think. You just smile and nod and ignore them all. It's incredibly liberating." I smiled brightly, and Jack burst out laughing.

"She's right there," he said, meeting my eyes. I felt a jolt. I didn't know who this woman was, or what she meant to Jack, but between the two of us, there was *something* going on. This party was probably not the place to get into details, but it wasn't a bad place to start.

Molly took her drink from Harry, carefully taking a bit off the top.

"You need to meet people," Jack said. "Bess says you didn't leave the house for weeks when you first got here."

"Bess? My landlady was talking about me?"

He made a face. "I asked." I wasn't sure how I felt about that but filed it away.

"True," I said. "There was a bit of a, ah, learning curve."

"Learning what?" Jack asked.

"How to live on my own."

Molly nodded. "Yes, that's a big one. How's it going?"

I thought. "Well, I've gone out, gotten a job, I'm fostering a few kittens, had people in my house for wine and coffee, so I guess I'm making progress."

"And now, look at you," Sandra drawled. "Getting all dressed up and crashing parties."

"She was invited, Sandy," Jack said dryly. "*I* invited her."

She stepped back, gave a bit of a shrug, then moved around Jack and out into the dining room.

He made a face. "I have to play bartender for a little. Harry is due for a break, and someone needs to keep the drinks flowing."

Harry grinned. "Just fifteen minutes." He winked at me. "Union regs."

Jack rolled his eyes. "Molly, can you play hostess for a bit?"

"Absolutely," she said, and I followed her back into the crowd.

Molly knew every single person in the room. "I've lived here my whole life," she explained. "And I'm very nosy." Everyone she introduced me to was pleasant, mildly curious about who I was and why I'd chosen Hills of Andrew. The crowd was diverse, but I expected that from theater people. It was interesting to me that the same stereotypes I would have encountered in a New York City party existed in such a small community: the flamboyant gay man, the very butch lesbian, the preppy woman in Lilly Pulitzer, the brooding black poet-type, the belligerent sister in a colorful headscarf, the gray-haired man in a corduroy jacket, requisite leather patches on the elbow, talking quietly about climate change to a bored-looking older man in a shabby cardigan and loafers.

"I'm thinking people are the same everywhere," I murmured to Molly.

She looked up at me, her eyes shining and slightly reddened from the drink. "I'd like to think so. But remember, you're meeting a very tolerant and empathetic crowd tonight. Jack is an exceptional person, and he attracts other exceptional people. Except for Sandra. She's a raging bitch." She drank off the last of her martini. "But even Jack knows there's a time and place for kissing ass. And the people at the library are all pretty open-minded about most things. But never forget, my dear, that you are a stranger, a northerner, and this is a very old, very small town. Old, small towns are slow to change, slower to accept."

"Dante Robinson said something very similar."

"And he would be one to know. "

I looked around the large, crowded room. "They live here alone?"

Molly nodded. "It was their father's family home, and when the grandmother died, Jack came down to sell it but moved in instead. Heaven knows why. Both he and Harry stayed here when they were kids. Summers and holidays, so they knew the house and knew the town." She looked around. "They've changed up things a bit, of course. But I know that all the monstrous dining room furniture stayed. And some of the upstairs bedrooms weren't touched. It's too big a house for two bachelors. There should have been lots of children sliding down that banister, but..." she shrugged. "Some people weren't meant to have children." She looked at me and raised an eyebrow. "You?"

I shook my head and sipped more of my drink. "When my mother died, I took up that role for my brothers. I couldn't wait to get out of all that. Then, when I got my restaurant, I took care of my employees. Kitchen help can be very temperamental. I have nieces and nephews when I feel like spoiling someone. One niece, Carla, well, I spoil her more than the others. She's beautiful and talented, but there are issues."

Molly made a clucking sound. "All God's children got issues." She turned her head. "Harriet made her shrimp dip. You need to taste this. Come on over and try it. And you should meet Harriet. She's a real character. And a very good cook. You had a restaurant? You could trade recipes. What kind of food did you cook?"

"Italian. Very old-school Italian. My grandmother's food."

Molly made a face. "There's no Italian restaurant around here. Not for miles. Did you want to open another?"

I finished my drink quickly. "No. I think I'm probably too old now. It's a lot of work."

"You can't be older than Harry, and he seems to do okay."

"It's complicated."

She pursed her lips. "I suppose so. Harriet, dear, meet Sara. She just moved here and is taking over for me at the library."

Harriet was short and very round, with large white teeth in a very dark face. She hugged Molly. "No one can take your place, Molly." She held out a hand and shook mine warmly. "But hello anyway. Sara, did she say?"

"For Sarafina."

"But that's a lovely name. Here, try some of my shrimp dip. It's one of the things I'm famous for."

She picked up a platter off a side table and held it toward me.

I took a plain cracker and maneuvered a bit of dip into the corner and took a bite.

"Oh, my," I said. "That's amazing," I told her, because it was.

She beamed. "Thank you. It's my secret ingredient that makes it so special."

I snagged another cracker and took a larger portion this time, chewing slowly. "There's a hint of curry powder in there."

Her smiled cracked. "How did you know?"

"She's a cook," Molly explained. "But I'm sure she'll keep your secret." She looked at me. "Won't you, Sara?"

I held up a hand. "I'll take it to my grave. I promise."

Harriet's smile returned. "That's some taste detector you got there. No one has been able to get that secret out of me in twenty years. You're a cook?"

A chef. Trained in New York City, Genoa, Italy, and Lyon, France. I smiled. "I'm kind of retired. Not cooking anymore."

Out of the corner of my eye, I saw Jack weaving his way through the crowd in the dining room.

He caught my eye and raised a hand.

"Your date is here," Molly whispered.

I stared at her. "This is not a date."

She shook her head. "Maybe not in New York City it isn't. But here in Hills of Andrew, this is a date."

Jack reached me, smiling. "Another drink? Or would you like the grand tour?"

I smiled back. "I'm fairly new here. You decide."

"Then both. Harry is back on duty. I'll take you around." He waggled his eyebrows. "Maybe I'll show you my etchings."

Behind me, I heard Molly whisper, "Told you so."

We finally made it up to the third floor of Jack and Harry Lockhart's house, where a small room with a low, sloped ceiling opened out to a small balcony overlooking the Chesapeake Bay. It was just big enough for a tiny table and two spindly chairs. We sat, sipping our drinks, watching as the half-moon rose over the water.

"I would probably spend most of my time right here," I breathed. "Just looking."

Jack nodded. "I do lots of thinking up here. We're at the widest part of the bay. Sometimes, you can make out the Eastern Shore." He pointed vaguely. "It's over there somewhere. But usually, it's like looking into the void: nothing but water and sky. It's a perfect spot for figuring things out." He was more relaxed now than he'd been earlier in the evening.

"Theater things?"

"And life things. Theater things are easy. You find the director, the money, and you try not to make any enemies. Pay the bills on time and keep on the good side of Actor's Equity."

I was surprised. "This is an Equity company?"

He nodded. "Yep. It took a lot of work to get everything just so, but The Northumberland County Theater Company is legit."

"And what does that mean, exactly?"

"A boatload of work, that's what it means" he said with a laugh. "The rulebook for Equity is a bear. And there's no downtime. We're either in production or in rehearsal or planning what's next and then there's fundraising and keeping the subscribers happy." He sighed. "I love it all."

"Did you always want to own a theater?"

He snorted and shook his head. "I had very little interest in anything to do with the arts. But when I came down here, the theater was up for sale. I knew I wanted to be in business for myself, and I thought, how hard can it be? So, I bought the building. That was the easy part. You've heard the expression, 'herding cats'? That's what came next. For about four years. I didn't know what I was doing, and it was driving me crazy, but once I figured everything out, well," he shrugged and I could see his smile in the darkness. "That was ten years ago. Now I can't imagine doing anything else. Even during the bad years, when I barely make enough to pay the bills. It gets in your blood. It really does. And the thing is, I hate people." He stopped, then chuckled. "No. That's not it. I'm not *comfortable* around people. Strangers. The best part about being an accountant was sitting alone at my desk, looking at numbers instead of faces. The fundraising is really hard for me, meeting strangers and," he faltered. "It's always been hard. So having the theater has forced me out of my comfort zone, although I still have layers of employees between me and the general public. But it's okay because it's a passion. That's very hard to explain to other people. The passion, I mean."

I nodded. "I understand completely."

He looked over. "What's yours?"

"Food. I trained as a chef. I worked in Italy, then New York. I had my own restaurant for years. It, well...it closed."

"You could start over here. I did."

I shook my head. "The joy is gone." My mouth felt suddenly dry, and I drained my glass. The bourbon was going to my head. I could feel it, the slightly fuzzy feeling. I put the glass down on the table and hoped I hadn't drunk too much. I didn't want to start saying things I shouldn't, not to this man who had peaked my interest during the evening "And believe me, I've tried to get it back. The closest I came was this week, actually. I made pasta for myself."

"And that was a big step how?" He asked, his voice genuinely curious. "I mean, even *I* can make pasta."

I sat back. "I hadn't cooked anything for myself besides eggs and toast or hot dogs and canned beans for weeks. Months."

"And you made pasta?"

"With garlic and onion and fresh tomato."

"How was it?"

"I couldn't eat it."

"Because?"

How could I possibly explain? "Because food and my family are intertwined. There's a big empty space where my family used

93

to be. The cooking part was good until it reminded me of what was missing."

"So maybe you need to find another passion, something that won't remind you of the past. Something that you can love without bringing back the hurt."

I stared. "That's very... astute."

He chuckled. "That's me alright. Astute. It comes from so much self-analysis. I'm practically an empath."

"Really?"

He threw back his head and laughed. That same laugh that had echoed through the library now floated out of the balcony, across Bracken Road, and off to the water. "No. I was just trying to lighten the situation. I didn't mean to start a conversation that would bring you down. I'm sorry."

I smiled back at him. "It's fine. I'm fine. I miss it. Every day. I loved to walk into my kitchen and start throwing things together. It was an amazing feeling, the creating part of it. Looking at a handful of *things* and putting them together and then sharing with other people." I shook my head. "I can't imagine anything else that could bring me that kind of joy."

"Maybe not do it for yourself, but other people?"

I shook my head. "I would never try to start another restaurant. It's so much harder now. And I'm getting too old. Restaurant life sucks the energy right out of you. You should know all about that."

He nodded. "Yes, I guess I do. Harry has it pretty easy, I would imagine. He has his smokers, buys his meat and produce, bakes his bread. The same crew has been with him from the start. They all know exactly what to do, even if he's not around. Which is a lot." He made a wry face. "Harry has a little drinking problem. He goes on binges every couple of months. Drops off the face of the earth for days."

I looked down at my glass. "I'm sorry."

Jack exhaled loudly. "It's no big deal. Not anymore. He used to be a junkie. Big time. When he was in the Navy. So, if he wants to go off and get drunk every once and a while, I'm fine with it. He's better than what he was."

We sat then, in silence, until I noticed people leaving his porch and getting into the cars along the edge of the road.

"Your guests are leaving," I said. "Shouldn't you be saying goodbye to them?"

He waved a hand. "They all know the way out. Harry will stop the ones who are too drunk to drive. Some mornings I walk down my hallway and every extra bedroom has someone crashed in it."

"Do you have these kinds of parties often?"

"I'm not terribly comfortable with all this." He waved his hand again toward his departing guests. "Harry says it's good for me to be uncomfortable once in a while, and he's probably right. Every couple of months it's somebody's birthday, or an anniversary, or Harry is just in the mood to cook up something that's not on his regular menu. A few months ago, he made a six-course dinner for about twenty people because he found an old Bon Appétit magazine and wanted to duplicate the menu. He's a little crazy like that."

I remembered that feeling. Wanting to try something totally new. And it wouldn't do to sit quietly in the corner of the kitchen. Productions needed an audience. "How was it?"

He laughed again, more quietly this time. "Spectacular. Sometimes that guy can really surprise me." He was quiet again. "You have any brothers or sisters?"

"Two brothers. Younger. We're not close." Not anymore.

He nodded. "Families are complicated."

"All relationships are complicated," I said.

"Not if we don't want them to be," he said slowly. "For instance, let's say we saw each other again. In a more... intentional situation. We could decide exactly what we wanted our relationship to be."

Molly had been right. He was interested in me, after all. He wasn't all that obvious about it. He acted like a man who had made up his mind and was being very careful about what came next.

"So, are we going to see each other again?" I asked. My mind was churning. He was bright and attractive, despite the initial nervousness. He didn't appear to have too much baggage, and it seemed to me he was being careful not rush into anything.

That was fine with me. I hadn't thought about being with another man in any way, shape, or form in months. I wasn't going to rush into anything, either. Knowing that this was going to happen slowly made me that much more interested in pursuing the relationship.

I felt brave asking him that question. I'd taken the biggest risk in months, ever since I threw everything I owned into the back of a car and started driving away from my old life.

He looked out over the bay. "This is a very small town, and I generally go to the library once a week. So yes, of course we'll see each other again. That's not the right question to ask. We are two adults who've been around this block. Many times. So, do we want to spend time together, just the two of us, knowing that something might happen? And if something does happen, are we willing to at least try to see it through?"

That was a lot. I took a breath. "Let's see if something happens. We can go from there."

He turned to me and smiled. "Okay. We can do that." He shifted a bit in his chair. "Of course, we have to resolve the Radagast situation."

"Where is he?"

"Shut in a bedroom with a bit of doggy Xanax."

"Well, I'm sure he and I will overcome our initial misgivings. I might even come to like him."

"But what if you decide you want to be a cat mom after all?"

I sighed. "In the past few weeks, I've moved into and decorated a totally new place, found a job, made some casual friends. I didn't intend to do any of those things. And just now I have agreed to go on a date with someone" I glanced over at him.

"That decision *was* intentional. I'm beginning to feel like anything is possible."

"Good. It's settled then. Rags and I usually take a long walk on the beach early Saturday mornings. Will you join us? "

A walk on the beach? It was something I wanted to do ever since I'd gotten to Hills of Andrew, that I wanted to do every day that I stood on my small patio and looked over the trees and streets and houses that lay between me and the Chesapeake Bay. Something I had not, until just this moment, had the energy to do.

"That would be lovely."

"We'll pick you up around eight."

"I'll be ready."

And I knew I would be.

Molly made no fuss about the party the next day. She simply asked if I had a good time. Then we spent the rest of the day working in the "Library of Objects", a collection of things also available for patrons to check out: a sewing machine, a digital camera, an electric keyboard, several iPads and a Kindle, a portable laminating machine, simple power tools. She carefully instructed me on each, and at the end of the day, I felt strangely empowered. I fought down the urge to bring home the drill and all its various bits and attachments, knowing that for the two pictures I had left to hang, it was probably overkill. Did I have anything to laminate? What about stitching up some simple drapes for the living room, now that the dusty and broken blinds were gone?

The possibilities seemed endless, and slightly exhausting. I opened up two cans of soup, made myself a tuna salad sandwich, and watched old *Cheers* reruns on my laptop, in between laughing at Shoes and Socks playing with the plastic tie from the bread that missed the garbage can.

Then I went to bed early so I could be fresh and ready for my walk along the beach.

Eight in the morning was sunny but cool, and Jack drove a twenty-year-old Jeep Cherokee down from Bracken Road to the county highway that ran along the beach. A few miles from Hills of Andrew, a large unpaved space appeared along the side of the road, on the opposite side of the water, and Jack pulled in, maneuvering next to a Honda SUV.

"Ready?" He asked. We had barely spoken during the ten-minute trip.

I nodded.

He got out, opened the back door, fastened the leash onto Radagast's collar, and the dog bounded out, his entire body wiggling with excitement.

"Sit," Jack said quietly, and Rags did, although his butt continued to make circles where it was in contact with the sand.

I stuck my hands in the pockets of my jean jacket. "So, I guess this is a favorite spot of his?"

Jack grinned. "We've been coming here a long time."

We crossed the highway and walked past a wooden fence, its vertical slats leaning slightly away from the wind off the bay, and down a few battered steps and to the beach.

It was breathtaking.

As a longtime lover of the Jersey shore in all of its beautiful and sometimes not-so-beautiful incarnations, the sight of the Chesapeake Bay, stretching out in a clear dark blue, was unexpected and stunning. The water was still, not the roiling waves of Seaside Heights. The sand stretched out as far as the beach in Wildwood Crest. The sea birds were as loud as the most aggressive gulls on Long Beach Island. The air did not smell fishy, like Tom's River, but briny and crisp. The sun had cleared the horizon and hung, brilliant gold, right above the line where water met sky.

"It never gets old," Jack said, raising his voice against the soft rushing sound of water on the shore, and the calling of the birds.

I had looked at this same bay many mornings since I'd been in Hills of Andrew. But standing so close to the water, with my feet in the sand, and the soft rumble of the surf as it slowly crept up the beach was a different experience.

"No," I agreed. "It never does."

He reached down and snapped off the leash. Rags did not bound away, but rather put his nose to the sand and began to work his way south, sometimes going up into the dunes, sometimes splashing in the water, but steadily south.

Then Jack and I began to walk. And talk.

The first production he had done upon reopening the theater had been Oklahoma, because he wanted a celebration as American as apple pie. I had seen the production on Broadway years before. We compared notes on the songs, the characters, the story. Then we moved on to movies. Then music. He liked Van Halen and Aerosmith.

We agreed to disagree.

"Ten favorite books?" he asked.

I shook my head. "Impossible. Ten favorite classics? Tearjerkers? Historicals? Biographies? Be more specific. Can you name your favorite play?"

He laughed. "Fair enough. How about favorite food?"

I shook my head again. "Once again, impossible." Nonna's gravy, brimming with meatballs and homemade sausage, that simmered all day long? Fresh made pasta with cracked black pepper and grated aged Parmesan? A perfectly roasted chicken with braised carrots and golden-brown potatoes? Grilled corn on the cob dripping with butter?

"For me?" Jack smiled. "Easy. A sliced tomato sandwich with Duke's mayonnaise and salt and pepper on Wonder bread. The taste of my childhood."

"The taste of my childhood was a roll of fried pizza dough dipped in marinara sauce, eaten like a popsicle."

"I played softball every day during the summers. We had a community playground in my neighborhood."

"Yes! The community playground. Did you grow up in the suburbs?"

He nodded. "Right outside of Charlottesville. You?"

"We moved out of the city when I was ten years old to a very quiet suburban town. My mother was lost without her family, public transportation and her favorite butcher right down the street. But we kids were in heaven. We went from playing stick-ball and hopscotch in the street to making lanyards and friend-ship bracelets at our playground. My brothers played football all year round. Once we moved, they could always round up enough neighbor boys to put together a skeleton team. It was pretty perfect for a while."

"For a while? What happened?"

"My mother died. When I was fourteen. Then everything was awful."

He stopped abruptly. "Oh, Sara, I'm so sorry."

I stopped too. The last time I had teared up remembering my mother's death had been twenty years ago. Now, it was just something that had happened to me, like starting my period or graduating from cooking school. It was a milestone, nothing more. The love I felt for her was abstract after so many years, nothing like the sharp and tearing pain of losing my father, which still felt like an open wound.

"I had to step into her shoes. My father just expected me to do everything she had done. Thank God I had my Aunt Celeste, or I would have been trapped there until my brothers married and moved out. And then I would have been expected to stay and care for Dad." I saw his shocked expression and shrugged. "Guilt. It's an Italian thing."

He shuddered. "Then I feel very lucky to be a WASP. Although there's a certain amount of guilt that goes along with that too. It shocked my father when I bought the theater. And disappointed. I was on my way to being a partner in a very big firm, and that was more important to him than my physical or mental health. And my actual happiness was never considered."

"Isn't it amazing the things parents do to their children in the name of love?" I asked, walking on.

"My first serious girlfriend had an abortion. I was devastated, but looking back now, it was the right thing to do. We were college freshmen, way too young. As I got older, I realized what a crappy parent I would have been. I'm pretty selfish. I probably would have been just as miserable to any child of mine as my dad was to me."

Rags ran into the water, chasing a gull. We stood and watched as he repeatedly jumped at the bird, which hovered in the air just out of reach.

"I think that seagull is seriously messing with your dog."

"I think you're right." He whistled sharply, and Rags came reluctantly out of the water and continued down the beach.

"Were you ever married?" I asked.

"Yes. Twice. Becca died of cancer. Maria was a simple case of bad judgment. I thought she loved me, and I was wrong. You?"

"Once. I met him when I moved back to the States. When I opened my restaurant, he jokingly started calling it 'the other man'. Eventually, he got tired of playing second fiddle, and I was so wrapped up in my success, I just nodded and signed the papers. He was a good guy who deserved better. I always knew he wanted a family. I never should have married him in the first place." I shrugged. "It was expected. Good little Italian girls got married and had babies. They didn't work fourteen hours a day six days a week." I smiled grimly. "I wasn't a very good little Italian girl. My brothers never forgave me."

"What the hell is wrong with your brothers?"

I laughed. "They were raised by a mother who refused to tell them they were ever wrong."

There was a bench set back by the dunes, and we sat.

"You owned a restaurant?"

"For almost fifteen years. And then, things just...happened. There was an electrical fire in one of the apartments upstairs and we had to close shop while the entire building was rewired. I started paying my staff out of my savings, waiting to reopen. Then, my landlord died, and his son wasn't sure he wanted to keep the building, so he kept delaying our reopening. For months. He finally sold the building and the new owner, well, he didn't want us anymore. I tried to find a new location, but I ran out of money, so that was that." I was pleased that I could say those words without my throat closing up and my chest tightening.

"That's gut-wrenching."

I looked at him. "Yes, that's exactly what it was. How do you know that?"

"Because that's how it felt in the middle of our third season when I thought I'd lose the theater."

Of course. We sat in a comfortable silence.

"I usually have a late breakfast at the cafe in town," he finally said. "They have excellent food for a place that looks like it was a set piece for The Andy Griffith Show. Would you like to join me?"

"That sounds lovely. Yes, I would." We turned and walked back to the car, not talking, just walking. Some people feel the need to fill the silence. Jack was not one of those people. Neither was I. Sometimes, you can learn a lot from a person by what they don't say.

The cafe on Main Street in Hills of Andrew looked like it belonged in a nineteen sixties sit-com. The floor was black and white squares of linoleum, the booths in red leatherette and the tabletops gray Formica. Rags lay down on the sidewalk outside the cafe, tied to a hitching post conveniently right by the door, and we sat at the window.

Th menus were long rectangular sheets, laminated, the prices crossed off with marker and new prices printed in red.

"Morning, Jack. Great day for a walk," the waitress said as she put down water glasses. She was fortyish and very pretty, dark hair in a messy topknot and soft brown eyes. She eyed me curiously but said nothing after asking if we wanted coffee. She came back with two mugs and poured. "Fresh blueberries for the pancakes," she said to me. "If you're interested. I know Jack isn't, because Jack always orders the same thing."

Jack nodded. "Absolutely. Hash and eggs. Over easy and rye toast."

The waitress nodded and scribbled on her pad, then looked at me.

I decided quickly. "Biscuits and gravy. Fruit on the side."

Jack grinned. "Going native?"

I nodded. "Yep. I've only heard the rumors."

"It's heaven," the waitress said. "It will also stay with you until next Tuesday. Southern food is famous for its, ah, staying power. You're new in town?"

"Katie, this is Sara," Jack said. "She's renting Bess's place on Bracken and working in the library. Sara, Katie is owner and operator of the Main Street Cafe. Married to Owen, fry cook extraordinaire."

I nodded. "Pleased to meet you."

She tapped her pencil against her front teeth. "So, you're the chef from New York?"

"Retired," I told her.

She nodded and hurried through the swinging doors at the back of the restaurant.

"Is that the word on the street?" I asked, half joking. "That I'm a chef from New York?"

He nodded. "You have to understand things in the Hills. Not much happens here. You're moving in on Bracken Road created a ripple of excitement the likes of which we haven't seen here since Charlie Birch got Annie Winesap pregnant."

I sipped the coffee. It was excellent. "Shelia's ex-husband?"

Jack spooned sugar into his cup and stirred. "Charlie is a real hound, but he's usually careful. The consensus is that Annie was tired of him catting around and pinned him down the fastest way she knew how." He made a face. "Charlie is the most charming guy you'd ever want to meet. Everybody loves him. He just can't keep his pants on."

I had lived for years with constant drama: the staff, customers, my family, the food community in New York. The gossip had always flown thick and fast, and I had tried to stay above it. But this small-town chatter presented itself as irresistible.

"Was he at your party?'

Jack snorted. "God, no. There was a chance that one of his old conquests would have been there. It would have gotten ugly fast if he'd been invited. And besides, he and I are in very different circles." He looked at me carefully. "He would have found most of my guests," he paused, thinking, "objectionable for one reason or another. He's something of a good ole boy." He grinned. "That's one reason he's Shelia's ex-husband. I think she thought she could change his way of thinking, but people like Charlie don't see any reason to change. It's one of the great failings of certain southerners."

I looked out the window. The street was busier now, people going about their Saturday shopping. Everyone swerved around Radagast, who lay close to the side of the restaurant, his head down, ears alert.

"I lived the first half of my childhood in an all-Italian neighborhood, then moved to a very white suburb. Going to school in New York was a real eye-opener for me. My parents weren't prejudiced, exactly. They just never felt the need to step out of their comfort zone. I can't recall a person of color ever being in my home growing up. Or a gay person. My Aunt Celeste came out, later in her life, much to the shock of all her sisters. Like, they never guessed why a beautiful woman like her never married. And she waited until her mother died." I sighed. "She's still a pistol, and one of the best people I know, but God, the histrionics."

Katie put our plates down in front of us, plain white dishes, mine filled with two fluffy biscuits smothered under a gravy that smelled of sausage and herbs. The fruit salad was all seasonal melons and berries. Jack's hash, I could see, was not of the canned variety, but actual chunks of corned beef, chopped rough, with diced potatoes, peppers and onions, and two of the most perfectly cooked eggs over-easy I'd ever seen.

"That bread," I whispered, "looks home-baked."

Jack picked up a half slice and poked one of the eggs until the yolk spilled onto the hash. "It is," he said, taking a bite then picking up his fork.

We ate in silence because our mouths were too busy with chewing. Biscuits and gravy, by the way, were heaven. When we were done, and our empty plates pushed to the center of the table, we both sighed happily.

"That is the second-best meal I've had here," I said. "The first being your brother's pulled pork."

Katie appeared and picked up the plates with a laugh. "We are constantly trying to best Harry," she said. "So far, we win because we have more than six menu items, but you're right, Harry's pulled pork is pretty spectacular. We don't even have it on the menu anymore because everyone knows where to go if that's what they're craving. Anything else? More coffee?"

I shook my head, as did Jack, and she trotted off.

"Thank you for a lovely morning," I said.

Jack smiled. "You're very welcome. I haven't had such a good time in quite a while. Usually, Rags and I are a silent and morose pair." He sat back. "What do you think?"

Good question. Was I ready to even explore the possibility of a relationship? Marco and I had been apart for a long enough time that the news of his marriage should not have hit as hard as it did, but I reasoned that my reaction was fueled in part by additional feelings of grief, guilt, and loneliness. The lonely part was slowly ebbing, as was the guilt.

"Who is Sandra, exactly?" I asked. I certainly didn't want to start anything with built-in complications.

He narrowed his eyes in puzzlement, then nodded. "Ah. Yes.

Sandra. She is Sandra Malinowski, or Sandy Mills, depending on whether or not she's on stage. She's territorial." He stopped, picked up his spoon, and twirled in between his fingers. "She has, for some time now, been suggesting that the two of us would make a perfect couple. I have, at the same time, been telling her that we'd be a terrible couple. She's too young and incredibly vain and needy. I have neither the time nor the patience for someone like her in my life. For some reason, probably because she's so beautiful, she doesn't believe me. While I find her physically desirable, that is not enough. I've told her that. Again, she doesn't believe me, so she tries to seduce me every time we're in the same room together. Luckily, that's not too often because I am, after all, only human." He put down his spoon. "I can understand the question. I hope my answer is satisfactory."

"You just sounded a lot like an accountant."

He nodded. "That's fair. I was one. For over twenty years. Sometimes, it shows."

I sat and looked at him, the broad shoulders beneath his corduroy jacket, the long slender fingers, the dark hair curling at his neck. "I think I like you, Jack Lockhart." I said. "And I also think I'm beginning to like Radagast."

He grinned. "Good thing you added that last part. I'm very much a love-me-love-my-dog kind of guy."

I grinned back. "Should I say the same about my kittens?"

He winced.

I laughed. "Too much too soon?" I asked him.

He shook his head. "Nope. I'm a big boy. I'll figure it out. Somehow."

We sat for a few moments, smiling at each other.

Something had begun.

I thought that maybe, just maybe, it was something I could finish.

Chapter Eight

On Sunday morning, I texted my landlady.

Can I put in a garden?

The house was on a fairly large bit of property. The one side, where the drive came in and the detached garage stood, abutted a vacant lot, all sand and brush and scrub pine, and beyond that a small ranch-style house barely visible through the trees. On the other side, a fairly new stockade fence separated me from my nearest neighbor, whose name was Linda. We had gotten into the habit of waving at each other, but nothing more. I was certain she had long ago decided that there was not a lot of satisfaction to be found in befriending a renter.

Bess Robinson texted back immediately.

Define garden. And where?

The patch of ground I was thinking of was barely twenty feet wide, a mixture of a pale green vegetation and dead brown patches that would probably start growing as the weather turned. What I wanted was something like the garden my father had treasured for years, and that I had tended to in the last two years of his life: rows of tomatoes and peppers, vining cucumbers and sprawling zucchini, potatoes growing in a large barrel, a pumpkin patch in one corner.

I want veggies and a few flowers. The strip between the house and fence. I'll have to turn the soil over and put in a lot of compost. There will be trellises

Excellent. Use what's in the garage.

Thank you. And I am fostering the two kittens.

She responded with a series of happy faces. What are their names?

Shoes and Socks

It took a few minutes for her response. You are ridiculous

Maybe I was.

I went outside and pulled open the garage door. I had looked in it a few times before. It was very neat and well organized, with a long workbench along the back where Dante had put the paint cans. Along the wall hung several rakes and a shovel, pitchfork and hoe. There was an electric push mower and a battery-operated weed-whacker in one corner. A substantial length of hose was coiled and stashed under the workbench.

I knew that I should start with the pitchfork, turning over the dirt and loosening up that thatched and tangled growth from last year, but did I really want to start that first thing on a Sunday morning? There was a fairly large and interesting-looking garden center not twenty minutes down the road. I needed inspiration. Once I saw all the lovely things I could put into the ground, I'd have all the energy and determination required for the several hours of the boring and back-breaking work necessary to prepare a vegetable garden.

I should have known better. When I returned to the house two hours later, I had twelve bags of organic compost, mulch, twenty-seven assorted seedlings and twelve seed packets. Thank God the Subaru had enough space behind the front seats. As I pulled up to the house, Dante's truck was in the drive. I parked the car and got out. I could hear some sort of equipment chugging along and followed the sound to the side of the house, where Dante was pushing a gas-powered rototiller through the matted dead grass and packed soil.

He stopped when he saw me and the sound of the rototiller geared down.

"I love you," I yelled.

"Love my aunt," he yelled back.

I unpacked the Subaru and placed all my seedlings on the ground, arranging they as I wanted to plant them in the garden. I looked quickly from where I had put everything in the front yard and looked over to the garden. Could I have possibly over-bought? Just a little?

By the time I had stacked the bags of compost and mulch, Dante had cut the engine of the rototiller and was pushing it to the front of the house. He stopped when he saw my rather grand display and whistled between his teeth.

"Should I do more?" he asked. "Maybe another six feet or so into the front?"

I nodded, wondering, exactly, how many people I was planning on feeding once all these vegetables started coming in. I was one person. I had three zucchini plants. Already I could see an overwhelming overage.

I went to the garage and brought out the pitchfork and spade. By then it was almost noon, and the sun was high and it was starting to get warm.

Dante had put the machine back into the truck and was crouched down, reading all the labels of my plants. As he straightened, he grinned. "Are you expecting company?"

"You will have noticed," I said, "not all of those are vegetables. I'm also planting lots of flowers. I love fresh cut flowers in the house."

"You will have more tomatoes than any ten people can eat in a season," he pointed out.

"I'll can them."

I heard a car pull into the drive, and looked and saw my landlady, Bess Robinson, get out of a sleek black Mercedes. She was dressed in a flowered dress and a large straw hat.

She approached, looked at me and smiled. "I don't make it a

habit of just stopping by to check on my tenants. I'm actually checking up on my nephew, to make sure he didn't tear up the wrong patch of ground."

Dante rolled his eyes. "That was years ago," he said with a laugh.

She glared at him. "And I have not forgotten. But it looks like you did it right this time." She took a few steps closer and examined my array of plants. "Will you be getting a roommate? Or six?"

"I'll can the tomatoes," I explained. "And I can roast the peppers and pack them in oil."

She made a kind of harrumphing noise. "I suppose. Well, at least you seem to be doing better than the last time I was here."

"I am," I told her. "Would you like to meet the kittens?"

She grinned. "I'd love to meet the kittens."

As we went into the house, I heard the familiar thump-thump, and Shoes skidded to a stop in the middle of the living room before darting off into the kitchen.

Bess looked around, her face lighting up. "Why, Sara, this is lovely. What a restful room."

I felt a small swell of pride. "Thanks. I like it. Shelia picked out the wall colors, and they're perfect."

Bess walked over and peered into one of the bookcases. "All your childhood favorites?"

I nodded. "Yes."

She nodded, then looked over at the watercolor on the wall. "Is that Harvey Hillman?"

"I think so. It's hard to read the signature. I know it's a local artist."

She continued to nod, as though to herself. "Yes. He's gone now, but he did wonderful pieces. I have one myself." She watched as two flying pieces of fluff streaked across the rug and careened off to the bedroom. "Well, they certainly seem very energetic. You said you were fostering them. You aren't going to keep them?"

I heard the now familiar thump-thump as they ran. "I think I probably will."

She took a few steps forward, looking around the dining room. "Is that one of Shelia's?", she asked, pointing to the near-empty China cabinet.

"Yes," I said.

"Good. It's important to support our local businesses."

"I'm thinking about taking one of Dante's classes."

She gave a short laugh. "Well, I hope you're a morning person. He starts most of his classes at the crack of dawn. He says it weeds out the curious, and that only the faithful would get up that early to stretch and bend."

Shoes stuck a cautious head around a corner and Bess bent down, making little kissy noises. Shoes backed off and vanished.

She straightened. "Not friendly. But then, they are cats." She smiled at me. "I'm so glad to see you settling in."

"Thank you. I'm starting to feel more comfortable here."

"Good. We can always use fresh blood."

She left then, and I ate lunch, then spent the rest of the afternoon working: spreading compost, turning it into the dirt with the pitchfork, and raking the plot even. I moved all my seedlings into the garage. I hadn't checked to see when the last frost was predicted, and even though the day had been sunny and warm, I knew that nights turned cold. I went inside and checked the planting tables. Yes, I was a bit premature, but in the next few weeks I could get everything into the ground.

The muscles in my legs and back started to ache, so I washed down Tylenol with some herb tea, crawled into bed early, and started reading *The Silmarillion*.

When my Aunt Celeste sent me an email early Monday morning asking me to call her, I knew it wasn't good news. She hated talking on the phone. Always had.

When I was a child, she always seemed glamorous and very

stylish: she wore mini-skirts and bright red nail polish when all her older sisters were still in house dresses. She was fifteen years younger than my mother, the youngest of the girls, and had defied all their conventions; she worked, never married, had her own apartment, went on vacations alone. Later, when she came out, it all fell into place for me.

Growing up, she had been the most beloved of all my aunts, not just because she was so different.

She was my champion, the only one to stand up to my father after Mom died. It was she who insisted he hire a cleaning person when she found me, late one Friday night, huddled next to the vacuum cleaner crying because I had to stay home cleaning instead of going out with my friends. She insisted that I learn to drive, and in the ongoing battles with my brothers when I was in cooking school, she shut them down with one withering look. She lent me the money I needed to go to Italy after I graduated. She was the first guest when La Cucina opened.

As I got older, she became more like a sister than an aunt, being only twelve years older than me. But she carried the authority of being 'Aunt', and she used her power to my advantage. She had, just before Dad got sick, retired from a life-long career in retail, and moved into a 55+ community where she ruled supreme.

But she hated talking on the phone, and had kept in contact with me through long, chatty emails and Instagram posts of her and her senior-living cohorts on various excursions.

I had just come in from work, my first solo day at the desk. Molly had hung back and let me take care of most of the patrons, and I felt rather tired but quite accomplished. The good-job vibe faded when I saw her name in my caller ID.

"Aunt Celeste? Hi, what's up?"

"When was the last time you talked to your brother? Vincent?"

I sighed. "It's been a while. Is everything okay there?"

I could hear her make a tsk-tsk kind of noise. "No. Carla is miserable. They are fighting all the time."

"About nursing school?"

"About everything. She has a boyfriend, you know. Or had. Her mother, God, Maureen is such a bitch, found Carla's birth control pills. So, of course Vinnie blew up, like he never imagined his twenty-year-old gorgeous daughter would *ever* think of having sex? Hadn't he and Maureen been going at it like rabbits in high school? Anyway, he threw away the pills like any responsible father would *and* forbade her from ever seeing that poor boy again. Because you know how often *that* turns out well."

I sat back on the couch and sighed. Shoes scrambled up my leg, batting at my phone with one tiny paw. "I'll call Carla tonight," I promised.

"You can't. They took away her phone. Apparently, they *threw* away her phone. I only found out what happened because she called me from her friend's phone."

I rubbed my forehead with the palm of one hand. "I'll call Vinnie then. And see if he'll let me talk to her. I can send her another phone, and I'll pay for it myself. And I'll add her to my plan. What a shitshow." I poked at Shoes with a finger and she latched on, chewing with tiny, sharp teeth. "How are you, Aunt Celeste?"

She made a snorting kind of noise. "Starting to feel my age. I have reached a point in my life where I can predict the weather by what parts of my body ache. Left knee pain? Rain. Lower back? Possible thunderstorms. Sinus pressure? Expect humidity."

I laughed. "Oh, come on."

"How about you?"

"Well, the job is so-far-so-good. And I met a man who's interesting and apparently interested in me."

"Well, of course he's interested in you! What man wouldn't be?" She said stoutly. "You're a prize, Sara. Don't ever forget that."

"Thanks, Aunt Celeste." I smiled as Socks catapulted into

the living room then bolted away. "I have kittens." I had called Dr. Rajani from work that morning and told him I would keep them.

"That sounds like you're putting down roots," she said slowly.

"They're kittens," I said. "I can stash them in a shoebox and take them with me when I go."

"*When* you go?"

I wrestled my finger away from Shoes. "If. Listen, I'll call Vinnie. Like, right now."

"Okay baby. Love you."

She clicked off and I took a deep breath, then called my brother Vincent.

He answered right away. "I bet it's not me you want to talk to at all," he snarled when he answered.

I bit back my anger. "Why, hello Vinnie. And how are you?"

I could see him in my mind's eye; pacing up and down the hallway of his house, phone at his ear and his other hand in the back pocket of his jeans, scuffed tennis shoes moving across gleaming hardwood floors, shoulders hunched.

"I shouldn't even let her talk to you," he said. "I can't believe a daughter of mine would sleep around with that worthless piece of —"

"I thought he was a college student."

"So? What kind of respect for a woman does he have if he's screwing her without so much as a ring on her finger?"

"About the same amount of respect you showed Maureen, I would think."

I waited, listening as his breathing got louder. "That was different. We got married."

"Oh. That's right. And you knew that you'd marry her, let's see, your junior year of high school? Or did you really think you were so good at keeping secrets that we all didn't know what you two were doing in the back of that old station wagon?"

He said something unintelligible.

"So, listen. Vinnie. I'm sending Carla a phone, and I'm

putting her on my plan. So, if you have any ideas about throwing her new phone away, just know that it is *my* property you'd be destroying. And since phones cost a small fortune these days, destroying it might be, I don't know...actionable?"

"You're still a real bitch, Sara. You know that?" Then I heard him yell for his daughter, and then came the sound of running feet.

"Hello?" Carla said.

"Hi sweetie. Listen, I'm going to send you a new phone. I'll have it on my plan, so your father won't be able to just do with it what he wants. I'll do it tomorrow, okay?"

Her voice was low and full of tears. "Oh, thank you Aunt Sara. This has been so awful."

"Oh, I know. And I'm so sorry about you and, what was his name? Justin?"

"Well, to be honest, he was getting to be kind of a drag," she said, her voice different now. "This whole thing just shifted the break-up from me to my dad, so, that part kinda worked out."

I snorted with laughter. "Okay then. And how is everything else? You're still drawing, right?"

"Yeah. When I can. These nursing classes are really hard. And boring. When I do sketch its usually in the middle of a lecture and it's usually of a human body with some terrible disease."

"Leprosy?"

She giggled. "Tumors are fun too,"

"Well, at least you're putting all the new knowledge to work."

"Thank you for the phone," she said, very quietly. "It's really weird to be without one."

"I can imagine. How are your brothers?"

She sighed. "They're fine. *They* have phones."

"I'm sure they do. And as soon as they're old enough, they'll have cars."

"I almost have enough for one." Right now, she was taking a bus to classes every day, and had to borrow her mother's car if she wanted to go anywhere. "It's not so much the car, it's the insurance that costs a fortune. And I'm not working all that much because of all my classes. And tips are, well, you know. Crappy. My life just really sucks." The tears were back in her voice. "Everything is awful."

"Oh, Carla, honey, it won't always be."

"I wish you were here," she whispered. "Remember when I would visit you in the city? And we'd go to all the museums?"

I almost choked on the rush of memory. I'd meet her at the Port Authority, and we'd walk all the way up Fifth Avenue to The Met. Afterward, we'd walk to have tapas at a little place we'd found. We'd take the subway downtown where she'd sleep in the guest room of the loft I shared with Marco. The next few days she'd be off on her own, crawling all over the five boroughs looking for museums, art galleries, studios. Then, in the evenings, she'd come back to La Cucina and sit in the corner table, eating and talking to the staff who had known her since she'd first come to visit at the age of eight.

That had been a lifetime ago, when La Cucina still existed and Marco and I shared a loft.

The last time I saw her, she was holding back tears and hugging me tightly. That was the morning I drove away from New Jersey.

"You know why I left?" I asked her.

I heard her sniffle. "Of course. I'd have been right behind you if I had a choice."

"Two more years and you'll be out of school and will have a job of your own and you can do anything you want. And believe it or not, two years isn't that long." No, it wasn't. The two years my father spent dying had flown past in a blur of stilted conversations, whispered, tearful phone calls, and endless meals prepared with all the love and hope I could muster, only to be pushed away with my father's sad smile of regret.

"Call me as soon as you get the phone," I told her. "Do you know my number, or was I just your number one contact?"

Her voice lightened. "I know it. I'm good with remembering stuff, you know that. My memory is all that's getting me through all this science stuff."

"Okay then. We'll talk in a few days."

I clicked off the phone and stared at the blank screen. She was trapped, kept away from her passion, just as I had been. Without Aunt Celeste, I would not have had enough money to finish cooking school or go to Italy. She had argued with my father, coolly shot down the arguments of my brothers, and never stopped telling me to keep going.

Carla didn't have that anymore. She'd had me. I paid for her art classes. Vinnie, of course, balked, then complained that he couldn't manage taking her to class every week. Maureen, he explained, was too busy with the boys. My father stepped up, and he drove her to and from her classes until he was too weak and disoriented from all the medications to drive anywhere.

She was alone, taking classes she hated, in a house that did not recognize her talent, her gift, her love. My heart went out to her, but I could not have stayed any longer. Not even for her.

I stood slowly and walked to the patio doors, looking out across the bay. It was quite dark.

Finally, I followed Shoes to bed.

I registered for Dante's introductory yoga class online, his first class of the day.

I had done little yoga in the past few years. I had done little of anything in the past few years. I sat and watched as my father got weaker and sicker, argued with my brothers, played canasta with Carla in the afternoons as Dad napped, and cooked.

I cooked for my father every day. At first, I remade every dish I knew, then tried variations of all the old recipes from my grandmother. Finally, I turned my hand to chicken broth with pastina, bread soup, barley, and beans. As his cancer got worse, he could digest fewer and fewer types of food, and in his last days, all his meals were sipped from his favorite mug.

But in the end, all the love and hope I'd poured into everything I made came to nothing, and after his death, I simply stopped cooking. I had lost my mother, then Nonna, the two people who had nurtured my love of food. I lost my restaurant. Then, the only one left to cook for had been Dad, and when he died, I felt like there were no reasons left at all.

Heading out at five thirty in the morning to drive down the coast road in the wan sunlight made me nostalgic for the days in NYC when I walked to class, when the city was just waking up, loud and alive; trucks rumbling by, street vendors setting up their wares, the ever-present sirens in the distance.

Dante's studio looked like it had been a gas station in a previous life. Where the service bay had once been, a single massive piece of glass let in the rising sun and the blue-gray water. He was across from the beach, with a few cars parked in front and the door standing open.

He grinned as he saw me and waved me in.

"Welcome. It's good to see you here. There will be about eight of us this morning. Is this your first yoga class?"

I shook my head. "Not at all. But it's the first in a few years, so I thought I'd go slow."

He made a face. "You'd be surprised how much is going to come back to you. Muscle memory is an amazing thing. Put down your mat anywhere, but it gets warm right by the window."

The class filled quickly in the next few minutes, and the music began, a sitar, I thought, a single instrument and a repetitive melody. He was an excellent guide. His voice was calm. His body, in loose linen trousers and a tight T-shirt, was beautiful to watch. He walked around to check each pose, offering quiet advice and an occasional hands-on adjustment.

He was right. I remembered every move, stretch, hold, release. My breath slowed and deepened; I felt a familiar sense of stillness. Not peace, exactly, but rest.

After, Dante nodded to me as I left. "Will you be back?"

"Yes," I said, and followed the women out into the now-bright morning. They did not chatter or gossip, as the women in my previous class had. We all just nodded to each other, got into our cars, and drove away.

I got home and arranged all my plants. I didn't put them in the ground — I was still afraid of a frost — but it was nice to see them, their pale green sprouts peeking out of their black containers, balanced on re-raked rows. Then I went to the back of the house and sat, watching the water, and waited for the unused muscles to start to ache.

I had taken my first yoga class in high school. I had taken it on a lark but ended up a believer. I'd taken some sort of a class since then, no matter how busy or complicated my life was, until a faulty wire in an upstairs apartment caught fire.

And La Cucina, and my life, went up in flames.

Chapter Nine

JJack Lockhart asked me out to dinner, and I said yes.

We had taken another beach walk, followed by another breakfast. The conversation was easier, and I felt a growing attraction to this quiet, odd man with a quick sense of humor and an easy, comforting manner. I relaxed with him. I felt safe.

He came into the library. He had another book on hold, this time an older biography of Mark Twain, and we chatted pleasantly for a few minutes before he asked me if I was free the following night.

"That's my work night," I told him. "Wednesdays. I start at noon and I'm here until eight."

"Then Thursday night? Thursday night is Marty's. That's good. Marty's is a great place to eat. I could pick you up, say, 6-ish? We could drive over to Reedville for some seafood."

Jennie Lee was watching closely, as was Rose. The library was short-staffed, and Rose often worked the desk during busy times, or when there were no volunteers to shelve books. I didn't want to give either of them too much to talk about. Besides, I told myself, this was dinner. Just dinner.

"That sounds great. Thanks."

He grinned, obviously not caring what assumptions if any, were being made, then left.

Rose sidled up beside me. "Many have tried," she murmured.

"Tried what?" I asked, all innocence.

"Now Rose," Jennie Lee chided.

"I'm just telling her," Rose said. She made face. "Jack Lockhart has been through a whole lot of women in the past few years."

"Yes, he has," Jennie Lee agreed. "It's called dating. And there are a whole lotta men in this town dating."

Rose chuckled. "Yes, there are. I'm amazed at the number of so-called eligible bachelors that haven't been snatched up." She and Jennie Lee exchanged a look, and they both giggled. "Or maybe not so amazed."

Okay then. Jack dated. He had mentioned two previous wives, and Sandy. Who else?

And did it matter?

I started checking in books, and Jennie Lee greeted a patron.

"Ah, good morning, Miss Bishop. Yes, I have your books right here."

I looked up. Martha Bishop, she of the true crime obsession, was somewhere in middle age, from forty-something to past sixty, with sharp dark eyes and a pinched face, her mousey brown hair hanging limp, pushed back behind unadorned ears. She narrowed her eyes at me.

"You're the new girl?" she asked.

Girl? Seriously? But I smiled and nodded. "Yes. I'm Sara."

"You like books?"

"Very much," I answered.

She took the stack from Jennie Lee and looked at each of the four titles carefully before nodding and handing me her library card. "I like true crime," she said.

"I can see that," I said. "Have you read *Helter Skelter*?"

Her face brightened. "No."

"It's old. It's about the Sharon Tate murders. Written by, ah, I think the prosecutor?"

She took her books from me and put them into a canvas tote, faded blue with a large 'M' in the middle. "I've never heard of it," she said slowly, as though challenging me. Did she think I'd made it up?

I went to the computer, and after a few seconds had the record on the screen. "We don't have a copy here, but I can request it from another library. Would you like me to do that?"

She nodded slowly. "Please. I'm running out of books to read here."

"We have plenty of books, Miss Bishop," Jennie Lee said reproachfully. "You've just read every horrific retelling of kidnapping, torture or murder that we've got."

Martha Bishop cracked a smile. "Yes, I have, haven't I? Well, ah, Sara, thank you for the suggestion."

"Not a problem. Enjoy your reading."

She sighed and patted her bulging tote. "I always do," she said, and turned away.

"If she ever tells us her husband is away visiting family, that's it," Jennie Lee said in my ear. "No one will ever find the body."

I choked back a laugh.

"Good job," Jennie Lee murmured. "And about Jack."

I turned and looked at her. "What about Jack?"

"Well, you know that he's a bit particular about certain things?"

I nodded.

She made a face. "I happen to think he's real particular about women too. That's all."

"Oh," I said, and I smiled through the rest of the day.

Jack and I ate at a small restaurant perched right on the water, under a dark green umbrella that seemed to serve no purpose except to look quaint. The days were getting longer, but there was no need to block the sun.

"It's to protect you from the gulls," Jack explained.

"Diving?"

"Pooping. There's a whole lotta bird poop that gets dropped around here."

I fought a giggle, then decided to let loose. "Seriously?"

He nodded. "Absolutely. Wait, here's the server. Hello, Jeff." He didn't even glance at the name tag. "Can you tell my friend here why you have the umbrella open?"

Jeff, looking barely old enough to serve the tray full of drinks he was holding, glanced around, then leaned down. "The gulls drop bird shit all over the deck here."

Jack looked smug. "Told you," he said to me. Then, to Jeff, "The usual."

"What's the usual?" I asked.

"Bourbon. Over ice," Jeff answered.

I nodded. "I'll take the same, thanks."

Jeff left, and I sighed, looking out over the bay.

"This is just beautiful," I said.

"And the moon is full tonight. It should be spectacular, rising over the water. I take it you're a beach person?"

I thought. "If you asked me a few years ago, I would have said I was a city person. One hundred percent. Now, who knows? Being a beach person sounds like a good idea. I guess you are?"

He nodded. "Absolutely. Give me three inches of sand and a ripple of water and I'm a happy guy. But city... New York, I take it?"

I sighed. "Yep. I loved every inch of it, right down to the dirty gutters and smelly exhaust and the rats in the subway."

He chuckled. "Not much to love when you put it that way."

I sat back and shook my head. "But there was also the energy, the people, the endless parade of music and art and theater. There was always something happening somewhere, any hour, any day. It was impossible to be bored. That's what I loved, despite the dirt and smell and rats."

He looked thoughtful. "All of that would make me crazy," he said. "An endless parade? No, thank you. The best thing about the beach is the solitude.

I laughed. "You've never been to the Jersey shore in the summer."

He shuddered. "I don't go to the beach in the summer. That's when I sit in my house and watch from the balcony."

Two glasses were set down in front of us. Jeff hovered, but Jack waved him away. He held up his glass. I lifted my glass and gently clinked his.

"Here's to a gorgeous moonrise," he said. "And to being able to relax."

I sipped, the bourbon sliding down my throat like warm honey. "I'm taking a yoga class. That should help."

"Dante?"

I nodded.

"He's an interesting man," Jack said. "It surprised me he stayed. It seemed to me that he would have had a warmer welcome in a more, ah, progressive area."

I looked at him. "Is this place really so conservative? I mean, it's *yoga*."

Jack shrugged. "Small towns like this one are slow to change. Eventually, all the old thinking will die out. Literally. But it will take time, and not even having a force like Bess Robinson behind you will make things go any faster."

"You know Bess?"

He nodded.

"Do you know everybody around here?"

He laughed. "Everybody knows everybody around here. Oh, Jeff. Excellent. What's good tonight?"

Jeff had two menus in his hands but held them to his chest. "The striped bass are still flopping, they're so fresh. But you know me, if there's trout on the menu, that's my go-to. Came in this morning. Caught off the Maryland side of the bay."

Jack looked at me and raised an eyebrow. "They grill the trout here. It's done perfectly, and I get all the side dishes."

Trout? I rarely ate trout, so I nodded. "Whatever he's having," I told Jeff, pointing to Jack.

Jack grinned, then turned to Jeff. "Lots of hush puppies. And greens. And slaw. You know the drill."

Jeff nodded and vanished.

"So. You're a regular?" I asked.

He shrugged. "If Harry doesn't cook, nobody cooks. I eat out a lot. And I go to the same restaurants over and over. I like the familiar. And they know what I like."

"I loved my regulars. I got to know their names, their kids' names. I saw families grow up right before my eyes, one Wednesday night at a time." I thought about Michael and Lois and their twins. Mr. And Mrs. Campanella. Bryce and Trevor. All the others who had their own night and time, their own table, and their own favorite dishes. I hadn't let myself think about them for a very long time, and the sudden swell of emotion caught me by surprise.

I downed the rest of my bourbon in one long gulp.

"I seem to keep bringing up unsettling subjects," Jack said slowly. "I'm sorry. I hope that, given time, I'll know what subjects to avoid."

I shook my head. "It's not like it's your fault. And I can't even give you a list of subjects to avoid, because I don't know what's going to break my heart all over again. Maybe 'break my heart' is too strong."

"If that's what you feel, then it's not too strong."

"You're a very observant guy," I said. I twirled the ice cubes around in my now empty glass.

"They look lonely," Jack said. "Those two melting ice cubes."

"They are. See? Observant."

Jack raised a hand and Jeff materialized. "Two more," he said, draining his own glass.

"You must also be a big tipper," I said.

He laughed. "Yes, I am. I can't cook to save my life and therefore grateful to anyone who was willing to feed me. And it just feels good." He made a face. "I don't have to worry about money. The theater is barely getting by. A couple of times things were *very* bad. Without my grandfather's money, I probably would have had to shut it down by now. That would have meant lost jobs, lost revenue for the shops and restaurants around the theater, lost advertising dollars. Generational wealth isn't all bad."

I eyed him. "Says the man with it."

"My family were merchants from Boston. They weren't directly in the slave trade, or cotton, or rum, although I'm sure all trade was interconnected at the time. They shipped lumber from New England logging camps to the Union Army during the Civil War. They were all very religious, so it's entirely possible they did not cheat the government too much. But they still made an obscene amount of money, which they then invested in railroads. There's blood on the money, I'm sure of it, so I try not to buy too many yachts or private jets. Harry, as you can tell, has no interest in the family fortune at all. I have a few cousins who arrive at family funerals in limousines, but we're not close."

"You don't have to explain anything to me," I told him. "I'm not a big believer in inflicting the sins of the fathers."

He chuckled. "I'm not either, but not having to work for my money breeds guilt."

I laughed. "Yes, I do know. Catholics are big on guilt. Which is why I'm practically a heathen."

He raised an eyebrow and smiled crookedly. "Does that mean dancing naked around a fire in the waning of the moon?"

Our drinks arrived, along with a small bowl of mixed nuts. I grinned down into my glass. He wasn't just a geek, there was humor, even whimsy there. "No. Naked dancing is only for special occasions."

"And where, exactly, can one find a calendar of those special occasions?"

I looked up and met his eyes. There was a warm feeling in the pit of my stomach that I welcomed. "I'm beginning to think that the odds of you seeing me naked have nothing to do with the waning moon."

His jaw dropped, then he sat back and laughed. "Thank God. A woman who actually shoots straight about sex."

"Were we talking about sex?" He was keeping this light. Good. "I thought you wanted to sketch me. Au naturel."

"I'm a terrible artist." He waggled his eyebrows. "But I could manage a bit of finger-painting."

Our food arrived, two plain white platters with a single, perfectly grilled trout lying down in the center. On one side were heaped crispy hush puppies, and the other side was crowded with small individual bowls: steaming greens, mounded slaw, lima beans swimming in fragrant liquid, macaroni and cheese.

"This looks amazing," I said in genuine awe.

"Those hush puppies are a religious experience," Jack said as he fluffed out his napkin and settled it on his lap. "And the lima beans are cooked in pot liquor. Do you know what that is?"

I arranged my napkin and shot him a look. "I'm a chef."

"I know. But I wasn't sure all your New York experience ever brought you up close and personal with southern cooking."

I flaked a bit of trout off the bone and ate it. It was delicious. I forked a hush puppy and blew on it before putting the whole thing into my mouth. It was almost too hot, but the roof of my mouth wasn't scalded, and the crunchy exterior dissolved into melting goodness.

"Oh, my," I said. I heard Jack chuckle and glanced up to see him grinning.

"Food distracted you from sex," he said. "Good to know."

"Food distracts me from just about everything," I told him,

and tried the mac and cheese. Then I forked a bit more trout, then the greens, followed by the slaw, then a bit more trout.

I glanced up and saw Jack watching me, his fork suspended. His eyes crinkled.

"Well?" He asked.

"This almost makes me want to cook again," I said, then immediately regretted it. The things I didn't want to talk about may have a constantly shifting list, but frozen at the very top was why I didn't want to cook anymore.

Jack met my eyes and said nothing.

That warm feeling in my stomach grew stronger, and right then I decided that yes, I would give this man all the time he needed.

Carla called a little after eleven. I was almost asleep, my laptop glowing faintly beside me on the bed. I answered the phone with a feeling of dread.

"Aunt Sara, oh, I really need to talk to you. I dropped out."

I took a breath. "Oh, Carla, why?" Even though she'd hated the classes she'd been taking, she'd been doing well.

"I just couldn't. We started going to the hospital and it was awful. I threw up my first day and, well... I couldn't go back. Yesterday I finally quit."

"What did your father say?"

She sobbed. "He told me to get out."

"Of the house?" I sat up straighter, clenching the phone to my ear. "He threw you out of the house?"

"I'm at Jenny's. I don't know what to do next."

I felt my throat tighten with anger. My brother was unshakable in his belief that he knew what was best for his daughter. Vincent steadfastly ignored the praise of teachers and others, including several local artists who noticed her and joined in the chorus singing her praises. He refused to acknowledge her talent.

My two brothers had been raised by a mother who assured them they were always right in everything they did and thought. After Mom died, and their care and comfort fell to me, I didn't have the heart to tell them that Mom had been wrong. So, the belief continued until they went from stubborn, disagreeably arrogant boys to stubborn, even more arrogant men.

"Carla. Honey, what did your mom say?"

"The usual," she sniffed. Of course. Vincent had married his high school sweetheart, who had never, in all their years of their marriage, said a word against him, not even in defense of her children. "Remember," she said in a small voice, "when you said I could live with you?"

"That was last year, before Dad died and when I still lived around the corner." It had been after a particularly violent argument between Carla and Vinnie. She had threatened then to drop out, and I had extended a tentative invitation, but Dad had said no, and I would not go against the wishes of a dying man. "I'm not in Jersey anymore. It's different."

"No, it's not," the pleading whine that I rarely heard crept into her voice. "It would be even better, because I'd be so far away from them. I'd get a job. Where are you, anyway? I bet there's an art school close by."

"No, Carla." It hurt to say the words. At one time, I had been strong enough to defy the wishes of her parents, but I hadn't been willing to defy the will of my father. "I'm sorry, but I'm really not in very good shape myself. It's been..." How did I even try to explain to her what I'd felt when I finally drove away from my father's house, the 'SOLD' sign in the front yard, leaving behind all that had made me what I was?

"Besides, this place I'm living in doesn't even have a whole lotta room. So, no." Actually, the little cape had a tiny back room, not to mention the entire attic space, finished, with dormer windows and a deep closet, perfect for a young girl who needed her own space. But Carla held anger and pain not so different from my own. The two of us together could be a disaster.

"I thought you loved me."

God, that kid knew how to hit hard. "I do. With all my heart. But no."

She hung up. I know that it's impossible to angrily slam down a cell phone, but somehow, she managed it.

I tossed and turned so badly that Shoes and Socks finally jumped off the bed in disgust, and I heard the thump-thump of their play long into the night.

The Hills of Andrew library was small, and everyone, even Rose, the director, put in time when and where needed. Jennie Lee covered the Children's department if either of the two regular librarians there were at lunch. Louise, the grim-faced office person who paid the bills, approved payroll and typed correspondence, also shelved books. I knew that once I became proficient at the tasks behind the check-out desk, I'd be pointed in other directions.

I didn't mind. I liked the library: the quiet, efficient work, the dedicated co-workers, the regular patrons who had, as I eased into my third week, engaged me in conversations about books.

After our dinner date, Jack had given me a cool goodnight kiss, and seemed not all that interested in advancing any other physical closeness. We spent another Saturday morning walking on the beach and having breakfast. When we parted, there was another kiss on the cheek. That warm glow was still there, growing stronger every time I was with him, but staying a respectable distance from my core. Which was fine. If I wanted sexual fantasy, I had Dante Robinson and his early morning yoga class, where I watched his smooth skin ripple across lean muscle and fine bone. I had decided that I would go every week.

Watching that beautiful young man was a high point of my week, and the yoga wasn't all that bad either.

Shelia Birch and I had breakfast on a Wednesday morning. She had asked me for lunch in a quick text, but I explained my work schedule, and told her lunch would be very short, so we settled on a breakfast on my late day. We met at the cafe in town.

She was already there when I arrived, chatting to Katie, and she waved as I came in. I smiled at Katie, asked for coffee, and sat back, looking at Shelia.

"Forgive me for being so forward on our rather short acquaintance, but do you consider this a date?" She was dressed is a very clingy dress, the same color of her blue eyes, under a short, fitted, linen jacket, sleeves rolled, exposing several thin silver bands on her wrists. She had on long earrings and a matching necklace of turquoise. Her hair curled, pushed up and held off her face by a single barrette, and her make-up was expert.

She blushed and looked down at her coffee cup. "No. Of course not." She looked up. "Too much?"

"Well, that depends. A little too much for breakfast with me. Where are you going next? Tea with the queen?"

She rolled her eyes and dropped her head back, shaking it. "I never get this right," she muttered.

"Never get what right?" I asked.

Katie, bringing me coffee and putting two menus on the table, snorted. "She's in love."

Shelia's head straightened, and her eyes flashed. "I am not," she said. "I'm just..."

Katie shook her head and leaned down to me. "She's in love. Why else would she get all dressed up to pick up her *dog*?"

She left, and I looked at Shelia. "Your dog?"

She picked up the menu and studied it as though she had never seen it before in her life. Her color had risen, and she was quite red-faced.

"Is this about the vet? Dr. Rajani?" I asked, remembering the reaction she had when I'd said he had dropped off the kittens. "Are you in love with Dr. Rajani?"

"Of course not," she snapped. "I'm thinking French toast, with berries. They use homemade challah bread. It's delicious. And smoked bacon on the side. You?"

I picked up the menu. "He is very attractive, as I said before, but I thought he was just an itch. I seem to remember you saying that..."

"Okay, you can stop now," she muttered from behind the menu.

I scanned the breakfast items. The menu was small, and I'd already knew and imagined what every item would taste like. In fact, I'd cooked every item. In my head, of course. My breakfasts were still toasted English muffins with peanut butter, except for the few I'd had here with Jack. "I'm sticking with the cheese omelet." I put down the menu. "If I have too many carbs, I'll fall asleep at work."

She put down the menu, and her color was back to normal. "Protein base. That's the trick." She looked up as Katie appears. "My usual," she said, handing the Katie the menu.

Katie wrote nothing down, just nodded. "And you?" she asked me. "Your usual? Cheese omelet, home fries and rye toast? Or biscuits and gravy?"

"I'm impressed," I said. "You're treating me alike a regular. Omelet please."

She grinned. "I'm a pro," she said, and turned away.

Shelia looked at me. "So, you've been here often enough to make an impression?"

I shook my head. "Just with Jack.

Her eyebrows shot up. "Jack Lockhart? He's brought you here for breakfast? Have you been on his beach walks with Rags?"

I sat back. "Is this routine of his written in stone?"

She nodded. "Oh yes. But I don't think he ever brought a date here. Not for breakfast. That was fast work."

I shook my head. "Not on my part. And besides, weren't we discussing *your* love life?"

She sighed and leaned forward. "I know what I said." She waved her hands, making air quotes as she spoke. "I don't need a man for anything. And I don't. But I think that Dev Rajani is the kindest, funniest, sexiest man I've ever met, and whenever I step into his office, I'm fourteen again; insecure, pimple-faced, and tongue-tied. It's actually a wonder I can even explain what's wrong with the damn dog. This time, it was easy. He lapped up half a jar of glaze I left open, so just a simple stomach-pumping situation and overnight observation. When I found Clive, I—"

"Wait. Your dog is named Clive? "

She shrugged. "Cody named him, and I cannot even begin to imagine how or why he picked the name. Anyway, when I found him, Clive, I mean, his nose was halfway into the jar and red glaze was *everywhere*. I was so panicked, I just scooped him up and rushed him over. I was dressed, of course, for working, in my usual baggy jeans and spattered oversized sweatshirt, with clay and red glaze and dog slobber all over my face. So today, I thought I'd show another side. That's all."

I nodded slowly. "Of course. Your evening-at-the-Ritz side?"

She closed her eyes and dropped her head to the table, her forehead making a dull thud against the Formica top. "I'm an idiot," she mumbled. She picked her head up. "I didn't use to be. I was, in a former life, practically a player."

I shook my head. "When you're a player, that's all it is. Playing. You don't care what the end result is. It's all about the game. Then when you realize the end result is *all* there is, everything changes. You can finally tell the wheat from the chaff."

"Farming? You're giving me *farming* metaphors?" She glared at me. "That's it?"

I sighed. "The hair and makeup are fine. Go home and change. There's nothing wrong with jeans if they fit like a glove.

You want to flaunt cleavage? That's fine too. Get a V-neck t-shirt."

She stuck her foot out from under the table. She was wearing shiny red stiletto heels. "So maybe change the shoes?"

I stared in wonder. "You can walk on those?"

She shrugged. "Not well." Katie arrived with the food.

"Sara here says I should change," Shelia told her.

Katie nodded. "Sara is a wise woman," she said, and whisked away.

We ate for a few minutes in silence, then I said, "I haven't seen Cody at the library."

She chewed and swallowed. "Thursday was the usual library day, but he wanted to take music lessons. Violin. Can you believe it? And the only day available for lessons was Thursday, so he's in a genuine panic because now he has to rearrange his whole week. He's a little, ah, anal retentive about stuff. OCD. Big time. Changes to routine are not welcome." She made a face. "It's really hard dealing with it all. And just when I want to shove him into the kiln, he says or does something to break my heart into a gazillion mushy little pieces."

She ate another forkful, then looked up. "And now for something completely different, I'm having a potluck dinner Saturday. Cody will be with his dad, so I get to play with other grown-ups. You can cook something and bring it over. And you can bring Jack. He's been to my place before, so he should be okay with coming with you. Tell him only eight people and he knows them all. Around six? They'll be a bunch of us. In the shop. We usually chat for about five minutes, eat and drink, and we're pretty much done by eight. We in the Hills aren't known for our late-night festivities. What do you think?"

My first thought was that I'd have to cook something, and my throat tightened, but this was an invitation from someone I was thinking of as a friend. I unclenched my jaw and nodded. "Sounds fun. Invite Dev."

She froze and stared at me. "What?" She croaked.

"Dr. Rajani. When you go over today, causally ask him if he has any plans for the weekend, and if he says no, invite him."

She still hadn't moved. Hadn't blinked.

"Think about it," I urged. "You won't have to entertain him. He'll be part of a crowd and you can kind of, I don't know, worm your way around him. You know?"

Her face softened. "That's kind of a good idea."

I grinned. "Yeah. I got a million of them."

She nodded slowly. "Okay. Thanks. And you'll be there?"

"Oh yes," I said. "With bells on."

Chapter Ten

❦

"Molly's last day is Friday," Rose told me. "We're planning on closing the library early and having a little send-off. All of us, the Library Board, a few regulars and maybe even the mayor. Have you met Sam Billings yet? He's a real character. You can make it?"

I nodded. "Of course. Is it a surprise?"

Rose cracked a smile. "In theory. But I'm sure Molly knows more about it than I do. We're asking all the staff to bring a covered dish."

I stared down at my hands. It was the second time that week someone had asked me to cook something. Shelia was having a potluck dinner. The library was having a small retirement party. Bringing a covered dish to either of those gatherings was not an unusual request. All I had to do was walk into my kitchen, take out a few ingredients, and cook something. It wasn't like I hadn't done that exact thing thousands of times before.

"Count me in," I said, proud of myself that the words didn't catch in my throat.

Rose's smile broadened. "Wonderful. I hope you bring something Italian with lots of cheese and sauce."

I nodded, a smile fixed on my face. "No problem."

"Good. Thanks," she said, and walked back to her office.

Italian? With lots of cheese? Lasagna, of course. Not what the restaurant had usually served, but the first lasagna I learned to cook, my grandmother's, with homemade noodles rolled thin with a narrow, marble rolling pin. The sauce cooked slowly with beef and pork that she ground herself, in slow turnings of an old-fashioned crank, seasoned with garlic and lots of oregano. Nonna made her own ricotta, and the mozzarella came from the small grocery down the street, small balls of it wrapped in plastic, still warm that she sliced then shredded with her hands. The old, large aluminum pan was wrapped tightly with foil, and then, in the last minutes, uncovered and sprinkled with freshly grated parmesan that turned golden and crisp in the hot oven.

I went to the grocery store that was located beyond Hills of Andrew, a large chain store that, at least, had a selection of cheeses that went beyond yellow and white American and Muenster. I would make the fresh pasta but bought ground beef and pork, canned San Marzano tomatoes, and splurged on two large, ceramic baking dishes.

I arranged the food on my counter. I'd make the sauce first. I'd brown the meat, then chop onions and garlic, then simmer everything slowly in my large, heavy pot...

I stared at the meat. I reached out and dropped in into the pot, hearing the sizzle as it hit the oil. I stirred and watched, then stirred some more. The kitchen slowly filled with memory: Nonna, bent and smiling in a housedress of faded blue and splotchy roses, my mother slapping away Dom's hand as he tried to snatch a piece of bread from the inch-thick board, my father sitting back in his favorite chair in the old apartment, a juice glass of red wine in his hand, listening to the Yankees game on a summer afternoon.

I couldn't breathe. I turned off the heat and backed out of the kitchen. I practically ran through the dining room and opened the sliding glass doors, and I stood outside trying to stop the ugly, gulping sobs as I stared out at the cold blue of the bay.

Finally, I went back into the house and dumped the half-cooked meat into the garbage, left the dirty pot in the sink and crawled into bed.

The next day after work, I drove almost an hour to the nearest Costco. My membership had lapsed, so I paid for another year and went to the frozen food section, where I found the pre-made lasagna. I bought two, along with a jumbo-sized box of oatmeal, and enough toilet paper to last six months. When I got home, I opened one container of lasagna and pried the frozen block of pasta and cheese out of the aluminum foil tray in had come in and forced it into one of the ceramic dishes I'd bought the day before. When it was all cooked, I let it cool on the counter. It looked homemade. I covered it with foil and stuck it in the fridge. I'd reheat it tomorrow at the library and no one would even guess, and I'd do the same for Shelia's potluck.

Molly followed me downstairs when I arrived Friday morning.

"Whatcha got?" she asked.

"Lasagna."

"Really? You made it?"

I couldn't look at her. "It's from Costco."

She nodded. "They make it pretty good.'

"I hope so," I muttered

"Wait," she muttered, wrestling me aside as she reached into the fridge. "This is all my crap, anyway. Might as well just toss it." She handed me an assortment of plastic containers of various sizes and shapes. One container contained one shriveled carrot stick. Another, an unidentifiable block of something heavy and a rather wicked-looking green.

"For God's sake, don't open any of them," she said sharply. "You might release some sort of mutated spore and wipe out all humanity. Just throw them all in there." She pointed to the garbage can.

"Shouldn't you try to recycle these?" I asked.

"That would mean opening them. Mutated spores, remember? The end of the entire world?"

I threw them into the tall plastic garbage can. "I would have pegged you for one of those 'save the earth' types, Molly."

She straightened, holding two stained paper coffee containers and a bent straw. "Honey, I haven't used a paper plate or plastic fork in years, but the safety of mankind comes first. There. Plenty of room now."

And there was. I put my covered pan on the bottom shelf.

"Don't you know how to make it? Lasagna?" She asked. "Seems to me that would be something, well, you know, that you'd be able to make yourself."

I closed the refrigerator door and nodded, sudden and completely unexpected tears coming to my eyes. More than tears. A large, gulping sob escaped my lips, then another.

"Oh, Sara, honey," she said softly. "I'm so sorry. What did I say? Here, sit a minute. I never meant to upset you."

I sat on the couch and covered my eyes with my hands, fighting for control, shaking my head sharply. "It's not your fault. Really. It's so stupid. See, I haven't cooked anything in a while. Months. Since October. And my grandmother used to make lasagna. From scratch. Even the pasta. But just thinking about it, it just —" I took a few deep breaths.

"Tell me," Molly said quietly.

"I was going to make it myself. I really was. I had everything lined up on the counter, but then I remembered Nonna. I remembered following her around the kitchen when I was a kid. She lived across the hall from our apartment. Nonna had a tiny gas oven, and she believed in cooking low and slow. In the summer, her apartment became so hot that we would all be forced out of doors. She baked her lasagna every week, doing all the prep work on Saturday so she could sit and enjoy her time, after mass of course, with all of us. We'd sit together and talk and laugh and the whole building knew what she was cooking. The smells were always so wonderful. We'd eat this huge meal, and her kitchen was so small we'd practically be sitting on each other's laps." I stopped and drew a ragged breath. "I just couldn't."

Molly sighed next to me. "Memory is a tricky thing. All those moments of our lives just sitting there, quiet, never meaning much. Then something happens, usually something so small we don't even realize what's happening, but it's like a finger stirring a pile of ashes, all sorts of things start flying around." She looked into my face. "What happened in October?"

"My father died."

"Ah," she said. "I bet that broke your heart."

I nodded. "It did."

"What about your mom?" She asked gently.

"Mom died when I was fourteen," I said. "I hardly even think about that anymore."

She looked shocked. "Really? But that must have been devastating. Unless, of course, you didn't like your mother."

"I loved her," I said. I hadn't thought about her or her death in such a long time. "We had just become close," I explained. "We lived in a four-family house, surrounded by her mother and two of her sisters. She was always with them. But when we moved out of the city, she was alone. Lonely. She started spending all her time with me. That's when we started moving closer. She didn't love cooking, not like I did, but we cooked together every night. She never learned to drive, so she was home all the time."

I shifted on the lumpy couch. "Then she got sick. She was sick for two years, and it was terrible. She was in pain, especially at the end. All those rosaries said for her recovery. All those unanswered prayers." I shook my head. "That's when I stopped believing. In the God, the Church, everything. My dad, he never stopped going to mass, but I, well, I just stopped."

He never questioned me about it. Never insisted, although he took both boys. I would stay with mom as she lay in her bed when they went off to church. She'd hold my hand and whisper,

"I'm so sorry." I'd ask her what she was sorry for, and that was when she would cry.

"I'm leaving you, and I just now got to know you," she said. "All those wasted years we could have had, and I sat on the front stoop with my sisters. I should have been with you. And now you'll have to take care of them, your father and brothers. It's a burden. You're too young."

I looked at Molly. "She was right. I was too young. I don't blame my dad, he was grieving."

"So were you," Molly whispered.

"I cooked. It was all I could do. It gave me strength, to do for my family. Especially my father. It showed him I loved him. And now he's gone and I just can't anymore."

"I'm sure he knew that you loved him."

"I'm sure he did. But I didn't do it for him. I did it for myself. If I showed him how much I loved him, then he wouldn't leave too." I shook my head. "But he did."

There was silence, and I heard Molly sigh.

"Well," she said. "You don't have to tell anyone where this came from. It's nobody's business. This is my party anyway, and I'm just glad you're here. And I'm sorry you're still so sad."

"It's been months. You'd think I would try harder to get over this."

She sat back and snorted. "Why? Why try to rush anything? It's your own heart that has to heal itself, and you can't rush something like that. I just hope you don't start crying again. God knows, Rose will probably call 9-1-1. The woman is hopeless in any situation that calls for empathy."

I looked at her. "What are you going to do, Molly? Have you planned your road trip?"

She looked thoughtful. "Barely. First, I have to clean out my house. I've got decades' worth of shit all over the place. I will not leave that mess to come back to after I'm done with my gallivanting."

"You're not afraid?"

"Of traveling alone?" She laughed and shook her head. "I'm a little nervous about driving into places I've never been and maybe meeting up with someone terrible, but I happen to think there aren't nearly as many terrible people as Dateline would have you think." She smiled. "I'm an optimist."

I took a breath. "I'd better get up there. *We'd* better get up there. Can't have you slacking off just because it's your last day."

She leaned over and kissed me on the cheek. "I want to see more of you before I blow this pop stand. I think I like you, Sara. We could even be friends. I've really enjoyed this time together. You're a smart girl. And you don't take shit."

I smiled. "I'd like that too. I could use a friend or two, and I'm feeling like I can open up a little again."

She lifted an eyebrow. "Like with Jack?"

I rolled my eyes at her. "Maybe. Let's get back to work."

It was a quiet day. Late in the afternoon, as we began to turn off the computers and shelve the last few books left on tables and countertops, I went downstairs to heat the lasagna. When I came back to the main level, Bess Robinson came through the front doors on the arm of a younger man - younger than her, at least. He looked mid-fifties, African American with gray cropped hair in a well-cut suit, wearing a straw boater, something I'd only seen in pictures.

"Sara," Bess called, "this is my cousin, Sam Billings, who happens to be mayor of Hills of Andrew."

He swept off his hat and stuck out his hand, smiling.

I reached across the counter to shake. "Mr. Mayor, it's an honor."

His handshake was the perfect politician's grip, strong and assured. "Always a pleasure to meet a new resident. And how are you liking our little town?"

"Liking it just fine, sir. You're here for Molly's retirement? They're all downstairs."

He swept his arm out, letting Bess precede him around the counter, and there was another flurry of activity as seven older folks came through the door, all at the same time. Each of them nodded to me as they filed by.

"The library board," Jennie Lee whispered as they passed.

"Do they always arrive like that? In a group?" I asked.

She choked on a laugh. "Why, yes. Now that you mention it, they do. It's like they wait by the door until they're all accounted for, then make an entrance."

Rose came hurrying out of the office, glancing around. She stopped and took a deep breath. "Italian? With lots of cheese?"

"As requested," I told her.

Then she looked around. "Are they here? "

Jennie Lee nodded. "Just went downstairs."

"Is the mayor here?" Rose asked.

Jennie Lee nodded again. "Just went downstairs," she repeated.

Rose didn't look nervous, exactly, just a bit ruffled. "I don't suppose our guest of honor is anywhere?"

"Molly went down a few minutes ago," I said.

Rose went from looking ruffled to slightly panicked. "She's down there? With the board? Alone?" her voice rose a few decibels. "And the mayor?"

Jennie looked hard at Rose. "Calm down. Bess is *also* down there. Molly can't do too much damage if Bess is by her side."

Rose signed and hurried towards the stairway to the basement.

I looked at Jennie Lee. "What was all that?"

Jennie Lee smirked. "The board has lots to say about where library funding goes. Several years ago, there was a church group that wanted us to remove certain books from the shelves. The board agreed with them and threatened to withhold money if we didn't do as requested. Molly organized the pushback in record time. Sam Billings wasn't mayor back then, but he was a selectman who was on the side of the board, and he was the object of quite a bit of Molly's ire. She has never forgotten, and neither has he, and God knows the board remembers everything. They haven't tried anything since. Molly put the fear of our Lord into them. Luckily, Bess has a talent for calming the waters around here. She's not a board member but donates lots of money, and nobody wants to cross her. She and Sam are opposites, politically, but they are also family." She shrugged. "Small towns can get pretty complicated."

"I guess," I said, shaking my head. I had already recognized several regulars who had gone downstairs, most of them with covered dishes, and the scent of baking lasagna mingled with other scents: fried chicken, baking apples, smoky bacon.

"How many people?" I asked Jennie Lee.

Jennie Lee looked thoughtful. "Probably a lot, but not enough. Molly has been a fixture in this town for longer than I've been alive, and she's meant a lot to many people around here. If it were up to me, I'd have a heck of a lot more than covered dishes and sweet tea. I'd have champagne and caviar because she deserves it, if for no other reason than all she's had to put up with all these years. Hills of Andrew can be an unforgiving kind of a place, even to its chosen few." She looked around at the now empty library. "I think we're all good but make the closing announcement anyway. I'll lock the back door." She turned away and headed to the back of the library.

There were eleven employees of the Hills of Andrew Public Library: reference librarians, the children's librarians, those of us who worked the circulation desk, office staff, cleaning crew. Various volunteers who came for a few hours a day to shelve books or straighten the magazines and newspapers. They were all there to say goodbye to Molly.

The assortment of food was impressive. My lasagna wasn't the only thing that had cooked all afternoon, and the casseroles ranged from ridiculous to sublime.

Jennie Lee talked me through, standing slightly behind me, her soft voice in my ear.

"Now, that fried chicken is Belle's. Grab a bit while you can. These greens right there? Only if you like your salt straight off the lick. There are more marshmallows than sweet potatoes in that dish. Just sayin'. Now that pie? Take a slice now cause it'll be gone in a flash."

We had set up two long tables in the hallway with folding chairs, and everyone settled into eating. The mayor seemed to hold court at one table, the board members crowded around, alternately listening and laughing. Bess sat beside him, occasionally shaking her head but laughing along with the rest.

Molly sat beside me, after working her way down the table where most of the library folks had gathered.

"It was wonderful, that lasagna," she said, sighing. "Best I ever had."

"Thank you," I said, and narrowed my eyes. I'd tasted it of course, and my taste buds and my brain collaborated on hundreds of adjustments: the texture of the pasta, the sweetness of the sauce, the finest of the ground meat, the quality of the cheeses, "You're just saying that, aren't you?"

She gave me a little smile. "Maybe. Someday, I want to taste your own version, okay?"

I nodded. "Okay."

"Sara?" Bess Robinson was standing over me. "The mayor would like to meet you,"

I looked up at her. "Really?"

She shrugged. "I've told him a bit about you."

I pushed away from the table and walked over to where Sam Billings was sitting, his head thrown back as he laughed. He stood as I approached, wiped his fingertips with a paper napkin and grabbed my hand with both of his. "Sit down, Miss Castellano, please. I understand you're a chef?"

I nodded and sat in the chair that Bess had vacated. "It's Sara, please. Yes. But full disclosure, I didn't make the lasagna. My recipe is very time-consuming, and..." I trailed off. I'd never had to apologize for anything I'd ever put before someone on to eat before, and it felt strange.

He shrugged. "I understand. A restaurant is quite different from a library farewell party. But you had a restaurant? Because if you ever decide to open one here in the Hills, I can assure you there will be no problems getting permits. We could use a nice white linen eatery on Main Street. The cafe is only open in the evening on Fridays and Saturdays, you know, and that pizzeria..." He shook his head.

I smiled. "I really don't think I'm the right person for that. Perhaps you can find someone else. After all, there was so much good food here today. That fried chicken brought tears to my eyes. And the lemon pie was amazing."

A smallish white-haired lady who had come in with the board raised a hand, looking delighted. "That was my pie," she said.

"Well, it was brilliant. I was never much of a baker, but I know a perfect pie crust when I taste one," I told her.

"Sam here says you're from New Jersey?" another board member asked, a rather grim-faced man with a bad comb-over and very white teeth.

"Yes," I said.

"Is that where you had your restaurant?" the man continued.

"This is David Jost," Sam Billings said. "One of our distinguished members of the library board."

I nodded. "Pleased to meet you, Mr. Jost. Actually, my restaurant was in New York City."

His eyebrows shot up. "New York? Really?"

"Yes." I didn't like this man for some reason. Maybe it was the comb-over. Maybe it was his rather smug attitude. "For fifteen years."

The older lady leaned forward. "And you gave it up to move here?"

I shook my head. "Not exactly. It closed, there was a fire... there was a lot."

Sam made a sympathetic noise. "Now that is a shame. But as I said, we in town would sure appreciate a nice place to eat."

I felt my breath quicken. "I'm sorry, but I've retired from the restaurant business. Too much work and too much risk. I think the library job will suit me just fine."

He looked at me closely then, his eyes shrewd. "I see."

"Sam," I heard Bess call. "Are you giving my new tenant a hard time about something? I can recognize the signs from here."

A look of annoyance flickered across his face. "Not at all, Bess. Just offering a suggestion, that's all."

I glanced over and gave her a quick smile, then stiffened as David Jost snorted.

"Just as well," he said. "I doubt you'll be setting down any real roots here, anyway. Your sort of person rarely lasts too long here in the Hills."

An uncomfortable silence settled around the table.

"And what sort of person am I, exactly?" I asked slowly.

David Jost leaned back in his chair, smiling faintly. "Most of us have lived our whole lives here. We're used to the way things are done, and we like the way things are done. I've found that folks coming down here, especially from a big city, always figure they can 'fix' things." He shrugged and looked at me, still with that smile. "We don't need fixing."

I took a breath. "Well, Mr. Jost, I don't think you have to worry about me too much. I just want to work, grow a garden, and maybe make some friends."

He nodded slowly. "Well, that certainly is good to hear, isn't it, Sam?"

Sam Billings nodded, then leaned over and took my hand again. "Absolutely. Once again, Sara, welcome to the Hills of Andrew."

I pulled my hand away and stood up, smiling brightly at everyone, especially David Jost. "It was a genuine pleasure to meet you all."

"The pleasure was ours," the older lady said. "I think you'll be a welcome addition to our library as well. We will all miss Molly very much."

Sam chuckled. "We'll miss bits and pieces of Molly. Sometimes, she was, well..."

"So I've heard," I said, the smile still pasted on my face. "And I think I can safely say that she not only taught me all I need to know about working here, but we both feel strongly about the same things. I can only hope to carry on in a way that would make her proud."

David Jost stopped smiling.

I turned and went back to my seat, my mouth in a tight line until I saw Molly give me a quick thumbs up.

There were speeches. Of course there were. Every board member had a fond memory, but as I watched Molly's face, I could see that her memory was not quite as fond. She finally stood up, and with tears in her eyes, said goodbye.

"This library has been my family for years, and you never really leave your family, no matter how badly you might want to," she said. There was a ripple of laughter, and I felt her words go right to my core.

"The world is not going to get any easier," she continued. "In fact, I think things might get pretty grim. But as long as there is an open exchange of ideas, a freedom to be our true selves, and a chance to see and understand another person's point of view, I believe we'll be okay. This library has always allowed those things to happen, and I trust it will continue even if I'm no longer here to kick ass when needed." She looked pointedly at Sam Billings. "Right, Mr. Mayor?"

Sam nodded, looking very serious.

"You and I didn't always agree," she went on, speaking directly to him now. "But we both love this place and want to see it thrive. And you can't thrive if you keep going back." She cleared her throat. "And now I want to thank you all for making this part of my journey blessed. I only hope my next steps will be as joyful."

I looked around at the tears in so many people's eyes. Here was a woman who had made a difference in people's lives. How lucky she was to have made such an impact.

We cleaned up quickly. There wasn't much food left over, and soon the casserole dishes were emptied, washed, and set back out to be claimed by their owners. Molly stayed to help after the mayor and board left, and finally it was just she and I, Rose and Jennie Lee, stacking the folding chairs and putting them back into the storage closet.

"Why are you still here?" Rose asked. "Didn't you just retire? Why aren't you home getting ready to knit something?"

Molly laughed. "Oh yeah, like that's what I'll be doing. No, when I get home, I have to sort my life into piles. What to keep and what to give away, and who the hell wants to do that? I'd rather fold metal chairs any day."

"I'll help you," I told her.

She tilted her head. "That would be lovely. And that way, you can get first dibs on all my valuables."

"And what valuables would those be?" Jennie Lee asked with a smile. "I've been to your house, you know. Are all those Rembrandts stashed away in the attic?'

Molly made a face. "I have nice things. I may not know exactly where they are, but I'm pretty sure I'll dig 'em up in time."

Jack and I had already decided that since rain was predicted for the weekend, I'd forgo the beach walk, and that he'd pick me up to go to Shelia's at six. "I can come by tomorrow, unless that's too soon?"

She shook her head. "The sooner I start, the sooner my house will be emptier and I can drive off with a clear conscience. But I should probably do an initial run-through by myself. Besides, don't you and Jack do a morning thing? Seems to me—"

"Are you kidding?" I stared at her. "We go for a walk on the beach with his dog. Does the whole town know?"

Rose looked sheepish. "There's not a lot to talk about around here," she admitted. "You won't believe the grilling I got from my church group when I hired you. Not a lot of strangers come to the Hills."

"And the tongues really start wagging when it comes to Jack and Harry," Jennie Lee said. "They spent time every summer here when they were kids. The whole town watched them grow up. Their grandmother was quite the queen bee around here for years, living in that big house all alone after her husband died. She even ran for mayor back in, what, the early eighties?"

Molly nodded. "Yes, I remember. She was quite the character, Gwen Lockhart. She was on the board before I started working here, and she ruled with an iron fist. Donated lots of money but she had some very peculiar ideas. In her later years, she became something of a hermit. She'd show up to church and sometimes at town council meetings to speak against one thing or another, but otherwise she'd just sit up on her little balcony day after day, just staring out at the bay. So when she died and those two boys moved in, well, let's say we all took a special interest. Still do."

"They aren't boys," I said. "They're two grown men."

"And maybe," Rose said, "in another ten years or so, they will stop being Gwen Lockhart's grandbabies."

I looked from Molly to Rose to Jennie Lee and back to Molly. "Really?"

Molly shrugged. "Small town. I tried to warn you."

"So, everyone knows that Jack and I have walked his dog on the beach, and that's a big deal?" I asked.

"A very big deal. Those two are at the top of the list of eligible bachelors here in Hills of Andrew. Course, Jack's got a few problems, and God knows Harry does too, but still."

The chairs were all put away and Rose flipped off the lights. We walked upstairs.

"Who else is on the list?" I asked.

"Well, you met one tonight. David Jost. He divorced Kathy, what, three years ago?" Rose asked Molly.

Molly nodded. "Yep. And she wasted no time getting the hell out of here. Back to Pittsburg, I think. Our own mayor, Sam, recently divorced, and he is considered quite the catch. There's money in there, you know. Sam is a lawyer. Real estate."

"And there's the vet. Dr. Rajani. Now, there is an attractive man," Jennie Lee said.

"What about Dante?" I asked. "Isn't he on the list?"

Jennie Lee laughed. "Isn't he a bit young? Not that I'm against May December romances, but he's also..." She frowned.

"You might not be his type," Molly said, smirking. "None of us have decided if he even *has* a type. He's kind of, well, all over the board when it comes to his, ah, friendships."

"Hard to pin down?" I asked with a grin.

"You could say that. And then there's Charlie Birch," Rose said. "Anyone who's lived here more than a month knows he's not for the long haul, although I think Annie may have finally got him. She's due next month, and once that baby is born, I think poor Charlie is going to have more to deal with than he bargained for."

We gathered our things from the back office.

"Thank you for the offer of help, Sara." Molly said. "I'll let you know when I need you. I know how to find you."

We walked through the quiet library to the front doors. Molly turned to look back into the darkness.

"I loved working here," she said simply, and pushed open the door and went out into the night.

Chapter Eleven

I spent the rainy Saturday alone. I cleaned and rearranged the books on my shelves. I listened to the 80's music channel, streaming through the little Bluetooth speaker I had tucked in my china cabinet, and sang along. I re-read parts of *The Swiss Family Robinson*. I tried to brush the kittens, but they were too interested in playing with the brush than letting me do anything useful with it.

I called Carla. During our last phone call, she had told me she was still living with her friend, looking for an apartment, looking for a job. She answered on the second ring, her voice low and tired.

"Hey, Carla, how are things going? How's the job? I know money is tough."

She sighed. "Yes. Still just waiting tables, but the tips are pretty good. Jenny's family is being real nice about me staying here, but," Her voice trailed away. "Daddy still isn't speaking to me."

"You daddy is hard," I said softly. She must have been feeling angry, frustrated and alone. "If you need money, let me know."

She was silent for so long, I thought she had hung up. "I guess I'm okay for money. I'm putting everything in the bank, trying to save for my own place. I've got a few leads, some friends looking for a roommate." Her voice got stronger, more confident. "Thanks, though. I know I can count on you. And Auntie Celeste has been great."

After we hung up, and I stared out my back sliding doors to the blue gray of the bay. She said she could count on me, but what could I do for her except tell her how much I loved her? How talented she was? How she should never give up? At her age, I had been on my way to Italy, taking the first step toward realizing my dream. How far away was her dream?

I shook off my feelings of sadness and guilt, and as the afternoon drew on, I forced the second frozen tray of lasagna into another ceramic baking dish and put it into the oven to bake, then showered and got ready for Jack to pick me up.

He arrived on time. He was good that way. My contribution to Shelia's potluck had just come out of the oven and was steaming hot, so I wrapped it in foil, then in a large bath towel to hold in the heat.

"Smells good," Jack said. "Is that something you made at La Cucina?"

I shook my head. "I tried to make this from scratch, but..." I told him about my disastrous attempt that ended with almost four pounds of partially cooked meat in the garbage.

"I can't cook anymore," I said, trying not to sound totally miserable about the very thought.

"That's not true," he said. "You said you cooked pasta, remember?"

I nodded. "Yes. But I couldn't eat. If I can't even eat my own food, how am I going to cook for anyone else? Because that was the whole point, cooking for the people around me. That was the joy, bringing something to the table that I had made just for them. And I can't do that anymore."

I carried the hot pan to his car and set it on the floor behind the passenger seat, then strapped myself in next to him. He didn't start the car.

"Why don't you try on a smaller scale?"

I looked at him. "What do you mean?"

He glanced at me, started the car, then backed out onto Bracken Road. "Cook something for me."

I stared out the windshield. The evening was closing in, but it was still light enough to see a break in the rain clouds off to the north. "I might be able to do that," I said slowly.

"Good," he said. "Next Friday night? You can try whatever you want. Plain pasta is fine, if that's all you can manage. Then we'll see where you go next."

I sat for a moment longer, thinking about Jack. I had thought about him quite a lot during the past week, and most of those thoughts left me with a cozy, almost happy feeling. And another feeling that I finally admitted to recognizing it for what it really was. I turned in the car seat and looked at him. "If I invite you over to dinner, and we have a good meal, and then we sit over espresso or wine, do you think you'll make a pass at me?"

He kept his eyes on the road. "I don't know. I'd be on your turf. Maybe you should be the one to make the pass at *me*?"

My jaw dropped open, then I burst out laughing. "Okay, Jack, you've got me there. I'll have to think about this. All of it."

He pulled into the long drive at Shelia's. There were a few cars already parked along the side of the drive, and all the lights in her shop were shining through the long windows.

He switched off the engine. "Here's the thing. Twenty years ago, we wouldn't be having this conversation because I already would have made my move. But I'm not thirty-five anymore. Or even forty-five and, well, let's just say I'm not quite the man I used to be." He squeezed his eyes closed. "That didn't come out exactly as I meant it to."

He turned in the seat to face me. "I have found, as I've grown older, that sex isn't the first thing I think about when I meet a woman like you."

"And what kind of woman am I, exactly?"

He looked at me for what seemed a long time before answering. "You're very different from the woman I usually want." His mouth twisted. "That came out wrong, too. Wow, I used to be so much better at this." He took a breath. "I have a type. Always have. Blondes. With long legs and lots of angles."

"Like Sandra?"

H grimaced. "Just like Sandra. But she comes with so much baggage." He frowned. "She's too much work. But if I were younger, she'd be exactly my type."

I spoke slowly. "I am none of those things."

"I know. But there's something about you." We held each other's gaze for another long minute. "What's your type?"

"Driven. Ambitious. Self-absorbed. I was always so wrapped up in my own career, I didn't want to have to put too much work into someone else's, so the more detached the man, the more attracted I was. Marco and I were together for almost ten years, but he travelled constantly. He had to for his job. We probably spent at least one week every month with him in another city. Or country. And during the weeks together, I was working six out of seven days. I told myself it made the time together that much more important." I stopped and ran ten years of my life with Marco through my head: sport-related galas, food-centric parties and festivals, all glitter and excitement and breathless anticipation of time finally alone. "But the truth was, we could have spent all the time we wanted together if we chose to. But neither of us did."

"You were married," he said. "What was he like?"

I sighed. "He was a genuinely nice and caring man who lived his life around me and my career. I worked in three different restaurants while we were married, and then I bought my own. When he finally had enough, I didn't even notice that he had pulled away. And when he was gone, I was relieved because I didn't have to choose between what I wanted and what he wanted."

"You wanted to cook," he said.

"Not just cook. There is so much more to having your own restaurant than that, but yes. Basically."

"And you can't do that anymore?" His voice was very quiet.

I shook my head. "No. Not lately, anyway." I tilted my head at him. "So, what do you think about now? Instead of sex?"

"A connection. Looking deeper. Peeling the layers."

"That sounds like work."

"It hasn't been work so far."

We stared at each other in the darkness until I finally smiled. "Well, then please. Continue to peel away."

Shelia's shop was ablaze with light, and as we approached, a burst of laughter came from inside. Jack stopped on the gravel path.

I had walked on a few steps before I realized he'd stopped. I turned. "You okay?"

He nodded, then ran his hands over his face. "I just need a minute."

I took a step back to him. "Shelia said to tell you only eight people, and you know them all."

"She did? Good. That's good."

"Listen, if this is too much for you," I began.

He shook his head. "No. I'm fine." He took off his glasses and rubbed his eyes. "I know that once I get inside, I'll be fine. But sometimes, taking that first step is tough."

I shifted the hot pan in my hands. "Why don't I just go in and put this down, and then I'll come back—"

"What? Oh, the pan. I'm sorry." He took the pan from me. "It's hot."

"Yes, it is."

Inside, her shop was warm and bright. Down the middle of the vast space was a long table, with mismatched chairs on both sides. It was set with white dishes and dark green linen napkins, an assortment of clear crystal glasses, and a line of simple white votive candles running down the center.

The door had been left ajar, and we pushed our way in. She scurried over and gave us both a quick peck on the cheek. "I'm so glad you're both here. This smells amazing. Did you make this yourself?"

"No," I answered. "I'm not quite there yet."

She nodded as she took the still-hot pan. "But you came, so you've come at least this far. Jack, it's good to see you. Is that wine? Oh, wonderful. You can introduce Sara around. You know everyone. I need to put this someplace warm."

There were the promised eight people in the room including Jack and me. I recognized Dante Robinson, Dr. Rajani, and Katie from the cafe.

Jack took my elbow. "Come on. These are all pretty good folk."

I looked around. "Isn't everyone in the Hills pretty good folk?" I asked, half joking.

He shook his head. "No. Your library board? I hear you met them yesterday. Some of them pretty much suck."

I looked at him, startled, but he was leading me to the noise and light. Soon I had a glass of wine in my hand, and Katie introduced me to her husband, Owen, a slight, balding man about my age whose eyes sharpened when he heard my name.

"The chef?" he asked.

I shook my head. "Yes, but I don't do much cooking anymore. In fact, I couldn't even manage to put together tonight's offering."

He looked at me steadily. "Sam Billings is all excited about a new restaurant in town."

I took a breath. "Yes. He mentioned that to me just yesterday. I assured him I was not interested. My job at the library suits me just fine."

The lines in his face relaxed. "It's hard."

I nodded. "Very hard."

"And you were in New York?"

I nodded again.

"That must have been a killer pace."

I smiled. "Yes, it was. Which is why I'm perfectly happy to just cook for myself these days," I lied, because I really hadn't even been doing that.

Katie elbowed her husband. "Told you not to worry until there was something to worry about." She grinned at me. "He's a Gemini," she said, as though that explained everything.

Dev Rajani saw me and smiled. He hurried over. "How are your new kittens? Have they adjusted?"

I nodded. "Oh yes. They are right at home."

"That is good. And how have *you* adjusted?" he asked, his eyes twinkling.

"Actually, very well. They are much more than I imagined, and in a good way."

He turned his eye to Jack. "Excuse me if I presume, but how is Rags? And has he met the kittens yet?"

Jack rolled his eyes. "Presume away, Dev. Rags is Rags, and yes, he's met the kittens. And they got along about as well as you can imagine."

Dev threw back his head and laughed. "Poor Radagast. He does not like anything smaller or quicker than himself. I think he has self-esteem issues."

Jack nodded. "I suppose that's one way of putting it. So, did you bring something for the potluck?"

Dev Rajani nodded. "Yes. Biryani. I rarely cook, because it is always just me at the table, but I enjoy preparing food for others. I made my mother's recipe. It is good to be reminded of home. Did you?"

Jack shook his head. "Nope. Just wine. I'm riding on the coattails of Sara here."

I braced myself for another 'And did you cook this yourself?' question, but Dev just sighed. "I would love to have someone I could ride on the coattails of. You are a lucky man, Jack. You and I both know the bachelor life is not as much fun as it's cracked up to be."

Jack laughed. "Dev, you're at least ten years younger than I am. Don't be so hard on yourself and lump us together."

Dev's eyes suddenly shifted away from us, and I turned slightly to see him watching Shelia as she came out of the back room. That's a good sign, I thought. Maybe my idea would turn out better than Shelia and I hoped.

"How long have you been in the Hills?" I asked.

His large, dark eyes came back to me. "Almost twenty years now. I was first a student, and I worked summers with Dr. Ashfield, who was very good to me. I began working in the kennel, then moved to the lab, where I helped the techs there. When I went to college, I worked every summer. He wrote my recommendation to Cornell for my veterinary degree. When I came back here, he hired me. Four years ago, I bought him out. He's retired now, in Florida, but he drives up every Christmas and he tells me what I'm doing wrong." He grinned. "He still has strong opinions."

Jack nodded. "Oh, yes. Ben Ashfield always thought of himself as the smartest person in the room."

"That's a great story, Dr. Rajani," I said. "I love stories like that."

"Thank you." His smile was brilliant. "But you must call me Dev. I feel strongly that, with two kittens, you and I will see much of each other."

"Fine," I said, and turned as Shelia announced dinner.

The food was set out in her checkout counter, hot dishes crowded on one side, the cold dishes at the end. There was quite the assortment, quite different from the decidedly southern leaning casseroles of the library party. Besides my lasagna and Dev's biryani, there was a thick lamb stew that smelled strongly of Mideastern spices: cumin, turmeric and cinnamon. There was a fragrant paella and baked beans I could tell had been slowly cooked for hours with salt pork and molasses. There was a long beef tenderloin, bright pink in the center, barely warm with a horseradish sauce that brought tears to my eyes as I sniffed the serving spoon.

I sat down next to Jack and stared at my plate. "Wow," I said softly.

Shelia, from the head of the table, laughed. "I know. I have great friends, don't I? I'm a terrible cook, but every month or so I eat like a king."

There was a murmur up and down the table as the conversation quieted and everyone ate. After a few bites, I lifted my hand. "Who cooked what?"

"Lamb stew," called Dante.

"We did the paella," Katie said. "Well, Owen did."

An older woman Jack had introduced as Margret waved her fork. "I did the beans. Soaked them all last night. They've been bubbling away since this morning."

I saluted her with my fork. "I can tell."

She tilted her head. "That's right. You're a cook, aren't you?"

"A chef," Jack corrected. "Ex-chef." He glanced at me, eyebrows raised as though to say, 'See? I pay attention.'

"I roasted the beef," Shelia said. "My mother told me I didn't need to be a good cook if I had five perfect recipes. Tenderloin and horseradish sauce are one of them."

"And it's perfect," Owen said.

"Yes, it is." Dev said. He was sitting halfway down the table from her. "Everything is quite delicious. Thank you so much for asking me here tonight. I hope my contribution is good enough to warrant another invitation."

Shelia turned bright pink. "Your contribution is marvelous." She stopped and gnawed her lip, and her cheeks grew a deeper red. "Really. You have a standing invitation. Come any time." She closed her eyes briefly, and I could only imagine her inner dialog: Too much? Too gushy? Would he misunderstand? Did she want him to misunderstand? The emotions flickering over her face would have been comical if I didn't understand exactly how tortured she must have felt.

Katie must have too. "Dev, maybe you can teach Owen a few tricks. The cafe hasn't changed the menu in months. What do you think, babe? Can we switch things up?"

Owen looked at his wife as though she suggested he grow another head, but it did the trick.

Dev turned to Owen, his eyes alight. "I would love to teach you a few recipes. I know the cafe is only open a few nights a week, but we can do an international night. What do you think? After all, our mayor is constantly trying to get another restaurant in town. This may satisfy him enough to get him to worry about something else, like our outdated record keeping at the town hall." He looked at me. "Do you know that the tax records have never been digitalized? That some little old lady sits in an office all day with a calculator and types out our property tax bills? And keep records in a large bound ledger?"

I shook my head. "Sounds very Dickensian."

He slapped his palm on the tabletop. "Exactly. She doesn't even have a laptop."

Margret spoke up from the other end of the table. "That's my sister in there, Dr. Rajani, and if you gave her a laptop, she wouldn't know what to do with it. Alice still has a landline, for God's sakes. She's a complete Luddite."

There was a ripple of laughter around the table, and Shelia's color was back to normal. The talk turned to the mayor, who, it seemed, was generally liked by everyone, mostly because there was no one else to compare him too, having been the mayor for the past twelve years.

"Term limits?" I suggested, and a rumble went up.

"This is why," Owen said with a rueful laugh, "folks here in town are wary of outsiders. All those new-fangled ideas. Laptops and term limits." He waggled a finger at me. "Don't say things like that too loudly."

There was general laughter, but I had a feeling he was not kidding nearly as much as I thought he was.

Dessert was a carrot cake and coffee, and, as Shelia promised, by eight everyone pushed away from the table and say goodbye. I was about to offer to help with clean-up when I noticed Dev piling a stack of dishes and leaning toward Shelia, asking her something that made her nod but also blush and gnaw her lip again. It looked like help was already being offered. I said goodnight, waited for Jack, who took a bit longer, and he drove me back to the house on Bracken Road.

"I was surprised to see Dev there," Jack said. "I didn't think he and Shelia were that good of friends."

"They aren't," I said. "But she has hopes."

I saw his eyebrows go up behind his glasses. "Really? Hmm." We pulled into the drive. "What are you doing tomorrow?" he asked.

"Planting my garden. It's time, I think. The plants have been sitting there for three weeks. If I wait any longer, they'll die in their little plastic pots. It's going to rain next week, so the timing is perfect."

"Ah." He sat, his fingers drumming on the steering wheel. "Do you need help?"

I looked at him, his profile relaxed and handsome in the dashboard's light. "No." I sounded too abrupt. "See, my dad and I planted his garden last year. It was one of the last really physical things he was able to do. So, I think I'd like to do this alone."

He nodded. "Yes. Of course. Look, I'm sorry. I don't mean to crowd you. And I know it sounds like I'm trying to insinuate myself into everything you do. If it gets too much, just tell me. Like suggesting you cook for me. That was really pushy, and—"

"Jack," I said, laying my hand on his arm.

He stopped and turned to me, and I leaned forward and kissed him gently on the mouth. "If I thought you were being pushy, believe me, I'd tell you. I loved cooking for my friends. I always felt so grateful to share something of myself with them. And I'd love to cook for you. So, I'll see you on Friday. After six is good."

He nodded, his eyes bright. "Wonderful. I'll see you then."

I got out and went into the little house. It was still early, so I opened my laptop and watched old Remington Steele reruns on YouTube. Maybe I should get a television, I thought, because my eyes got so tired of watching the small screen. I thought about what I might cook for Jack, something simple but elegant. And I thought of the way his mouth felt against mine, cool and slightly roughened, and I kept thinking about that for a long time.

Chapter Twelve

Monday night after work, I went to Molly's house. She called at the library, asked if my offer to help still held, then suggested I come for dinner.

"You'll need sustenance to tackle my living room," she said. "I have stuff."

Her house was within walking distance of the library on a quiet street that was lined with leafing trees and small homes that all looked to be built possibly in the forties: small bungalows with wide porches and detached garages behind tidy, fenced yards. Her house was bright yellow with white shutters and an emerald green door. When she opened it, I walked into a tiny foyer, the staircase in front of me, and off to the left, behind a graceful arched opening.

"Oh," I said, and stared.

Bookshelves took up every vertical space that was not a window. There were also piles of books under the windows, and beside overstuffed chairs and on the top of tables. In front of all the books on all the shelves were things: ceramic kittens, small, framed photos, flowerpots with dangling vines, chess pieces of all colors and made of different materials, what looked to be tiny trophies and candlesticks with half-burned tapers.

"I know," Molly said. "Don't look too hard. Come this way."

Opposite the living room was a small dining room with a breakfront packed with china plates and more books, but the cherry table was bare and gleaming, laid for two, and the walls here were hung with watercolor seascapes.

"Sit," Molly said. "I have a casserole. Would you like some wine? Brandy? A shot of whiskey perhaps?"

I sat. "Wine would be good," I said, and she vanished behind a white swinging door.

There was the slow tick of the clock that stood in one corner. The oak floors were bare and gleamed faintly, the china plain white with a gold band. I flipped over the plate. Lenox. I picked up a fork. Sterling. The wine glass was a pattern of Waterford crystal I recognized but could not name.

She came back through the door with a tray that she set on one end of the table.

"It's cassoulet," she explained as the steam rose from the squat ceramic pot. "It needs to sit for a few minutes. Here." She poured red wine into my glass, then hers, then sat down. "Thank you for coming. It's going to be harder than I thought to sift through all this crap."

I lifted my wineglass and sipped, then held the glass up. "Crap is stuff you get at the Dollar Store," I said. "Waterford is not crap."

She sighed. "I know. But who even wants this kind of thing anymore? Do you want wine glasses that cost eighty dollars each to replace? I have three nieces that I offered all of this to, and none were interested. They have dishes from Ikea and acrylic goblets that go into the dishwasher and never crack." She sat back. "Do you like plants?"

"Plants? Well, I spent all day yesterday putting in seedlings and sowing flower seed into the ground."

She shook her head. "No. Houseplants. Have you seen it in there? Tarzan could swing from some of those pothos plants. What am I going to do with them all?"

I thought. "Hills of Andrew doesn't have a garden club?"

She rolled her eyes. "Lord, yes. All those women talk about are orchids. Who the hell wants an orchid? I've killed off at least a dozen but give me a good Heartleaf Philodendron or ivy and I'm golden."

"You could donate them to the library?" I suggested.

"Rose would kill them. She'd hover over them and overwater and over prune and they'd die from too much attention," Molly said. "How's the wine?"

I took another sip. "Very nice."

"Yeah, I like it. It's from what's-his-name-The-Godfather."

"Coppola?"

"Yeah. That's it. He's good at wine too." She took a healthy swig. "What's going on with you and Jack?"

I shrugged. "I like him. I may like him a lot. I'm attracted to him. Very much so, and he's attracted to me, and I think we'll both be exploring that soon. But I think right now he wants more out of this relationship than I'm comfortable with."

"Why aren't you comfortable?"

"I'm just not ready to trust a man in my life. I'm barely comfortable with two kittens. It's still hard for me to look ahead and think about for the long-term. So many of my plans ended up in ashes. I'd just as soon stay untethered."

Molly looked at me steadily, then lifted her shoulders and sighed. She stood to spoon the cassoulet into my dish, then hers. The woman obviously knew how to cook, because the cassoulet was delicious: chicken falling off the bone, the sausage lightly spiced but full of garlic, the beans with just a hint of resistance as you first bit in, then melting away to a silky richness.

I tilted my head at her. "You southern women really know how to cook."

She grinned. "Yes, we do. And not just fried chicken and greens, although we're good at that too. My mother's family was French, and I learned how to bake a baguette before I learned how to bake biscuits. More wine?"

I nodded, and she poured.

"I just worry about Jack," she said, picking up a thread of conversation I'd almost forgotten. "Everyone worries about Harry, and God knows there are plenty of reasons, but Jack is a rare man. I simply adored his grandmother. Gwen had a special spark. Jack has it too, but it's quieter. You have to spend time with him to really see it. He's dated a bit, but no one really stuck, and I appreciate that in a man. The willingness to wait."

"Or is it the inability to commit?"

She shook her head. "No. I can see where you might think that. He's a man who knows what he likes. He's crap around strangers, and he's not happy about new things, or changes, but he knows how to wait for what he wants."

I shook my head. "I wouldn't hurt him."

She set down her fork. "Now, what makes you say a thing like that? You could very well hurt him. You wouldn't mean to, I'm sure. No one sets out to break someone's heart. Well," she rolled her eyes and made a face. "Not most folks, anyway. But things happen. You're walking along and suddenly, bam, life changes. You see something, you meet someone, you hear a thing and all at once, everything is different from the way it was just five minutes ago." She pointed her fork at me. "Whoever broke your heart, do you think he did it on purpose?"

I took a breath, then let it out slowly. "No. He just said he met the love of his life."

"See? Shit happens all the time, despite our best intentions. If he hadn't met this love of his life, you would be happy up there in New York, right?"

I fiddled with my fork. "Probably not." I stopped, because the words came out involuntarily. "I don't think we would have survived my dad's illness. Marco wasn't giving. He would have resented the time I spent away from him, and, well, I don't think we would have ended well."

"You look a little surprised, Sara."

"I am," I admitted. "I've spent so much time hating what he

did. I've never really thought about what we might have become had things been different."

"Well, crap." Molly suddenly muttered.

"What?"

"Forgot the damn bread." She stood and hurried back into the kitchen, returning with a basket of sliced bread, obviously homemade.

"Here. You need this to sop up all that goodness on the bottom of the bowl," she said.

She was right. All that goodness needed sopping up.

After dinner we went into her living room and she began to take apart one of the floor-to-ceiling bookshelves. She was unsentimental and very methodical. There were four large cardboard boxes stacked in the corner, each clearly marked.

"This here is a trophy I was given by my fourth-grade class in 1987. They were a lovely group of kids. See, 'World's Best Teacher'. That goes in the throw-it-out box. Can't imagine anyone in the world wanting it. Here are all my Agatha Christies. They go for the book sale. But not these. Nobody buys Danielle Steele books around here because everybody already owns them. All these pictures? Just take them out of the frames and we can donate the frames to the church, and I'll look through the photos later. Most of those folks are dead now, but I may want to remember some of them. This snake plant? Had it sixteen years. You want it? You can't kill it."

When I finally left, it was after ten o'clock. I had a plastic bin holding eight plants, and a beautifully illustrated copy of Black Beauty. We had cleared out an entire bookcase. I was tired and worried about what the cats would think of all the plants, their vining leaves hanging down from the tops of my shelves and china cabinet. If they were at all interested, I didn't notice. I was too busy sleeping.

"I want you to know," Martha Bishop said, "That this book was fascinating. Thank you so much for recommending it." She slid *Helter Skelter* across the top of the counter, smiling.

"That was fast," I said.

"I couldn't put it down," she said. "Any other suggestions?"

I thought, then went to the computer and typed. "We don't have anything by Edna Buchanan," I told her. "I can get something from another library, and if you like her, there are quite a few books by her we can get."

Martha nodded, checked out another book by Ann Rule, and left.

Behind me, Jennie Lee snorted. "That woman needs no more suggestions, Sara. As it is, we all fear for her husband's life."

I smiled. It had been a quiet week. I'd gone again to Molly's and helped her with more bookshelves, attended to another yoga class, and stared at my newly planted garden through three days of light, steady rain. Now it was Friday, late afternoon, and Jack was coming to dinner. All I had to do was cook it.

I'd done my shopping the night before, so I went straight home, changed out of my skirt and sweater, put on jeans and a light t-shirt, and wrapped an apron around my waist. I listened to Frank Sinatra, my mother's favorite, as I laid out the ingredients, took a deep breath and began.

First the chicken. I cut each breast in half and pounded each piece between plastic wrap. I laid them in a pan, drizzled olive oil, smashed several cloves of garlic to sprinkle on top, then squeezed lemon juice over it all.

I wiped the counter clean, then scrubbed it dry. I measured flour right onto the counter, making a small bowl in the center of the mound with my hands. I broke the eggs in one at a time, stirring with my fingers as I added salt and olive oil, then another egg and more stirring, until it all came together in a smooth ball. I kneaded it until it felt ready, then cut it in small sections with the largest knife I had in the drawer. I scraped the counter clean of all the sticky bits of dough and re-floured it and rolled it out with the same worn, marble rolling pin Nonna had used, until the pasta was a thin, long stretch across the counter. I floured it again, rolled it up, then took the next piece until the counter was full of mounds of coiled pasta. I sat back and brushed the flour off my hands. I felt the need to reward myself for a job well done. I also wanted a bit more courage, so I poured myself a little bourbon and drank it down quickly.

Shoes had been sitting on the stool in the kitchen, watching every move with interest. "It has to be rolled thin," I explained to her, "because you don't boil fresh pasta for long. Three minutes, tops." I took a roll of pasta and with a long, thin knife, sliced through, making neat, even coils. Then I took the mass in my hands and tossed it into the air, and all the thin slices separated and fell onto the floured counter.

"That's how you do it," I said to Shoes. I reached for some more bourbon, realized it was maybe not such a good idea, and set the empty glass in the sink. I finished slicing the rest of the pasta, tossing it several times in the air to separate the pieces. Then I scooped it all up, shook off as much of the flour as I could, put it in a large bowl and cleaned the counter again.

"At La Cucina," I said as Socks snaked around my ankles, "I had Martin, whose only job was to make pasta. All day, every day. Different thicknesses, different shapes, whatever I needed for the menu. But I loved making it myself."

I turned back to the chicken, let the oil and lemon juice drain off the breasts, and dredged each piece in panko crumbs flavored with fresh parsley and finely grated Romano cheese. I put them on waxed paper on the counter and looked sternly at Shoes and Socks.

"You stay away," I warned them.

Socks twitched her nose.

I cleaned the broccoli rabe, tossed it with oil and smashed bits of garlic, spread it on a sheet pan and stuck it in the hot oven.

"I bet they can smell this meal on Main Street," I said to Shoes, then walked across the kitchen as the doorbell rang.

Jack had two bottles of wines in one hand and a bouquet of daisies in the other. "Let me guess," he said. "Something with garlic?"

I took the flowers. "How did you know? Please come in."

"I wasn't sure," he said, holding up the bottles, "so I brought red and white."

"White with dinner. And maybe the red after. We'll see."

"How is it going?" he asked, following me through the living and dining room.

I knew what he meant. "Well, a little bourbon helped. Can I pour you a bit? Or maybe wine would be better. But we'd better get to the kitchen. I don't trust the cats. They've never been tempted by real food before."

Sure enough, as I approached the kitchen, Shoes launched herself at the counter.

"Hey," I yelled, and she turned, literally in mid-air, and hit the floor, looking offended.

I didn't have a vase, but I pulled out a mason jar and arranged the daisies. It had been a very long time since someone had brought me flowers.

Jack surveyed the cluttered counter. "This looks complicated."

I shook my head and opened the white wine. "There's ice in the fridge if you need it. And no, it's not that complicated."

He took the glass I offered him and peered at the bowl of cut pasta. "You made your own?"

I nodded. "I figured if I could get past that, I'd be good. So, it looks like nothing will end up in the garbage tonight."

He nodded appreciatively and then perched on the stool and watched as I set the water to boil and heated oil in my cast iron pan.

"Tell me about this food," he said.

"Well, chicken cutlets are a thing. Or at least, they always were a thing in my house. The thinner and crispier the better. My grandmother always had a plate full of cutlets in her refrigerator. They went into sandwiches, on top of salads, made into chicken parmesan, everything. And pasta is pasta. This pasta is going into a recipe I learned from a seventy-three-year-old chef in Genoa. Very simple. Peasant food, he called it, because everyone had stale bread and garlic, and olives could literally be picked up off the ground. And the broccoli rabe is because my mother read something about how important B vitamins were, so we had something green with every meal." I poured myself some wine.

"So, I guess this means what, a breakthrough?" He was twirling the wineglass between his palms.

"If you do that," I told him. "You will actually make the wine warmer. White should be drunk slightly chilled, not heated through."

He made a face. "Sorry. Can I help? I saw the table was set, but maybe tossing something? Slicing something?"

"Yes, Thanks." There was a long loaf of bread I'd gotten at the grocery. I pulled it off the top of the fridge and laid it on the counter. "You can slice," I suggested, and pulled my bread knife from the drawer.

"Whoa," Jack said, sliding off the stool and coming closer. "That's some knife."

"Tools of the trade," I told him, and unfolded a linen towel into a small straw basket. "Slices in there, please."

I checked the oven, tossed the broccoli rabe, and closed the door. On schedule. I looked at the oil in the pan. There was a faint shimmer. I picked up a breaded cutlet from the wax paper and slid it in. A sizzle. I slid in another and checked the pasta water. Just simmering.

Jack had arranged the sliced bread in a pattern, a coil that began at the outer edge of the basket and ended dead center, with only one slice, an end, left over. I raised an eyebrow. "That looks like something an accountant would do," I said.

He looked at his creation and frowned. "Is it wrong?"

I shook my head and laughed. "No. Not at all."

He was standing close, the bread knife in one hand and a silly look on his face. The kitchen was warm and smelt of garlic and oil, bread and Romano cheese, and there was a crackling in the pan as the chicken browned. I leaned forward and kissed him, lightly, on the mouth. I just wanted to feel that again, to see if he felt like I had remembered, if his lips were really that soft.

He stepped in closer and his arms went around me in a sudden clench and the kiss became something very different - not questioning, but insistent. The knife clattered to the floor, and I sensed a cat jumping away, but I was too intent on the feel of his cotton shirt under my hands, the pressure of his mouth on mine, the coolness of his tongue as our mouths opened.

There was a sudden pop and hot oil shot from the pan onto my arm and I jerked away.

He stared at me, slightly out of breath. "Hot," he said.

I nodded. "Yes. I need to turn the chicken."

"Oh. You meant the oil?"

I nodded and tore my eyes from him, grabbed the tongs and turned the breasts over. "Yeah. That too."

He picked the knife off the floor and put it in the sink, took the basket of bread in both hands and went to the dining room. He came back in, picked up his wineglass and perched back up on the stool.

"Need," he cleared his throat. "Need help with anything else?"

I glanced at him and didn't even try to hide my smile. "Any more help like that and we'll burn down the kitchen."

He grinned. "Maybe after dessert," he said.

The clocks had been turned ahead the week before, so it was still light out when we were done eating. We had finished the white wine, and Jack opened the red.

"Should it breathe?" he asked.

I shrugged. "Probably. Would you like a tour of the garden while we wait?"

Outside was warm, and the air smelled like rain. We had gone out the back, around the small patio, and looked at the neat rows that took the whole of the side yard.

"How many are there of you again?" Jack asked.

"I wasn't sure of the risk factors," I said defensively. "You know, groundhogs, crows, rabbits, that sort of thing.

He walked along the side of the house and looked at where the bed extended through the front yard, almost to the road. "Zombie apocalypse?" he suggested. "And what's there? Nothing's planted. Is that where the magic beans are going?"

"No. I planted flowers there. Seeds. So that whole bit there will be zinnias, cosmos, celosia, daisies, all sorts of annuals. I love fresh flowers. We had them at every table in the restaurant all year long."

"I have rather a gray thumb myself," Jack said, squatting next to a row of tomatoes plants. "But even I recognize there are enough tomato plants here to feed a small island nation."

"I'll can them."

He straightened. "And do what with them?"

I opened my mouth, realized what I was about to say, then looked at him. "I'll cook with them."

He raised his eyebrows. "How about that? A week ago, you said these plants had been here for three weeks. So that means *four* weeks ago you knew you were going to be cooking again." He tapped his forefinger against his temple. "The subconscious is a powerful thing."

"Maybe." I looked at my plants. The steady rain had done its work, and they stood, bright green and leafy in the dimming light. "I wish I knew what my subconscious had to say about you."

He ran both of his hands through his hair, mussed it, then smoothed it back off his forehead.

"That day in the library, when I first saw you," he said, "you looked so tired. There was something in your eyes that seemed like you were on the very last stretch of road. It struck me so strongly. And there was something so attractive about that. No, that's the wrong word. Compelling. That's it. Compelling. Because you were doing your work and you looked up at me and even though I was having trouble putting together a coherent sentence, you were smiling and talking and I thought, I don't know what she's been through, but it's been awful, and she's still being nice. Still reaching out." He licked his lips. "I thought you were a woman I needed to know more about."

He stuck his hands in the front pockets of his khaki pants. The light had started to fade now, and I could barely see his face, but he held my eyes.

"And the more I find out about you, the more I want to know. I feel you're this bottomless well of strength and will and kindness. That's all I've been able to see so far but, God, Sara, I feel like I could spend years of my life finding out more. I know this is fast, but I'm not a kid anymore. Neither are you. We both know what's real when we see it. So let your subconscious think about tonight. How we shared a fabulous meal and an equally fabulous kiss and how I stood here ankle deep in tomato plants and bared my soul. And then let me know what you want to do. I'll be right up the street." He took a breath so deep his shoulders lifted, and his chest stretched out, and then he turned and walked quietly across my yard to the drive, out to the street, and disappeared up Bracken Road.

I went into the house and cleaned up. It felt comforting, the automatic motions of scraping the plates, stacking the cutlery in the dishwasher, rinsing out the wineglasses. I put the leftovers in glass bowls, covered with plastic film, and sat on my couch and texted Maribeth.

I just cooked dinner for a man

Shoes jumped up on the couch. I stuck my index finger under the fabric of my t-shirt and moved it across my stomach. She pounced, her tiny claws digging through the fabric. My phone made a noise. Maribeth was requesting FaceTime.

I opened the screen.

"What did you cook?" she asked.

I smiled. Although I hadn't mentioned a man in my life since Marco, she knew what was really important.

"Cutlets," I said. "And broccoli rabe. And pasta with garlic and olives."

She grinned. "Didn't you make that same meal for Leo and me once?"

I whooped with laughter. "How did you remember that?"

She waved a hand. "Sara, honey, I remember every meal you ever cooked for me. Who's the guy?"

"His name is Jack. He came into the library. He's also my neighbor. He invited me to the party,"

"Oh, right. So, I guess you made an impression?"

"I guess. He says he wants to spend the next years of his life finding out all about me."

She was silent. Then, "He really said that?"

I nodded. "Yep."

"That is, without a doubt," she said slowly, "the sexiest come-on I've ever heard in my life. "

I nodded. "Yeah."

"So did you immediately tear off his clothes and have crazy monkey sex?"

I shook my head. "No. Because he said he wanted me to think about what he said, and then he left."

She held up a finger, signaling me to wait. I watched as she got up, then watched her empty chair until she sat back down, martini in hand.

"He left?" she asked.

"Yes."

She took a gulp. "What are you going to do?"

"I haven't known him all that long," I said slowly.

"Yeah, but you're not twenty anymore. You're old enough to know what you want without having to overthink it to death."

"That's kind of what he said."

"So?"

"I'm just finding my footing here. I'm trying to go slowly."

"There's slowly, and then there's stupid," she said wryly.

I sighed. "I hate this FaceTime crap," I muttered.

"Then can we come down and visit you?" Maribeth asked. "Leo and me? His calendar is filling up and if we're going to have any time for ourselves, it has to be soon. Would you mind? Or we would interfere in your 'taking it slowly' life plan? Tell me the truth. You know I wouldn't take it personally."

"I just started my job, so I can't really take days off, but if you want to come, I'd love to see you both," I gushed. I didn't even think. I missed Maribeth so badly it sometimes hurt, and she and Leo were delightful company. "Of course, now I have to buy another bed."

"If you like," Maribeth offered, "I can have something sent down. Leo just signed with a mattress company. Well, mattresses, among other things. Every company is a huge conglomerate. I think they also manufacture pantyhose."

I laughed. "No, thanks. I think I can find something here. It's not quite the boondocks. There's a mall and everything."

"So where are you again, exactly? We need to Google places to go and things to see."

"Hills of Andrew. Virginia. On the Chesapeake Bay."

"Hills of Andrew. That is a fabulous name for town. Is it wonderful?"

I thought for a minute. "I think it is. I also think I'm still in the honeymoon phase, but so far, so good."

"We can be there in a week. Is that enough time to buy a bed?"

I laughed. "Yes. Oh, Maribeth, thank you for coming down. I really, I mean..." I could hear the emotion creep into my voice. She could too.

"You're on the way back, honey. Maybe not to who you used to be *exactly*, but that's not a bad thing. To do that, you're going to need just as much help to look behind you as you'll need looking forward. That's why if it's too soon, you just tell me."

I shook my head. "No, it's not too soon. And I want you to meet Jack."

"I can't wait," she said. "But do you really need my approval?"

"No. But you have the best BS meter I've ever seen."

She made a face. "Not really."

"Yes, really. You never liked Marco. Remember?"

"I liked him well enough. I just thought you deserved more. And I was right, because, in the end, he wasn't good enough."

"No," I said faintly. "He wasn't."

"Do you think this Jack person is?"

I nodded slowly. "Maybe. Yes. There's something about him that's...different. And special, I think."

"Well, when Leo and I get down there, we'll make him run the gauntlet."

I laughed. "Please don't scare him off. He's not what you would call a people person. Promise to be good."

She downed the rest of her drink. "Oh, honey. I'm always good. Let me talk to Leo and I'll get back to you in the next few days. You're sure about the bed?"

I nodded. "Yes. Oh, Maribeth, I'm so glad you're coming."

"I love you, honey, and I can't wait to see you."

"Me too."

I hung up and sat, took deep breaths and felt a mixture of happiness at the thought of seeing Maribeth again, and dread at what feelings her presence would coax back to the surface, feelings I was trying so hard to bury as deep as I could.

There were still bad nights when I couldn't sleep. There were still moments of such crushing grief that I sat on the couch, stared out the window, and struggled to just breathe. I was still so angry at my brothers for sitting back and watching me wrestle with Dad's illness and death, never offering help, and worse, never thanking me for taking on such a crushing burden. I mourned the loss of La Cucina. I mourned the loss of Marco, who I had loved so fiercely. And I mourned the loss of the joy I had felt for years in a kitchen, a few ingredients spread out before me and nothing to guide me but my memories and my heart.

But now there was Jack, and just knowing that seemed to bring a lightness.

Chapter Thirteen

I spent Saturday morning at work. The library was only open for half a day, so I drove over to Molly's after closing. When I called her that morning and asked if she needed help, she said yes.

"Do you have an extra bed?" I asked her when she opened the door.

"I got three. What size you are looking for?"

"Full size is good." I followed her down the hall. The living room looked much different than it had on my first visits, the shelves empty, boxes stacked waist high. The only furniture left was her couch, an ottoman, and her television, sitting on the floor, cable wires snaking across the room.

We went upstairs, and she pointed to a room at the end of the hall. The bed was simple, almost Craftsman-style, made from plain oak planks.

"The bed comes apart pretty easy," she said. "Mattress is brand new, too. Swear. I bought it six years ago, but nobody ever slept on it."

"It's perfect," I said.

"I can have Fred Nealy bring it over to you. He's been helping me a lot. He's got a truck, and he's been taking loads to

Brewster's. You expecting company?"

I nodded. "Friends from New York."

"Why, that's grand. Good for you." She looked at me shrewdly. "I hear you had company for dinner last night."

I almost choked. "Are you kidding? Does anything happen in this town without everyone knowing about it within twenty-four hours?"

She shook her head. "Nope. Not unless you're very sneaky. Other folks' business is the main form of entertainment around here. Haven't you figured that out yet?" She raised her eyebrows. "Did he spend the night?"

"What? You don't know? There seems to be a serious gap in your intelligence. You need to check your sources a little more carefully," I said.

She gave me a hard look. "A simple yes or no would be so much easier."

"Well, you're not getting one." I sighed. "Since we're here, want to work up here? "

"It's supposed to get hotter today, and this room only has the one window."

"I changed out of work clothes. Let's go."

We emptied an oak dresser of old magazines, two sets of faded bed linen, and four boxes worth of woolen sweaters.

"All of these were hand-knit by my Aunt Helen. She was a dear woman, but never did understand that I hated the feel of wool on my skin. She sent me one of these for Christmas every year for decades. I never wore them. You into wool?"

I shook my head. "No, thanks."

She chuckled. "Yeah, I don't blame you. They're also kinda ugly. But how about this dresser? Matches the bed."

"Sure."

There was a voice downstairs, calling Molly's name, that got louder as we heard feet on the stairs. Bess Robinson came into the room.

"I told you I'd help you today," she scolded. She looked quite different in faded but well-fitting jeans and a t-shirt adorned with bright pink flamingos.

Molly shrugged. "I'm not about to turn down extra help. And she's taking this bed and dresser off my hands."

Bess looked at me. "For the small bedroom?"

I nodded. "Company coming."

"How lovely," she said. "Okay. What's left?"

I listened to Bess and Molly chatter back and forth, town gossip, a few shared remembrances. It was obvious they had known each other for a very long time, and their friendship was not a casual one. We finally went downstairs to dinner, cold ham and potato salad, after which Bess looked into the living room and put her hands on her hips.

"What are you going to do when you come back? Live in an empty house?"

Molly stood beside her. "Well, by the time I get back here, I'm probably not going to want to be going upstairs to bed. My knees are already complaining. Lucky for me, I put in the downstairs bathroom. I'll maybe just make this the bedroom and forget all about upstairs."

I watched from the dining room as Bess shook her head. "What am I going to do while you're off traveling the world, Molly?"

Molly stepped back. "Good Lord, Bess, what do you do with me *these* days? Every time we get together, we just sit and complain about being old. You can find someone else to do that with."

Bess snorted. "You know what I mean. It's only a matter of time before they start talking about banning books again. Who's going to help me with that?"

Molly turned to look at me. "You up for a fight?"

Bess raised her eyebrows. "Sara might not be here. Isn't that right Sara?"

Molly frowned. "And why wouldn't you be here?

"She's the type that wants to just pack up and leave if she wants," Bess said wryly.

She remembered that? From all those weeks ago? "It's just that at this point in my life," I explained. "I'm not very comfortable being tied down to anything."

"What the hell does that mean? Don't want to be tied down to anything? Too late, little girl." Molly waggled her finger at me. "You've got friends now, and garden, I hear. That's roots. And Jack Lockhart has lost his head over you. Better take advantage of that man. There aren't too many like him left around in this world. He's reason enough to stick around."

By the time I drove home, it was growing dark. I looked at my garden again. Yes, there were definite shoots coming through the ground. And roots?

I looked up and down Bracken Road, straightened my shoulders, and walked to Jack's house.

He was sitting on his front porch, Rags at his feet. The dog's ears pricked in interest, but he didn't move. Neither did Jack. He watched as I walked through the gate.

"Hey," he said.

I stopped at the edge of the porch. "Hey yourself. So listen."

He leaned forward. "Would you like a seat?"

I shook my head. "No." I took a breath. "I really like you." I stopped.

"Go on," he said.

"Remember when we talked about how sex isn't the first thing you think about anymore?"

He nodded. "Sure do."

"Have you been thinking about it at all?"

"Oh yes. I certainly have."

"So maybe we could, you know, plan something. Make it sort of an event."

He looked thoughtful. "Are we talking about a live band?"

I snorted. "No. But I think we should go for a certain mood."

It was hard to read his expression, but I thought he was smiling. "Maybe some soft music instead?" he suggested.

I nodded. "That might help. And candles? A little cliched, but that's because it usually works."

"And wine. Just to, you know, loosen the old inhibitions. Or we might smoke something? Snort something? I don't think we've had the chemical dependance discussion yet."

I shook my head. "Pot puts me to sleep, and I learned early the downsides of speed and coke. Besides, I don't think my inhibitions are going to be much of a problem."

"Okay then. Your place or mine?"

"Mine." I stopped. "This is kind of a big deal for me."

"I figured. It's kind of a big deal for me, too."

I waited. "That's good to know," I said.

"Will I be staying the night?"

I thought. Did I want to stay tangled up in him all night, wrestling the covers, fighting for space between his body and the kittens? "I'm not sure."

He chuckled. "That's fair. When?" he asked.

"Tomorrow night?"

He shook his head. The light was fading now. "I have a meeting Monday morning in Newport News, and I have to leave at the crack of dawn. Monday night?"

"Okay. I'll cook again."

He shook his head. "No, it's my turn." He grinned. "I'll ask Harry for something special."

"Good. Well. I'll see you Monday night."

"Yes. You certainly will."

"Is this weird?" I asked.

"I think so. I've never actually scheduled first-time sex before. In the past, it was usually a little more spontaneous."

"Yeah. Me too. But it's okay, right?"

He nodded. "Fine. Seriously, I don't care. I'm still pretty much focused on a positive conclusion." He grinned.

"Good night, Jack."

"Good night, Sara."

I turned away and walked back home. Shoes and Socks raced around the living room, careening off the walls, obviously sleeping the day away while I'd been gone. I sat on the couch and watched them until the smile finally left my face and I could even think about getting some sleep.

"Why are you so happy?" Jennie Lee asked me.

"Why do you ask something like that?" I asked. "I'm usually happy at work. Unless Mitchell Cunningham is here."

She snorted. Mitchell Cunningham was a regular who came in a few times a week to sit and read *The New York Times* and complain that the newsprint stained his fingers and why hadn't we figured out a way to keep that from happening.

She shook her head. "No, this is not your usual happy. You getting some money or something?"

I shook my head.

"Another date with Jack?" she asked with a grin.

"Maybe. But if the answer *is* yes, is there anything I might do to keep the whole town from knowing every detail before the library opens tomorrow morning?"

She laughed and shook her head. "Sorry, no. But if you have any special plans, and you want to let me know ahead of time, so I can at least prevent any false rumors."

I shook my head. "No, but thanks."

"But you are seeing him?" she asked.

"Dinner," I said. And sex. Hopefully, really nice sex. No, *not* nice. Hot, hungry, can't-even-wait-until-all-the-clothes-are-off sex.

"You're blushing," she murmured. "Whatcha plan on eating?"

"He's bringing something," I told her, trying to keep my voice even. "He said he'd get Harry to cook."

She set the pile of books she was holding on the counter and folded her arms across the top of them, her eyes dreamy. "One time, we had this big old ice storm, and the power was out every-where, but we had generators, so we kept the library open so folks could warm up and charge their phones and such, and Harry said we deserved a treat. He cooked this pot of Jambalaya and brought it in here for all of us. It was without a doubt the best thing I'd ever eaten. That man is a magician."

"I know. I ate at his barbecue place the first week I was here."

Jennie Lee shook her head. "He goes on a wild bender every once in a while. Poor Jack usually waits a couple of weeks before trying to hunt him down and bring him home."

I leaned against the counter. "Where does he go? Harry?"

She shrugged. "Usually down Newport News. There's a lot of military down there, and I think Harry still keeps in touch with guys from his Navy days. Lucky for all of us, his people at the restaurant know how to keep things going. Andy has been with him back in that kitchen from the very beginning, and I think that Hattie and her daughter have been running the counter for about five years now. It kinda sucks for all involved, but Harry usually comes up with something new for the menu, which is always a good thing. I still remember when he baked that blue-berry cobbler. It was only for a month or so, when the berries were in season, but my, that was a good summer."

"Sounds wonderful."

"Did you bake? I know you were chef, but cooking chef things and baking are two different things, aren't they?"

I nodded. "Yes. Very different things. We had a pastry chef for all the desserts. Carmen. She was with me for years." I stopped. Last I heard, she and her husband had moved to upstate New York and opened a tea shop, complete with fresh-baked scones and fairy cakes, just like traditional teas in England.

"What?" Jennie Lee asked.

I shook my head and rearranged my face. I thought I was over feeling sad and guilty that I couldn't have been more supportive of my staff. They had been like a second family to me. But when the money ran out, they all scattered, trying to find another foothold in a post-La Cucina world.

That afternoon, Cody Birch came into the library. I hadn't seen him since that day in his mother's shop, but he came right up to me and said hello.

"Hi, Cody. It's good to see you here."

"Hi," he said in a breathless kind of voice. "Monday is going to be my new library day."

"That's great," I said. "I work every Monday, so if you need help with anything, just ask."

He nodded. "Thank you. So, did you ever get to see the fossils I was telling you about?"

I shook my head. "No. I hate to say it, but I forgot all about them, and I don't go downstairs very often."

"Well, I could show you them. Now. I'm going down to use the computer in the kids' section because they don't mind so much if I make noise. Do you want to come?"

I glanced over at Rose, who was staring at the computer screen, pretending not to hear every word being said. "I'll be back in a few minutes," I told her.

She smiled and nodded, and I followed Cody down the narrow back stairs to the lower level.

The children's librarians had made the downstairs a real haven for the kids who found their way there. There were brightly colored posters everywhere, a long table with a weekly craft the kids could take home, and a large story circle with bean bags and stuffed animals large enough to serve as chairs.

Along the back was the Discovery Wall, and it was there that Cody led me, past the display of schoolbooks and slates from the last century, past the models of snakes and grasshoppers, to the long glass cases at the end of the row. There, he explained in excited detail all about the arrowhead collection that had been found right there in Hills of Andrew, as well as the fossils that had been dug right out of the ground as they excavated the site where the library now sat.

"These are really cool, Cody. Thank you for showing them to me."

He was leaning over the cases, careful not to touch the glass. "What I really want is to see the dinosaur bones at the Smithsonian or in New York. Do you know that in the Museum of Natural History, there are whole rooms filled with dinosaur bones?"

I nodded. "Yes. I lived in New York. I've seen them. They are pretty amazing"

"That's what Dr. Dev said. He saw them too. He said we could all take a trip up there to see them. That would be really cool."

I looked down at him, curious. "You mean Dr. Rajani?"

He nodded. "Yeah. He was over again last night. I think Mom likes him."

"Do you?"

He shrugged. "He's pretty cool. I mean, we talk a lot about animals. He's really been good to Clive, cause Clive does some really stupid things sometimes."

"Cody, we all do some really stupid things." I reached down and gave him a quick squeeze on his shoulder. "Thank you for showing me all this. I probably never would have even noticed all this without you."

"Are you going to stay here?" He asked, looking up at me, his eyes wide. "My dad says you're going to get tired of Hills and you're going to find someplace better to live."

I stepped back. "I don't think your dad has the correct information," I said slowly. "I like it here just fine."

He nodded. "Me too. I think Hills of Andrew is about the best place in the whole world to live. But you lived in New York City, and I bet that was a pretty great place to live too."

I smiled. "Yes, it was. But things change, Cody. That's the one thing you can always count on. It may be the only thing you can count on. Things change in heartbeat." I ruffled his hair. "I have to get back to work. Thank you again."

I walked slowly up the steps, and for the first time that day, I wasn't thinking about Jack. I was thinking about Shelia and Dev Rajani, and how I should touch base with her to see how things were going. And I needed to find out about Charlie Birch and why he'd be telling his son I was leaving, and who else had he been telling?

Upstairs, Rose was still staring at the computer screen. "He's a really smart kid, Cody," she said.

I nodded. "Yes, I know. Do you know his dad?"

"Charlie? Everybody knows Charlie," she said. She took her eyes off the computer to look at me. "Why?"

I shrugged. "Just curious. I haven't met him yet."

She made a face. "That's because you're not twenty-something and dumb as a post. That's his usual style. If you were, believe me, you'd have met him."

"Yes, I've heard of his reputation."

Rose turned to face me. "Most things you'll hear in this town are a mixture of what's true and what people want you to think is true. In Charlie Birch's case, most of it is true. But be careful. You think Molly Packer is some great person who everyone loves, but even she has another side. Folks just don't talk about it is all."

"You mean about her being a lesbian?" I asked. Since Molly had been so forthright about telling me she'd been in love for years with a woman, I assumed it was not a state secret.

Rose shook her head. "Stuff like that doesn't matter to folks as much as you might think. All of us have an odd duck in the family." Her face got a suddenly sly and secretive look. "Maybe you'll never know all about her."

She turned back to the computer.

Before I could ask her anything else, the phone rang, I answered it, and there was a sudden flurry of activity, and then another, and by the time my shift was over, I realized I hadn't had a single thought about Jack in hours.

But all the way home was a whole other story.

It was a gorgeous evening, so I set my dishes on the small bistro table I had bought on Sunday for the back patio. I had also invested heavily in large white candles and a few ornate candle holders that I placed around the table and chairs. Then I went into the bedroom and placed a few more candles. I searched in my dresser until I found a small scarf and draped it over the lampshade. Too much? I sighed and put it back in the drawer. Next, I'd be regretting I didn't have black lingerie and fluffy, high-heeled slippers.

I glimpsed myself in the mirror. My hair was behaving. I hadn't changed from the dark blue jersey dress I'd worn at work because it clung just enough to my curves to give the illusion of an hourglass figure, although I reasoned that my appearance was secondary at this point. I know, at least, it was for me. He could show up wearing a torn t-shirt and baggy running shorts and it wouldn't matter — I'd just want to tear them off. I smiled at myself in the mirror. It felt good to want something — someone — again.

I scooped up Shoes and Socks from where they were curled up, sleeping at the foot of the bed. I tossed them to the floor in the hall and shut the door. The last thing I needed, on top of everything else I was feeling anxious about, were two playful kittens racing around on top of the bed in the middle of some serious whatever.

I'd left the door open, and as I walked back to the living room, I could see him coming down the drive, a red-and-white medium-sized cooler in one hand, and large, commercial style insulated food carrier in the other. I held the screen door open for him and as he came through, he stopped in front of me. Our faces were a few inches apart. I saw my face reflected in the lenses of his glasses and the smile in his eyes. There was the smell the scent of slow-roasted chicken and garlic and thyme.

"You smell delicious," I said. I could feel my smile grow as he nodded.

"Thanks. I slaved all day over a hot brother. He wanted to know if we were having sex before or after dinner, and when I said didn't know, he told me he was worried about the honor of the Lockhart name."

I grabbed the cooler out of his hand and led him into the kitchen. "We'll debate the success or failure issue later on tonight. Is that coq-au-vin?"

He put the carrier on the stovetop. "Yes. With a salad of spring greens with a simple dressing of oil and lemon, with a bit of balsamic. For dessert, a rustic apple tart."

"Dessert? He really thought about dessert?"

He looked at me in mock horror. "When I'm carefully planning a seduction, I consider every possibility. For all I know, it could be the sweet mingling of apple and flaky pastry that will open the floodgates of passion."

I snorted. "Planning a seduction? At this point, the only foreplay I need is a peck on the forehead."

He grinned and leaned over, giving me a quick kiss on my temple. He went to open the carrier, but I grabbed the front of his shirt with both of my hands and pulled him close and kissed him, hard, on the mouth, and he kissed me back.

My arms went around him, around his waist, pulling the thin cotton of his shirt with my fingers so I could feel the smooth coolness of his skin. His mouth never left mine as his hands pulled up the jersey of my dress, and my fingers fumbled with the zipper of his khakis. He pushed me against the kitchen counter, lifting me, his hands now under the dress and pulling away the thin nylon panty. I closed my eyes, dimly aware that the front door was still standing open, and that both the kittens were somewhere in the kitchen, tumbling from one corner to the next.

I could feel him, hard against the inside of my thigh, when he stopped. "I need a condom," he choked.

I shook my head. "No. It's okay," and I reached down to guide him inside of me, and I wrapped my legs around him, pulling him in closer, and leaned my forehead against his, locked his eyes, and we moved, slowly at first until I felt the heat begin, and I shifted a bit, and then again.

"Are you good?" he whispered. "What do you need?"

I leaned back and pushed myself against him until I came in a rush, and as I fell against him, he finished with a few quick thrusts and I realized he'd been waiting for me, and I wrapped my arms around his neck and buried my face in the hollow of his shoulder and waited for my breathing return to normal.

He stepped back, tucked in the front of his shirt, and buttoned his khakis. I slid off the counter, adjusted my panties, and smoothed the front of my dress.

We looked at each other for a long time, and we both began to smile.

"Not bad," he finally said.

"Yeah," I agreed. "I think you can tell your brother to stop worrying."

And then, we began to laugh.

Dinner was delicious.

We ate on the back patio as the evening darkened, drinking light white wine and laughing a great deal.

"I like the candles," he said.

"I feel like I wasted a lot of money," I said ruefully.

He shook his head. "Not at all. I'm touched that you went to the effort. It means a lot."

"I've even got some for the bedroom," I told him. "And four hundred thread count Egyptian cotton sheets."

"Wow," he said with a grin. "Four hundred? I feel very special."

We ate the apple tart in the living room, sitting on the couch, he at one end, I at the other, turned so we faced each other, legs intertwined.

"So where did your brother learn to cook?" I asked him. "In the Navy?"

Jack shook his head, took a bite of tart, chewed, then swallowed.

"He learned to bake in the Navy. He worked in the kitchens on ships for years. Later, he met some guy in rehab. A Creole? From New Orleans, anyway, and Phil, that was his name, took him under his wing. Harry worked with him for like eight years, then when I moved in here, he came up from Shreveport and opened his own place."

"How long have you lived here?"

"Ten years. But Harry and I both spent lots of time here when we were kids. Whole summers with Gra'mere. That's what we called her. Gwendolyn Lockhart was never anyone's Granny."

"You two are on the list of most desirable bachelors around here. I got quite an earful from the ladies at the library."

He laughed. "I bet you did. Our exploits have been the topic of many a dinner table conversation, I'm sure. Two rich, single men rattling around in a big old house with more rooms that we know what to do with." He waved his fork. "She's still there. Gra'mere. Harry and I, we can both feel her. Not to get all weird or anything, but there's a certain comfort we both feel in that house. Maybe it's just all the good memories, but I know I couldn't imagine living anywhere else."

Shoes had been sitting quietly along the back of the couch, right over Jack's shoulder, and now she stretched a paw down and snagged a bit of apple off his fork. Jack turned to stare at her.

"You little thief," he said, laughing.

"They don't get people food in their bowls, so they've taken to trying to swipe it off my fork. They're getting good."

"Rags has only tasted three things that were not made for

canine consumption: bacon, oranges and Fritos. All accidental ingestions, but the scent of bacon can send him into a frenzy. Oranges, not so much, but Fritos? He can hear the bag crinkle from three floors away."

I laughed. What an easy, lovely conversation. When was the last time I just sat and talked with a man like this? With my brothers, the undercurrents were treacherous: Dad's dying, the will, the family obligations, my obligations, real and imagined. It had been exhausting. And Marco and me. Had we ever just chatted? There was always something going on with the restaurant, with one of his clients, a sports scandal, a strike, something. Always drama. And arguments. Marco and I could argue about anything, and often did. With him, I always felt like I had to defend my work, my staff, my family. I was always on guard, and any slight or criticism would quickly dissolve into a war of words. After such arguments, we would make up by having sex; frantic, urgent sex that left us both physically satisfied, but I always felt that whatever caused the argument was left unresolved.

Jack nudged my hip with his foot. "What? You look a million miles away."

"I was. I was thinking about how easy this is. And how it's never been easy for me before."

"The truth is," he said, and I could almost see him choosing his words, "we have no reason for this *not* being easy. We really don't know each other that well. We've never disagreed over something we both feel strongly about. We seem to be on the same side politically, and that's huge, and we have broached none of the big topics."

"Like what?"

"Like, college basketball or the NBA?"

I stared. "You're a sports guy?"

He grinned. "See? I can tell by that tone, we're on the brink of something contentious."

I laughed. "I lived with Marco DePaolo for ten years."

He sat up and set his now empty plate on the coffee table.

"The sports agent Marco DePaolo? Who repped Vinny Conway and Lloyd Kenshaw and Delray Owens?"

I nodded. "Yep."

"So, I won't have to explain my obsession with spring training or the NFL draft picks?"

I shook my head. "Nope. Been there, done that."

He eyed me curiously. "Didn't he just get married?"

I nodded. My throat did not close up. There wasn't a prickling of tears behind my eyes. My breath did not quicken. "He married the girl he cheated on me with."

"Tennis player, right?"

I nodded and finished my apple tart.

"What was he like?" Jack asked. "I guess what I mean is, what were the two of you like?"

"We were a hot celebrity couple," I said. "In New York City, food and sports are very big deals. We fed off each other's energy. But we weren't very, how can I explain this? Deep? I mean, we were together for ten years, but I never met his youngest sister. He visited with me to my family for holidays and such." I smiled. "He really liked Carla. He knew her best, because she'd come and stay with me for overnights."

I felt a pang. My poor Carla. I needed to call her again to check in...

"But he was never *invested*," I continued. "And to be honest, I didn't care much about his family or his friends either. My friend Maribeth, when she met him, said she could see why I loved him, but she couldn't see what was holding us together. I did love him. Very much. But she was right. Maybe I loved the idea of him more than anything else, because there wasn't enough between us to keep him faithful. To make him stay."

He watched me steadily. There was something in his eyes. Not pity. Sadness.

I cleared my throat. "What was your meeting about this morning?"

He grinned. "Very graceful change of subject. I'm talking to a syndicate who owns a chain of theaters in the southern part of the state. They're thinking about transitioning to live venues. I may be interested in investing."

I raised an eyebrow. "Building an empire?"

He shrugged. "Maybe. If nothing else, it would make my father proud."

"And that's important?"

He shook his head. "No. But it would be nice, I guess. He's turning ninety. We don't get along," he said rather grimly. "He didn't get along with Gra'mere either."

I lay my head back and closed my eyes, listening to the sound of the wind outside the house. "I'd like you to stay over, but I'm fairly certain if you do, the whole of Hills of Andrew will talk about it over breakfast tomorrow."

He laughed, and I opened my eyes. He shook his head. "Your neighbor is a lovely lady. An actuary with a very large insurance company. She works from home mostly, so now she spends half her day looking out the window, hoping to catch sight of something interesting. I'm sure your arrival has been the most exciting thing that's happened to her in months, and I can guarantee that she's got one eye fixed on your front door right now. If I don't leave soon, yes, morning coffee will be very chatty here in the Hills."

"And you're okay with that?"

He shrugged. "I pay no attention. If someone finds my life so fascinating that they need to monitor my every move, that's on them. I work very hard at controlling the things I can, but some things are out of my reach. Those things I make myself let go. Or I'd be really crazy."

"Then you might as well stay."

He cocked his head. "You don't mind the gossip?"

I signed. "I'm a stranger from New Jersey, which may as well be New York, I guess, and I'm working in the library and I'm friends with Molly Packer, who I take it has a bit of a reputation around here. On top of all that, I'm in one of Dante Robinson's yoga classes. I'm already a hot topic, so what's a little more fuel on the fire?" I moved my foot and placed it, very delicately, on the V of his khakis. "Maybe snagging one of the town's most eligible bachelors will give my reputation a boost."

He grabbed my foot and pressed it harder against him. "Are we going to be spontaneous again? Isn't that a waste of all those candles?"

I grinned. "I'm sure we can find some use for them another time."

"Should I take off my glasses?"

"Probably."

And we began again.

Chapter Fourteen

W ednesday morning, I came out of yoga class and tried to ignore the fact that every single woman in class stared at me as though seeing me for the first time, although I'd been there every week for over a month. Dante flashed a grin and gave me a quick thumbs up. Apparently, I'd been right. Boning Jack Lockhart added to my street cred in a big way.

I heard the little jingle on my phone, announcing a text. I glanced down. It was Aunt Celeste telling me she was going to call me that evening, and what time would be best? I hoped it would be good news this time. I texted her back that now would be just fine.

It only took her a minute.

"Aunt Celeste? Hi, what's up?"

"Hi Sara," she said, her voice husky from fifty-odd years of Newport Lights. "It's about Carla."

My heart sank. I leaned against the car door and took a breath. "Now what?"

She sighed. "You knew your asshole brother kicked her out?"

"Yes. I've spoken to her. She sounded okay."

"Well, she's not. She's been living with me."

"With you?"

"Carla had camped out at various friends' houses, but that got old," she went on. "She's been trying to get a job and an apartment, but let's face it. It's northern New Jersey. You need to be making at least 70K a year to afford a decent one bedroom in any kind of safe neighborhood. Going out on her own was out of the question. What was I supposed to do, let her camp out on Bloomfield Avenue for the rest of her life?"

"What about the cousins?" I asked. I had over twenty cousins, all scattered across New Jersey. The sisters had been, after all, raised Catholic and had children regularly. As kids, we had been thick as thieves, but after my family had the audacity to move to the suburbs, I saw them less and less. We were not close. I had seen some of them at my father's funeral months before and was impressed mostly by the total lack of family connection.

"Oh, come on, Sara," my aunt said. "You know the only one who ever cared about Carla was you. Besides, Vincent still has the golden boy aura clinging to him. He was the oldest of the cousins, and they all worshipped him. They still do, and none of them will go against him."

"I was the oldest," I reminded her.

"Ah, yes. But you were only a girl," she said.

"True."

"She can't stay with me," Celeste continued. "She's too young to be a resident, and as a visitor, she has to move out after thirty days. I could try to bluff my way through, but there are rules here. She's only been here a week and they're already making noises. The Association can take action to evict me."

The silence between us lengthened.

"Sara?"

"Listen," I finally said. "I'm still getting used to living this new life. I'm finally comfortable with the job, and I've made some friends. I've even met a man." How could I explain to her how I felt? "Having Carla here would be a whole other thing, and I couldn't..." I couldn't what?

"You're the one person in this family she would want to live with. Where else can she go? She's homeless." Her voice was tired. "She can't stay here, Sara. Even if it *were* possible, I'm too old to do this again."

I closed my eyes. I knew what she had meant by that. She had stepped up for me when I was desperate to find a way out of a situation that would have crushed any of the dreams I had for myself. I never knew what it had cost her, all those whispered arguments with my father, the sudden appearance of money that opened so many doors.

I did not want to be responsible for anyone else. Which is why I chose a job I could leave behind me when I walked out the door. Why I rented a place I could leave at any time. It was enough that I had the kittens to care for, and I still sometimes panicked because I was afraid I'd forget to feed them.

I opened my eyes, staring across the water, but visualizing my niece. I was her godmother and standing up for her was the last time I'd been inside a Catholic church. She had been a tiny, dark-haired, red-faced ball of energy then, and she had changed little in twenty years. Now she was tall and beautiful, and desperately unhappy, homeless and practically alone.

Just as I had been just months ago.

"This is a lot, Aunt Celeste."

"I know. It's so much to ask. And I know what you've been through, Sara. But she's out of options."

I looked up and down the empty beach road. I had an entire attic, with dormered windows looking out over the bay. With some paint and a few pieces of furniture, it would be a perfect space for a young woman who needed lots of space for paper, easels, and paints.

"Yes," I said at last. This was my family, and as much as I had lost most of the connections of my past, I still had a future.

"I'll drive her to you," Aunt Celeste said. "Unless you're in

California, that is. I'd love to see you again. Besides, I went through the house and I found a few things your brothers had left behind. Things of your mothers. I'll bring them down for you."

"I said yes. You don't have to bribe me," I accused, and she laughed.

"I know." She stopped, then said quietly. "You won't regret this."

"I'll call her," I said. "I promise."

"Okay, Sara. It's the right thing to do. For the both of you."

She hung up.

As soon as I got home, I called Jack.

He was there in minutes. "You okay?" he asked.

I shut the door behind and reached for him, pulling him close. He stood there, his arms around me, not saying anything. Waiting.

"I have a niece," I said at last, stepping back.

He nodded. "Yes. She's an artist, right?"

I took his hand and led him into the dining room, and pointed at her sketch of Madam X, framed and sitting on a shelf. "She drew that."

He nodded. "I've seen that. I didn't know that was hers."

I let out a slow breath. "She's my heart, she really is. The daughter I never had. And my brother who, in case I hadn't mentioned before, is a stubborn, arrogant jerk who insists his talented daughter be a nurse instead of what she was obviously born to be. He threw her out of his house. She's been living with my aunt."

I'd been staring at the floor. He put his hands on my shoulders and gave them a shake.

"And?"

I lifted my eyes. "I guess she's going to move here."

He looked at me intently. "That's great. Where's the *but?*"

I smiled. "You always know when there's a *but*." I brushed his hands from my shoulders. "I don't know. I'm just now feeling good about things. The job, the house, you... I still feel like I need time to settle into all of this and I don't know how I can do it with a broken twenty-year-old hanging on me."

He turned me and pushed me gently to the living room and down on the couch. He sat next to me and took both hands.

"Why do you think she's broken?"

I thought. "I don't know, it's just the first thing comes to mind when I think about her. She's been in nursing school for two years, doing something that she has hated, not being able to do what she loves, having to live in a place where everyone around her is telling her she doesn't know her own mind. How can she not be broken, even just a little?"

He nodded. "Okay, if that's what it's been like for her, you're probably right. She might very well be broken. But if she comes here and lives with you, won't all that go away? Won't she be fixed?"

I let his words sink in. "Maybe." I closed my eyes and took a few long breaths. "It's just that I like not having any commitment to anything. Right now, everything feels good, but if something changes, I know I don't have to stay in a place that's making me unhappy. I can just pick up and leave and try again somewhere else. I don't *want* to be that way, but it's freeing to know I'm not tied to anything anymore. It's like I spent the whole of my life bound to a place or a person or a job, and now that I'm not, it's really powerful. With Carla here, I lose that, and I don't want to lose it. I like that feeling too much."

I opened my eyes and the darkness in his hit me like a blow to the throat. I realized suddenly what it must have sounded like to Jack, this lovely man who had just opened himself up to me and I had let him in, wholeheartedly. And now, just a few days later, to say something like that...

"I didn't mean you," I whispered. "I didn't."

"Oh?" His voice sounded odd, cold and very far away.

I stared down at our hands. His fingers had loosened around mine. "We're so new," I said. "I still haven't figured out where you fit into my life. It's like I found a shiny treasure that I don't know what to do with yet. I'm still carrying you around on the outside, trying to find a perfect place to fit you in."

I looked up again, and his eyes behind his glasses had softened. "If this is too much," he said, "if *I'm* too much, tell me now. Please. Because the longer we go on..."

I shook my head. "You're not. You're not too much at all. I'm sorry I said those things, because it really was not about you. In fact, I think you may be exactly what I need."

He brought both of my hands up to his lips. "I get it, I really do. But you planted all those tomatoes, remember? You're going to have literally hundreds of them out in your garden, waiting. Your subconscious was talking to you. It's all part of you working your way back to the person you used to be. Or at least, a version of that person."

I narrowed my eyes. "Have you been talking to Maribeth?"

He looked understandably confused. "What?"

I shook my head. "Nothing. It's just that a friend of mine said kind of the same thing. You'll meet her. She's coming for a visit and she can't wait to meet you."

He cocked his head. "You've been telling your friends about me?"

I nodded. "She says she's going to make you run the gauntlet."

"Ah." he frowned. "What does that mean, exactly?"

There was real concern on his face, and I reminded myself that for Jack, the idea that I wanted him to meet someone new was probably uncomfortable enough; to even joke about running a gauntlet probably ramped up his anxiety even more.

"She was just joking, Jack. It's a silly phrase. She just wants to meet you."

"And what about Carla?" he asked.

I thought. "Carla needs to go to classes, or maybe enroll in a fine arts program somewhere. She's so talented, but that's not enough. All artists need discipline. Talent isn't enough. You need to channel it, make it work for you."

"Like cooking?" he asked.

I smiled. "Yes. Anyone can follow a recipe. Anyone can create a recipe. But you need to hone your skills, cultivate your palate. And you have to be open to learning. It doesn't matter how good you are, there's always someone who can teach you something amazing."

"So, there's a plan?"

"I guess. I need Dante to paint the attic and get a bed up there. Maybe Maribeth and Leo can help. Leo is a decorator. I bet he'll have some good ideas." I looked down at our hands again. "Thank you."

"For what?"

"For coming over when I called. For listening to me say all the wrong things and not walking away. For accepting my stupid apology. For making me see beyond my own selfish needs."

"You're welcome."

I tilted my head at him. "So, maybe I could light a few candles?"

"Is that code for 'How about a tumble?'"

"Maybe?"

He grinned. "Light them suckers up."

The call to Carla was brief and tearful. Once she realized I was serious, she began to plan: what to bring, how to get her things out of her fathers' house, if she should even tell him what was happening.

"You have to tell him," I said. "He needs to know where you are, and that you're safe."

"He doesn't care," she mumbled.

"Of course he does," I shot back. "He may be an idiot, but he's still your father. And he's my brother. We're already as far apart as I ever imagined we'd be. I won't hide anything from him and make things any worse."

Despite my words, when Vinnie's number flashed on the phone the next day, I almost didn't answer. Let him leave a message, I thought. I really couldn't think of anything I wanted to say to him. All of our conversations since dad's death had ended in an argument. But—

"Hey, little brother, how are you?" He hated being called the little brother, and I realized it was probably the wrong way to start the conversation.

"Did you really tell Carla she could live with you down there?" He barked.

Oh, boy. I took a breath to steady myself. "I'm doing great. Thanks for asking. And you?"

"I do not want my daughter living with you. She belongs at home, and I do not appreciate your undermining my authority by enabling her disobedience."

"I'm not enabling anything, Vinnie. I'm offering my niece a roof over her head because apparently, you won't."

"No. Of course she can live under my roof. What has she been telling you?"

"That you threw her out because she dropped out of school. She never wanted nursing, and you knew that, and you forced her into doing something she didn't want to do, and when she couldn't take it anymore, instead of offering understanding and empathy, you kicked her to the curb. That's what she told me. Was she lying?" I kept my voice even, holding back the anger.

"It's not that simple."

"Yes, it is. She finally broke free and you're pissed as hell because you've lost control. If she wants to live with me, she can, and for as long as she likes."

There was a long string of expletives. Then I heard him take a deep breath. "You always did exactly as you pleased, Sara, with no thought to how it would affect anyone else. Why did you always think that was okay?"

I closed my eyes and counted slowly to five before speaking. "I guess for the same reason you always did exactly as you wanted, Vinnie, with no thought to how it would affect anyone else. I could never understand why you thought there were two sets of rules, one for you and one for everyone else."

"I'm talking about *my* family. You are interfering."

"You think that because you are my brother, I should do what you want, even if I disagree? Are you kidding? Because the only person in our family who had a right to tell me what to do was Daddy."

There was silence. "My daughter is creating a divide with her selfishness, and you are helping her. Are you really willing to do that?"

My mind went back to myself at seventeen when I stood up at the dinner table and told my father that I wanted to learn how to cook, because that was what I loved. I had been sick at the thought of even discussing the possibility with him, but when I received a letter saying I had gotten the scholarship I'd applied for, I knew there were no more excuses left to hide my plans.

"What do you mean, you got a scholarship?" My father had glared at me. The idea that I had gone ahead and done something without asking his permission was beyond his grasp. "You filled out all that paperwork by yourself and didn't even tell me?"

I lifted my head and gripped the edge of my chair with trembling fingers. "I was afraid you'd say no."

He threw down his napkin and shook his head. "Of course, I'd say no. Go to New York every day? Are you crazy? What about your brothers?"

"My brothers are old enough to take care of themselves."

He shook his head. "Vincent, yes. What about Dom?"

Dominick lifted his head. "I'm old enough. I don't need no one watching me."

"See?" I said. "He's just a year younger than I was when Mom — when I started babysitting. Or Vinnie can take care of him."

Vinnie snorted. "I can't. Football after school."

"There," my father said. "He is busy after school."

"Well, he can quit football. I had to come straight home. I wasn't allowed to join the Italian Club or the Cooking Club or the Ski Club or anything, so now he can give something up."

My father's eyes narrowed as the boys raised their voices in protest. "Your place is here, Sarafina. Your job is taking care of this family."

I felt tears swell behind my eyes. I stood so suddenly that my chair fell behind me, and the clatter caused a sudden silence. "That was Mom's job," I said, my voice cracking. "And I'm not her."

The silence stretched for what seemed like hours.

"You forget yourself," my father said quietly.

"No, Dad. I'm your *daughter*. Maybe you're the one who forgot."

He leaned forward, putting his elbows on the table, burying his face in his hands.

"That's a shitty thing to say," Vincent muttered.

I glared at him. "You forgot too. You and Dom both. Every time I asked you to help me, to set the table or take out the garbage or put away groceries, you know what you'd say? That was *Mom's* job. And then you'd walk away." I leaned across the table, my voice rising. "I wasn't Mom. *I was never Mom*. But all of you — "

"Sara, be quiet," my father interrupted.

"How am I going to start living my own life, Dad, if I'm stuck here trying to live Moms?"

We stared at each other across the dinner table, dishes empty of food, remains of pasta and salad in large white bowls, my mother's silverware scattered across the stained tablecloth.

"I want to get a job this summer. I already talked to Lucco's, the pizza place. I can wait tables there, earn enough money to pay for my bus and all my supplies. I'll be done with this program in three years, and by then Vinnie will be in college and I can get a full-time job in a restaurant, cooking. It's what I love,

Daddy." My voice broke. "Please. You know it's what I love. Please?"

He took a deep breath and looked at his sons. "I guess we're going to have to learn to do laundry," he said at last.

The room exploded in noise as the two boys began to argue. I bent and picked up my fallen chair, and sat down, smoothing the tablecloth with now-steady hands.

"Thank you," I said.

My father smiled. "And if you need help with the money, you just let me know."

Relief flooded through me, and I sat back.

Vincent glared, his breath coming in short, angry snorts. He looked at me as though he hated me.

But not Dominick. "You'll be good at that," Dom finally said. "Cooking, I mean."

He had been right.

And now, Carla was taking the same steps. And history, as it often does, was repeating itself. My brother Vincent once again refused to understand.

"She wants to do what she loves, Vinnie. Maybe you don't think she'll succeed. I know you're only thinking about her future, but this is *her* success or failure. This is her heart. Daddy let me follow my heart, remember? If you won't do that for your daughter, I will."

He was silent.

"Vinnie?"

"Don't make her hate me," he said quietly.

"Only you can do that."

He hung up.

Chapter Fifteen

✿

Maribeth called on me on my cellphone. "We're here. We found the key under your pot of parsley and your house is adorable. I take it we're getting the smaller bedroom?"

I laughed. "Yes, sorry, but I'm not giving up my room for anyone, not even you. I still have a few hours left of work. Can you find your way back to Main Street? There are some really cute shops and the food at the cafe is great if you guys are hungry."

Maribeth snorted. "Leo is always hungry, you know that. We'll walk around your little town and see if it's really worth that fabulous name. And we met your cats! Very energetic. Leo wants to know about your garden. Are you planning on opening up a produce stand?"

"It's a labor of love more than anything else," I explained.

"We can come to the library if you like, or would you prefer a more private reunion?"

"No, if you're in town, come and find me."

"Oh, my God! I just looked out of your back door. That view! Oh, Sara, honey, of course you love it here. Okay, Leo's making noises. We'll see you soon."

Jennie Lee looked over. "Your friends are here?"

I nodded. "Yes. They drove down part of the way yesterday. Leo is a real history buff. They hit a few Civil War battlegrounds.

"Well, there sure are lots of them here in Virginia. Gonna take them to the Hills Museum?"

I stared. "There's a Hills of Andrew Museum? Why did I not know that?"

She laughed. "Because it's only opened every other weekend for about five minutes, but it is interesting. Do you know Louisa Meredith? She's on the board, baked that amazing lemon pie at Molly's send-off? She's the docent there. You can call her, and she'll let you know when you can come."

"I'll do that. They're going into town, taking the tour, and then coming here."

Jennie Lee rolled her eyes. "Well then, they should be here in no time."

They came in just before closing. Maribeth strode through the front door, dressed all in white with a large straw hat on her head, and she looked around like a queen surveying her domain. Leo was behind her, slender and dark-hired, his pale skin slightly flushed, dark eyes wide.

Maribeth held her arms open. "I love this town," she announced. "It's just like in the movies. I want to meet the down-on-his-luck baker and the shy wallflower who rescues cats."

I flew from behind the counter and she rushed forward and swept me into a hug. I felt tears start, stupid tears because I was so happy to see her, and to feel the familiar strength — how many times had she been there for me, her arms around me, keeping me upright when I felt like I couldn't take another step?

"Now Sara," she whispered in my ear, "we're making a scene."

I pulled away from her, laughing now. "I don't care. I'm already the number one object of gossip in this town. What do I care if they have something else to talk about?"

I stepped around her to hug Leo and kiss him on both

cheeks. "It is so good to see you! Leo, are you at least trying to keep her under control? I bet she wants to buy the bookstore."

Leo flashed a smile. "Yes. And there's a vacant storefront she said would make an excellent ice cream parlor. If you're not careful, she'll turn your sleepy little town into a major tourist attraction."

Jennie Lee, from behind the counter, waved at me. "Go. I'll get Rose to help me close up. Honest, Sara, go with your friends."

I smiled thankfully at her. "This is Maribeth and Leo, from the wilds of Manhattan. Ladies and gentlemen, this is Jennie Lee, my coworker."

"Welcome to Hills of Andrew," Jennie Lee said.

Maribeth looked around. "This library is just as perfect as the rest of this town. Sara, you must love working here." She closed her eyes and inhaled deeply. "That smell is just heaven."

I turned her around and pushed her toward the front doors. "Go back to my house and wait for me. I'll follow in a few minutes." The two of them waved at Jennie Lee and left. I couldn't keep the smile off my face.

Jennie Lee laughed. "You are going to have a great time with those two," she said.

I nodded. "I know. And I can't wait."

I grabbed my purse from the back office, hurried out and drove the quick ten minutes home. They had let themselves in and were sitting on the back patio. Maribeth had found the cocktail shaker, and it sat on the dining room table.

"Cocktails before dinner?" she called from outside. "I have martinis ready to go."

I dropped my purse on the couch and walked out to the patio. Facing east, I didn't get to see any sunsets, although the few dawns I'd been awake for were spectacular. Even so, the view took away your breath, the pale water turning gold as the sun went down until the line between the sea and the sky blurred brilliant orange.

Maribeth was sprawled on one of the plastic deck chairs I'd bought for their visit. "Seriously, a drink, but we're starving. What are we having for dinner?"

I had planned so many things: pasta with roasted peppers and sun-dried tomatoes, chicken in white wine with gnocchi, pan-fried white fish with capers. But I was suddenly frozen on my feet. I stared out over the water.

"Maybe we could drive up for seafood," I said. "There's a great place right on the water. Jack took me there, and you'll love it."

Maribeth turned slowly, looked at me, and nodded. "Sure, Sara. That sounds just fine."

Leo opened his mouth to say something, saw Maribeth's expression, and snapped his mouth shut.

They'd been driving all day. The last thing either of them wanted to do was get back in a car to drive another half hour or so to eat, but the thought of going into the kitchen struck me numb. I felt angry with myself. I thought I had gotten over that feeling. I thought I had been making so much progress.

"Okay," I said. "Give me a minute, okay?"

I turned and raced back into the living room, hating myself. I couldn't even cook for my oldest friend. What kind of coward was I, anyway?

"Sara?" It was Jack's voice, coming from the front door. I walked over.

He was standing on the front stoop, holding two large paper bags by their handles. I could smell barbecue. Harry's barbecue.

He held out the bags. "I know it's your first night with Maribeth, and I thought you might not feel like cooking something."

I opened the door and took the food from him. "Oh, Jack, thank you. Thank you so much. Do you want to come in? I know Maribeth wants to meet you, and — "

He stepped back so quickly he almost tripped off the step. "No thanks. I don't feel like running any gauntlets tonight." He took a deep breath and forced a smile. "Harry sends his regards."

He backed away and hurried up the walk to the drive and then disappeared down Bracken Road.

I carried the bags to the dining room table and lifted out the foil-wrapped pan.

"What is that?" Maribeth called. "I smell something amazing."

"It is amazing," I told her.

She came in and peeked into one of the bags. "Who brought this?"

"Jack," I said.

"And he didn't even want to stay and eat with us?"

I took a breath. "Let's have that drink first, and I'll tell you all about it."

I called Celeste to tell her she and Carla could drive down in the next few weeks.

Maribeth had stared at me while I explained the situation, mouth tight, not saying a word until after I had poured out the whole story. Then she shook her head.

"Sara, I know you think she'll be too much. That she will cut a slice out of the life you're building here. That she'll force you to reassess how you want the rest of that life to look. But she is your family and you love her and she needs you. This is the right thing to do. Stop overthinking."

And she was right.

Dante painted the attic with all the leftover paint, creating a patchwork of green and white among the dormers and angles. Leo's eyes glinted when he looked at the room and forgot about Civil War markers and historic battlefields. In the course of their stay, he combed every antique shop, thrift store and second-hand furniture barn in a one-hundred-mile radius, bringing back an ornate iron bedstead, dozens of round mirrors he painted stark white, a long table for drawing, an overstuffed chair for dreaming. When he was done, the attic was just right for a young woman in need of her own space to rest, heal, and grow.

The second night they were there, I invited Jack over for drinks. He stood outside my front door, pale as a ghost. "I'm usually not such an idiot about this," he said. "It was just a terrible day, and I'm tired and stressed out. The idea of new people is just terrifying."

Maribeth and Leo were on the back patio, martini ingredients at the ready.

"You're not an idiot," I said gently. "I know how you feel. Sometimes I — "

"No. You don't know how I feel," he said, his voice tight. "I know they're good friends of yours, and I know they are probably going to be smart and funny and I'll probably end up loving them both, but at this moment in time the thought of meeting them makes me want to vomit."

I stared at him. I glanced over my shoulder at the two people waiting on the patio, closed the door quietly behind me and led Jack out to the drive.

"You are absolutely right. I don't know how you feel. I'm sorry I said that. And if you're not ready to meet them, you can wait."

"It's just that I'm stressed right now."

"Okay. Like I said, you can wait. They'll be here all week." I took his hands in mine and rubbed them gently. "You can wait."

He took a few long breaths. "Some days it's just hard."

"Okay."

He closed his eyes. "Just drinks?"

"Or not."

He opened his eyes and cracked a feeble smile. "Oh, no. There needs to be a drink."

He followed me through the house and out the back sliding door.

Maribeth looked up, shading her eyes against the setting sun.

"Hello there. I'm Maribeth and this is Leo. Pour something and have a seat."

"Can I pour for you?" he asked.

"Of course. How polite." She smiled.

Leo, on his first buying excursion, had brought back a wicker bar cart that was now parked on the patio. Jack busied himself with the ice bucket and cocktail shaker.

"My brother is much better at this than I am," he said. I heard the tension in his voice. "I mean, anyone can mix a drink, I guess, but some people have more flair. I just throw everything together and hope for the best."

"Well, whatever you do, don't add too much vermouth. That would be fatal." Maribeth said with a chuckle.

He froze and looked over at me. "Fatal?"

I walked over and took the shaker out of his hands. "Let me. You sit. You're my guest too, after all."

He stepped back, rubbing his palms against his thighs. "Thanks." He cleared his throat and looked at Maribeth and Leo. "And how are you liking us so far?"

Leo smiled. "The shopping is fabulous, and the view here is divine. Good company, good food and a cocktail at the end of the day is all I need to be happy."

Jack's shoulders relaxed. "That sounds like an excellent world view."

"We like it," Maribeth laughed. "Oh, thank you, Sara." She reached out and took the drink from my hand. I poured one for Leo, and then for Jack. He took his and downed it in one long gulp.

Maribeth raised an eyebrow. "Are we really that intimidating?"

He cleared his throat, set down the glass and took off his glasses. "No. It was a difficult day," he said stiffly. "I have a leading lady who seems to think her leading man is a hack. I had to go to rehearsal and deliver the equivalent of a strongly worded letter. She feigned outrage. I did not have to feign anything." He waved his glasses for emphasis. "I hate confrontation, especially with people I know I'm going to have to interact with for an extended period of time."

"You can't fire her?" Leo asked.

He rolled his eyes. "She's equity. She has to commit a felony before I can do that."

"What's the play?" Leo asked.

"*Guys and Dolls*," he answered, putting his glasses back on.

"I love that show," Maribeth exclaimed. His eyes brightened and his whole demeanor slowly changed. He pulled up a chair and sat, relaxed now, and he and Maribeth began talking about theater in general, *Guys and Dolls* in particular, and after almost an hour of non-stop conversation he suddenly looked around as though surprised at where he was.

"Is anyone hungry?" he asked. "Tonight is diner night. We can take a run out to Burgess."

"Diner night?" Leo asked. "There's an official diner night?"

He grinned. "Yes. When you're someone like me, there's an official diner night."

We rode out to Burgess to an old-school diner, complete with chrome stools at the counter and pink neon signs that flashed 'OPEN' and "Fresh Baked'.

The next day Jack gave them a tour of his theater and let them sit in on a rehearsal of *Guys and Dolls*. I was at work, so I only got a second-hand account of their day, but that evening Leo asked me if I knew what a treasure he was.

"Granted, he got off to a rocky start," he said. "But good men do exist." He grinned. "It looks like he's one of us."

"Everyone keeps telling me," I laughed. "The entire world thinks he's practically perfect."

Maribeth raised an eyebrow. "He's not perfect," she snapped. "There's bound to be a flaw somewhere. I mean, besides the social anxiety. Which, I have to admit, he handles pretty well. But I don't think he'll break your heart. In fact, he may be half-way in love with you. He's got a whole lot more invested in this than you do, and that's not a bad position to be in." She smiled rather slyly. "He didn't even ask too many questions about your, ah, past. And I could tell he was practically bursting with curiosity. He's a patient man."

"Yes. I know. This relationship is becoming something very different from what I'm used to."

The three of us were sitting in the living room, Maribeth and Leo sitting together on the couch.

Leo leaned forward, curious. "And is that a good thing or a bad thing?" He asked. "Because sometimes different is uncomfortable."

I shook my head. "I'm not uncomfortable. Not at all. But I'm a much different person who I used to be. I'm more cautious. So his patience *is* a good thing." I flashed a smile. "I remember how excited I was with Marco, how he swept me off my feet. We had sex, like, two hours after we met."

It had been at a fundraiser for a food bank, and we'd been seated next to each other by chance. The attraction was obvious and immediate. After an hour or so of verbal foreplay, I went and found an employee restroom, texted him the location, and we had sex standing up in a small, tiled room, fluorescent lights flickering, my back pressed hard against the porcelain sink. We saw each other every day after that, unless he was traveling, until I moved in with him six months later.

I blinked back the memory. "I was braver then, and more willing to take a risk. These days, everything is measured differently, especially my willingness to let anyone get too close."

Leo's eyes widened. "And how close, exactly, has he gotten?"

I actually blushed. "It's good," I told them. "Still new, but good."

Maribeth clapped her hands. "Well, bravo Sara. Welcome back"

One night, we cooked steaks on the new Weber charcoal grill I bought for the patio. I baked potatoes and Leo made a huge salad and a berry tart for dessert. We went up to Reedsville for a dinner of fish on the bay, Maribeth laughing at the gulls. Jack invited us all to dinner with Harry, who fed us fried chicken with biscuits, slow-cooked green beans with salt pork, and potato salad. We had bad pizza and beer at a place in the mall. And on their last night, I cooked chicken with lemon and mushrooms, finished with white wine, and served over homemade pasta.

Maribeth sighed as she pushed her empty dish away. "That was wonderful, Sara." She smiled. "Like the old days."

I shrugged. "Almost."

Leo shook his head. "No. Not almost. I ate this at La Cucina more than once. It's just the same."

"I can't believe you're leaving," I sighed.

Maribeth sipped her wine. "To be honest, that double bed in there is killing me or I'd be tempted to stay another week. Next time I offer to send down a mattress, say yes."

Leo laughed. "I can still make the call if you like."

I shook my head. "No. I think that bed is fine for the rest of the mortal world. I feel certain none of my future guests will have any complaints." I looked at both of them. Leo was lounging in his chair, a hand draped over the back of Maribeth's, his fingers gently playing with the ends of Maribeth's hair.

"I'm so glad the two of you are still so in love," I said.

Maribeth smiled. "Yeah. Me too. I think you're going to be good here, Sara."

I nodded. "There's a whole lot to living in a place like this that I will never get used to. And there are things about living in the south I can't understand. But I'm not afraid here. I think I can be happy here."

Maribeth raised her wineglass. "Then that is enough."

Dr. Rajani's office was set back off the highway, a long rambling ranch house with a graveled parking lot in front and a large side yard surrounded by a chain-link fence. As I pulled up, a pack of dogs on the inside of the fence barked. Inside their carriers, Shoes and Socks hissed madly.

The front office had a row of chairs that looked like they came out of a fast-food restaurant. Behind a counter and a sheet of Plexiglas from the COVID days, an older woman looked up from a computer.

"Yes?"

"Sara Castellano? With Shoes and Socks."

Her face lit up. "What great names! Yes, he'll be out in a minute. Have a seat."

I did, at the far end of the room, away from a youngish man with a golden retriever at the end of a red plaid leash sprawled on the floor. The dog lifted his head up long enough to look in my general direction, then went back to his blissful napping.

Dev came out a few minutes later, nodded his head at me, then dropped down on his knees and the golden lurched to his feet and crawled into Dev's arms.

Dev rubbed various doggy body parts while having a conversation with the owner. "He will be operated on this evening, and of course, he will stay overnight just to make sure there are no unusual reactions. Sometimes things happen, but I wouldn't worry. I'll call you after surgery, and tomorrow morning. He may have to stay an extra day, but I doubt it." He stood and took the red plaid leash, shook the owner's hand, and tugged gently on the leash. The huge dog followed easily.

"Please, come this way," he said to me. "Go into room two. I'll be there in a minute."

Room two had a stainless-steel table and a set of steel shelves with various medical-looking things organized behind glass doors. I put both carriers on the table and peeked in at the kittens. Neither of them was happy.

Dev came in and took my hand with both of his. "And are you still liking them?" he asked as he carefully pulled Shoes from the carrier. The kitten immediately stretched out but made no attempt to jump out of Dev's hands.

"They are much more than I imagined," I said honestly. "I was expecting two stuffed animals who ate and pooped, so every day has been a revelation."

He grinned as he put the kitten on the table and made a quick examination: eyes, teeth, ears, heartbeat, a few pokes in the belly, nodding all the while.

"Very good," he said, then called for someone named Lucas. A young man who looked barely twenty came through the door, took Shoes, and disappeared.

"And now..." He pulled out Socks, who was not as compliant The kitten hissed and tried to wriggle out of his hands, but he was patient, talking soothingly to the animal as he poked, prodded, and finally called for Lucas again. His assistant appeared, Shoes in hand, and they switched cats. Dev pushed Shoes into the carrier.

"They appear to be doing very well. You obviously are an excellent cat mom. Please keep them as house cats, as there are many cats running around with diseases and you do not want a sick cat. Believe me."

"I'm keeping them inside, but they can be pretty persistent. Every time the door opens, they appear from nowhere."

He laughed. "Yes, I'm sure. And are they getting along any better with Rags?" His eyes twinkled as he spoke.

"We've decided to just keep them apart," I told him. "It's easier that way."

Lucas reappeared with a furious Socks. Dev took the kitten from him, gave Socks a gentle shake and put him back into the carrier.

"By the way," he said, "thank you."

"For what?"

"I understand that it was your suggestion that I come for potluck?"

I tried to keep from grinning, but I wasn't succeeding. "How's that working out for you?"

He had a brilliant smile. "It's very interesting that you can know a person for many years and not know what to do or say to move in the direction you want to go. Sometimes all you need a little change of scenery and suddenly everything is different."

"Well, I'm glad I could be of assistance. To both of you."

He folded his arms across his chest. "How are you getting along here? It can be hard for a newcomer. Sometimes people are very reluctant to accept strangers."

"How was it for you?" I asked.

He shrugged. "I had Dr. Ashfield to run interference. I'm sure that not everyone here wanted a man of my background to take over as the local vet. People are very particular about their animals. But Ben was very firm with them, and he faced down all their silly arguments as to why they should go elsewhere. He kept his practice intact, even though many of his clients did not want to continue when I came on board. There were a few very hard years. Now, I am accepted by most of the people here, although there are still some people who will not walk on the same side of Main Street as me." He made a face. "There will always be people like that. I have learned they are not worth my energy."

"And then there are people like Shelia."

That smile reappeared. "Yes. Indeed. And how is it for you?"

"I have a few people to run interference as well. Molly Packer. And Jack."

He nodded. "Jack and I once tried to go golfing together. It was a ridiculous exercise in ineptitude. We ended up being friends, anyway." He leaned forward and dropped his voice. "Don't ever let him cook for you. Leave that to Harry."

I nodded. "Noted. Thanks."

When I had the cats stowed in the back of the car, I called Jack. "Just letting you know that Shoes and Socks are healthy and will probably outlive us both."

"Thank God," he laughed over the phone. "I was concerned."

"Dev Rajani warned me to never let you cook for me."

"He is a wise man. But I'm not too bad at grilling things. Was that a Weber I saw on your patio the other day?"

"Yes. The charcoal is right there if you want to start the coals. I'll stop and pick up something."

"Already did. Just burgers, but can you do hand cut fries?"

"Hey, what do you think I am? A chef? Of course. I'll be home soon."

He was waiting for me on the patio, and as the coals went from black to white-hot, I prepared the potatoes and sliced onions to grill alongside the meat, and he talked about his day: the rehearsal, the difficult leading lady, the mysterious footlight that refused to stay lit.

"These fries are trickier than you might think," I told him, so we went inside. I heated oil and cooked the potatoes, then raised the heat under the Dutch oven.

"Start the burgers," I told him. I stood alone in my kitchen, except for Shoes and Socks, who watched with interest as they did every time I stood at the stove.

"If you're waiting for something to drop, you're wasting your time," I told them. Shoes snaked around my ankles as I gently moved the potatoes around in the hot oil. "I know you're traumatized, but no people food."

When the fries were done, I pulled them out, put them in a basket lined with paper towels, and sprinkled salt.

"These burgers are perfect," Jack yelled from outside.

"So are these fries," I yelled back.

We ate on the patio, not talking now, just eating and gazing at the water. When we were done, Jack sat back and sighed.

"This good eating is going to do a lot of damage to the local economy," he said. "I am single-handedly responsible for keeping several area restaurants in the black." He stretched out his legs. "I need to walk Rags. Care to come along?"

"Absolutely." We cleaned up quickly and went back to Jack's house, where Rags greeted him as though he'd been gone for years. The walk up and down Bracken Road was quiet. There was not much traffic in the evening.

"Wait until June," Jack said. "We get lots of summer people. I don't know if you've explored down this way much, but there are all sorts of bungalows and three season houses. There's a little enclave, right by Dante's place, where forty or more families come down every year. Some of these little houses have been in passed down father to son since the twenties. The whole town changes. It's not a resort vibe, exactly, but the population increases enough to notice, and all the small businesses make enough to coast through the winter."

"I never thought of this place as a resort or vacation kind of place," I said. "Although with that gorgeous beach, I should have known."

"Harry and I came down every August, right before going back to school. We hated the idea of coming down because we'd been with our friends all summer, but once we got here, we were so happy. We went to the beach every day, played baseball in the evenings, ran around until late with all the locals. Gra'mere didn't want us mingling with the summer people. She was a bit of a snob, my grandmother. But the local kids all liked us well enough. Sam Billings and I used to get into all sorts of trouble."

"So, it wasn't such a big decision to move into her house?"

"No, it was. I had a whole life in Charlottesville. A house, friends, a career, my parents." He watched Rags as the dog burrowed into a small bush. "I guess I was ready for something else."

"Did you find it?"

He nodded. "Yes. Of course, buying the theater really turned my life around. It's a continual learning process. Not just the business side, that's the easy part. But there's a real challenge in the artistic side to it. That's what I love. Otherwise, I'd probably have set up an office in town and would still be doing taxes and monthly reports for local businesses. Not that that would have been a bad thing. In fact, it would have been much easier. All numbers and not so many people." He made a face. "The complete change of course made me stretch in ways I wouldn't have otherwise. It's still hard. Some days, it's almost impossible. But was the best thing that ever happened to me." He looked at me. "Until now."

My mind jumped to familiar words that were at the tip of my tongue: Don't. I can't be counted on. I might not stay. But as I stood there, I realized those things were not as true as they had been just a few weeks ago.

"Leo seems to think you're one of the good ones," I told him.

He grinned. "He and I got along pretty well. Maribeth was a harder sell. She's very protective of you"

I nodded. "Yes. Her feeling is that you have a flaw that will soon rise up and show itself. But then she feels that's true of just about everyone she meets, so don't take it too personally."

"I won't." We had turned around and were back in front of his house. "Harry is spending the night at a friend's. Poker night, and he doesn't drive when he knows he'll be drinking."

"Is that an invitation?"

"Absolutely."

I spent the night in Jack's king-sized bed, broad windows open to the Chesapeake Bay, the sound of the wind and the water and the reflection of the moon filling the room with soft light. At some point in the night, he got up and opened the door, and Radagast jumped into bed between us, his nose pressed against the back of my neck as I slept.

Chapter Sixteen

y Aunt Celeste still looked as beautiful and vital as
she had always appeared to me: her figure trim, hair
a careful mix of gray and ash blonde, cut short and
impeccably styled. But as she got out of the car, I saw something
I had never seen before, or, perhaps, never wanted to see. She
moved slowly, as though against a hard wind or through deep
water. Her movements were careful and deliberate as she got out
of the car and pushed the door shut. She raised a hand to me,
and I saw her smile, but as she lowered her arm, she winced.

I stepped out of the front doorway, ran across the small yard
and around the front of the car. I practically threw myself into
her arms. She smelled of Chanel #5. She always smelled of
Chanel #5, but there was something else that I recognized as the
faint whiff of some medication seeping up through her pores.

I was suddenly afraid I was squeezing her too tightly, and
stumbled back, but she held me.

"Oh, my darling girl, it is so good to see you," she whispered
into my ear, and then let me step away.

Her eyes were bright, the laugh lines deep and the paren-
theses around her smiling mouth pronounced. She wore much

less makeup now, but her lashes were long and dark, her mouth
bright red.

"You look good," she pronounced. "Much better than last
time I saw you, that's for sure. Your short hair suits you, as does
the gray." She leaned down to peer into the car. "Carla, come on
out, sweetie."

I watched as my niece climbed out of the passenger side of
the car. She was beautiful, with long dark hair pulled back off her
face, her large eyes shining.

She was staring at my front lawn, with the extra bit of garden
edging its way forward. "This looks like Grandpa's yard," she
said, and something pulled sharply at my throat.

"Yes. My landlady let me put in a garden," I told her as I
walked around the car toward her. She stood hesitantly in front
of me for a moment, then her face crumbled, and she stepped
into my arms.

"I didn't mean to plant quite so much." I said over the top of
her bent head, trying to keep my voice light. "You'll have to
help me."

She was sobbing quietly, and I looked over her head to Aunt
Celeste, who put her hands to her lips as her eyes filled with
tears.

After a moment, Celeste stepped to the back of the car and
opened the trunk, carefully taking out suitcases. Carla was still
in my arms, but her sobs had quieted, and she snuffled against
my shoulder.

"Thank you, Aunt Sara," she said, her voice muffled. "Thank
you so much. I didn't know what I was going to do, and..."

I pushed her away and looked into her tear-stained face. "It's
all good, Carla. You're here now. We'd better help Aunt Celeste
with the luggage," I suggested, and stepped back to look more
closely at the girl's face. "You're up on the second floor, all by
yourself. I hope you like it."

She smiled. "Well, I just left the most accommodating
senior living community in all of New Jersey. Trivia every

Thursday night. I doubt you can compete with that, but I'll try to adjust."

I laughed. "This small-town living is going to take a bit of getting used to. But you'll be fine." I grabbed her by the shoulders and looked into her eyes. "We'll be fine."

She walked to the back of the car and picked up two suitcases and headed toward the door.

"Take mine, would you, Sara? These old bones aren't nearly as strong as they used to be," Celeste said, her voice sounding tired. I met her eyes, then turned and watched as Carla half dragged, half carried her bags through the door.

I turned back to Celeste. "Are you okay?" I asked. "You look..."

She shrugged. "I'm finally feeling my age. It's a terrible thing, to suddenly be one of those old people you've tut-tutted about your whole life. I hope I'm not on the second floor."

I shook my head and headed back into the house, Aunt Celeste behind me. As I came through the door, I could hear Carla thudding up the stairs. I took my aunt's suitcases into the small back bedroom, then went back to the main part of the house.

"I always wondered what a place of your own would look like," Celeste said. She was in the middle of the living room, and she looked around, a small smile on her face. "I like this." She walked further in, stopping before the large china cabinet. "Blue Willow? I should have guessed. And that piece there is lovely."

"Done by a woman here in town," I told her. "An artist."

She turned to look at me. "A friend?"

"Yes, actually."

"Good. Well, where am I?"

"You're sharing with the cats," I told her, and lead her back to the small bedroom.

She followed, dropping her tote bag on the floor and taking in the simple oak bed, the plain white coverlet and colorful quilt. "Where are your cats?" she asked.

"Hiding. But they'll eventually show themselves. They played in this room a lot when it was empty, and were quite put out when I put the bed in."

She opened one of the suitcases I had put on the bed. "Let me unpack. Then I need a quick nap. Driving is tiring for me these days, as is pretty much everything I do."

I looked at her, concerned. "Are you okay?" I asked again.

She flashed a smile. "Yes, I'm fine. There's so much they don't tell you about getting old. I guess they figure you should be grateful to not succumb to the alternative, but let me tell you, it sucks. Things stop working, things start aching, there are creaks and crackles everywhere. Not for the faint of heart."

"You're not that much older than me," I said, doing the math in my head. She wasn't yet seventy.

"So be warned. Things happen slowly, then all at once." She leaned forward and pushed a curl behind my ear. "Do it all now, while you can."

"Do what?"

She grinned. "Everything. Now shoo. See to Carla. She was very unhappy for a long time, and that does bad things to a person. But you know all about that, don't you?"

I nodded and headed upstairs.

I had left the windows open, because the air got stale upstairs quickly, and I could feel the breeze as I climbed the stairs. The room was simple but calm, and, I thought, lovely. The rag rug covered the floor, the green spread was smooth on the iron bed, colorful pillows plumped along the back.

"Oh. Oh, my. Aunt Sara, this is beautiful."

I grinned. "Isn't it? You know Leo? Maribeth's partner? They were down here last week and Leo did this. I thought it was just right for you. He'll be thrilled that you like it."

She had dropped her suitcases on the floor and stood farther into the room, taking in the long table right under the dormer windows. "The light is just perfect," she said, wonder in her voice.

"Yes. It's south-facing."

"And there's so much storage," she said, running her hand along the top of the long walnut cabinet tucked under the slope of the ceiling. "I couldn't ask for anything more. Really." Her lips trembled.

"Carla?"

"You know Dad told me not to come home," she said, her voice flat and cold.

"I know." I moved to the sagging, overstuffed chair by the window and sat down.

"And of course, Mom just sat there and nodded."

I said nothing.

Carla opened her suitcase and stared into it as though she'd never seen it before. "I mean, where did they think I was going to go? They knew I couldn't afford an apartment, so what did that leave? The street? They would rather see me living in a cardboard box than even try to understand what I wanted to do with my life." Her voice was still flat, but I saw the anger in her body, in the stiff movements. "And they're mad at me, because I found another way. I didn't have to come crawling back to them, and they're furious. At you, too."

I nodded. "Your father and I had a conversation. He was not happy with me." I chose my words carefully. "Your father is hard sometimes."

"He's impossible," she muttered. She sat down on the bed and looked at me. "Was Grandpa like that?"

I shook my head. "No. Vincent takes after my mother. My father..." I stopped and swallowed a wave of emotion. "He wasn't always on my side. He was hard, too. Very old-fashioned. It probably never occurred to him I wouldn't want a life just like Mom's. But he could see past that when it counted." I smiled.

She nodded. "Yeah. I loved Grandpa a lot. He never said a word against Dad, but he'd take me aside and buy me ice cream when things were bad. Even when I was all grown up, he'd buy me ice cream. I could have used a good, stiff drink, but no." She made a face. "Ice cream. And he always said something that made me feel better."

"Yeah," I said softly. "That sounds about right."

She looked around the attic. "This should work well. As a workspace, I mean."

"I guess all those boxes in the back of Celeste's car are art things?"

"Oh, yes. Many art things. I literally had to sneak into the house when Dad was at work and get all my stuff out of there. I paid for it all. It was mine, but Dad threatened to call the cops. Seriously. I bluffed and told him I had the receipts. That shut him up." Her voice was angry again, but there were tears there, too. "Why is he such an asshole? Uncle Dom isn't like that."

"I don't know, honey. He was our mother's favorite, and he never let us forget it. It was hard on him when she died."

"It was hard on all of you," she shot back. "And *you're* not a jerk."

I laughed then. "And you've never lived with me. You may change your mind after a few weeks."

She looked very serious. "No, I won't. I am so grateful to you. And I promise, you will not regret this. I bet you were probably enjoying your new life. I thought about that, what it must be like to start your whole life over again, to be anyone you wanted. And then I come along and spoil it all for you."

I shook my head even as I acknowledged the truth in what she said. "You're family. You're not spoiling anything."

She leaned forward. "Really?"

I nodded. "Really. We have to decide about some dinner and then we'll come back here and figure out what to do next. I have a list of schools down here to look at. It's too late for the fall semester, but you can apply for the winter term. And we have to talk about a job."

She nodded solely. "Absolutely. But... are there, like, buses? I don't have a car."

I hadn't thought of that. "We'll figure it out." I got up and kissed the top of her head. "We'll figure everything out."

We went downstairs, and I heard noises coming from the small bedroom. I watched Carla walk back outside then went down the hallway to find Aunt Celeste sitting in the middle of what small floor space was available, with Shoes and Socks scrambling all over her, careening around the room, jumping on the bed, then diving back into her lap.

"They're marvelous," she said with a laugh. "Are they always this entertaining?"

I watched them in wonder. They usually hid away when people came to the house. During the week that Maribeth and Leo were here, Leo insisted I had magic cats because they disappeared at the sound of strange footsteps. "You must be a secret cat person," I told her. "They are just now getting used to Jack being here."

She looked up with raised eyebrows. "He must be over here often? I hope we're not going to cramp your style."

I shook my head. "There's always his place if the urge gets too much."

Carla stuck her head in the room. "What urge?" she asked. Then, upon seeing the kittens, thankfully switched gears. "Oh, aren't they cute! Who are they?"

I made introductions. Shoes and Socks had stopped their raucous play when Carla entered the room, but at least there was no hissing or arched backs.

"Let's get all this baggage unpacked," Aunt Celeste said. "I don't travel as well as I used to and need a nap. And then, if you don't mind, can we go down to the beach? I've never been to the Chesapeake Bay, and I feel an urge to get my toes wet."

"Sure," I said. "I can pack some sandwiches and wine and we can have a picnic. The water is still a little chilly, but toes should survive." Jack and I had taken off our shoes earlier that morning, and the cool water swirled around my ankles as we walked, Rags racing in and out of the gentle waves, covering us with droplets every time he shook his shaggy coat.

Much of what Carla had brought with her were art supplies, and they were heavy. I helped where I could: hanging her clothes in the closet while she carefully organized her dresser. Finally, she shook her head and sat back on her heels.

"I'm done. I'll figure the rest of this out tomorrow."

"Fine. Let's see what Aunt Celeste is up to."

Aunt Celeste was still napping, faint snore coming from the small bedroom, so Carla and I went out to the back patio. She walked to the edge of the property, where the yard began a sharp incline to the sandy lot below and spread her arms wide.

"I'll come out here every day to paint and never make the same picture," she said. "This is glorious." Then she turned around and caught sight of the garden.

"We'll can all the tomatoes," she said, moving slowly between the rows. "But what are we going to do with all this zucchini? I think you went a little crazy here, Aunt Sara."

We. She said we. I was still struggling with the idea of this young woman living in my house, moving freely in and out of my day-to-day life, but she had already decided.

We.

The next day, Aunt Celeste drove to church.

There wasn't a Catholic Church in Hills of Andrew, and she had to drive almost twenty miles to Our Lady of Sacred Sorrows, but she didn't miss mass if she could help it. While she was gone, Carla and I worked in the garden until Jack came by.

I had texted him earlier, asking when he wanted to meet my family, and he had texted back at once.

As soon as possible

His response surprised me a little, but I wasn't about to argue.

He had Rags with him. Carla eyed the dog with some skepticism until we were sitting on the back patio and he jumped up into her lap. Until that moment, I never thought of Rags as a lapdog, but he squirmed and wriggled until he found a comfortable spot on her long thighs, then settled his face in her neck.

She looked at Jack. "What am I supposed to do now?"

Jack laughed. "You now have the most valid reason known to man for not doing anything. Dog on lap. The universal excuse."

She lifted a hand to scratch under his chin, and Rags sighed audibly.

"What are your plans?" Jack asked her.

She glanced at me. "A job. Then art school, I guess."

"It's too late for you to apply anywhere for the fall term," Jack told her. "But you can apply for winter admission. If I were you, I'd look at SCAD. Savannah College of Art and Design. That you already have college courses under your belt will really help. You'll need to find recommendations, particularly from former art teachers."

I looked at him. "How do you know about SCAD?"

He shrugged. "When you told me that Carla was coming down here, I asked Shelby, my artistic director, for some advice. He also suggested that you work with him this summer, but you'd be an unpaid intern. And you'd mostly be painting back-drops. Very dull."

"How much is tuition?" I asked.

He made a face. "About forty grand a year."

Carla turned pale. "But that's ridiculous."

He shrugged. "Not according to Shelby. He says that's actually reasonable for art schools. And there are lots of scholarships available. Applying for them is kind of a full-time job, he told me, but that's how he did it."

Carla looked at me, her face puckered. "That's a lot of money."

I nodded. "Yes. And I'm pretty sure your father will not be of any help."

Jack shrugged. "It's something to think about. There are other options, of course."

Aunt Celeste slid open the glass door from the house. "Why, hello," she said to Jack.

He stood and grabbed Rags' collar as the dog slid off Carla's lap and lunged. Aunt Celeste never flinched but crouched down to hold out a hand. Rags sniffed and began to wag his tail.

I got up to close the door behind her. The last thing I needed was for one of the kittens to slip outside, or worse, have Rags catch their scent and tear into the house after them.

Aunt Celeste stood and held out a hand to Jack. "Hello. I'm Celeste. I'm so glad to meet you at last."

I could see Jack pull himself straighter and he smiled. "The pleasure is mine. Welcome to Hills of Andrew. Sara said you went up to Our Lady of Sacred Sorrows? That's a pretty ride."

She settled into a chair and kicked off her shoes, wiggling her toes. "Beautiful. This whole state is one giant postcard. This view alone is worth the trip."

"How long will you be staying?" Jack asked.

I looked at her, waiting for an answer. Of all the things we had talked about the night before, her departure had not come up in conversation.

She shrugged. "I hate to think about the long drive back to New Jersey alone. I may stay here for a week or maybe two, as long as Sara doesn't mind."

I shook my head. "I don't mind at all. You and Carla can get to know the neighborhood. I have to work, and I'm still helping a friend clean out her house, so you two might be on your own for a bit."

She waved a hand. "No problem. We can fend for ourselves."

Carla looked uncomfortable. "I have to find a job."

Aunt Celeste glanced at me, then nodded. "Of course. There's quite a nice little Main Street here, lots of shops. We'll find you something, I'm sure."

Carla fidgeted in her chair. "Art school is really expensive."

Aunt Celeste nodded slowly. "Yes. I imagine it is. But you already have two years' worth of college behind you."

Carla made a face. "Biology. Anatomy."

"But also English and basic math and social sciences. They will all transfer. And your GPA was quite good." Aunt Celeste leaned forward. "You'll be fine."

Carla's face relaxed. "Maybe."

Celeste stood and motioned to Carla. "Come inside. I stopped at a farmer's market on the way home. Help me unpack."

Carla and Aunt Celeste went inside, and Rags settled himself at Jack's feet.

"She's a stunner," Jack said.

I nodded. "Carla was always a beauty."

He chuckled. "I meant your aunt."

I threw back my head and laughed. "Yes, her too. I come from good genes."

He laughed with me. "Good to know. Now I see what I can look forward to in twenty years."

I reached over and grabbed his hand, shaking it until his eyes were straight on mine. "Do you really think that far ahead? "

His smile faded. "Sometimes. Don't you?"

"I..." I stopped, then began again. "When I first got here, it was one day at a time. Seriously. That's why this house didn't get painted. I had no furniture. I lived out of my boxes and suitcases because I couldn't imagine my life moving ahead in more than twenty-four-hour blocks. Bess, bless her, knocked me past that. When I started working, I imagined my life in week-long chunks because I had my schedule, and I knew where I would be and what I would be doing. Then I met you." I stopped again. "It was frightening to think that there might be something in my life again that was going to make me think about the long term."

"And now?" he asked quietly.

I searched those lovely, kind eyes. "Now I don't feel the constant urge to flee. Because that's what it was. I was waiting for something to happen that would make me drop everything, jump back in my car, and just go. I don't feel that way anymore, and it's partly thanks to you."

"But you can't imagine twenty years from now?"

I looked past him at the clear blue of the sky and the rolling shimmer of the Chesapeake Bay. "Actually, yes. Sometimes I really can."

Chapter Seventeen

Aunt Celeste had stopped by the library. To check the place out, she said with a grin, while Carla walked up and down Main Street, looking for a job. I introduced her to Jennie Lee. They started to talk, and twenty minutes later were still at it.

Molly came through the front doors in a rush, in faded jeans and a scruffy t-shirt, a smudge of dirt down her cheek.

"Sara, this is an emergency. I told Fred Nealy to come by Wednesday to pick up more of my stuff, and I thought I could clear out the attic, but I can never do it alone and if he doesn't come Wednesday, it will be at least another week before he can bring the truck and you know I have a schedule."

I frowned. "You have a schedule? Are you kidding? Since when?"

"Since I decided I wanted to be on the road by Memorial Day."

"That's just a month away."

"I know. That's why it's an emergency. Can you come by after work and help? Please?"

"Molly, this is my aunt, Celeste Pugliese."

Molly hit her forehead with the palm of her hand. "Right. Your company. I forgot. Okay, that's fine, I'll — "

"I can come by tomorrow after work," Jennie Lee offered. "And I can bring James. He's been grounded for the week and won't be going anywhere, so he may as well be useful."

"And *we* can come tonight, can't we Sara?" said Aunt Celeste. She turned to Molly. "I don't want to keep Sara from doing anything that she would normally do. And I love climbing through other people's attics. Any ghosts up there?"

Molly laughed. "Maybe. Nobody died there while I owned it, but I bought it from Hester Marks and we never figured out why her husband just up and left in the middle of the night."

Celeste looked delighted. "Excellent. What do you think, Sara? Carla and I will be glad to help."

I shrugged. "Sure. Why not?"

Molly grabbed Aunt Celeste's hand with both of hers. "Thank you. And I'll feed you. I can put together a big old meatloaf easy enough, and mac and cheese."

Aunt Celeste raised her eyebrows. "You're talking my language. "

"Perfect," Molly said. "And Jennie Lee, I'll have something for you and James tomorrow. The least I can do is feed all you kind folks for your time."

Jennie Lee laughed. "Whatever you were going to make for us, double it. James is fourteen and has a wooden leg."

Molly blew her a kiss and scurried out.

Aunt Celeste looked at me. "And she is?"

"I took her job," I explained. "She retired so she could drive across country and see everything she missed when she was young. She's selling her things and emptying out her house, because she plans to live a simpler life when she finally gets back."

Jennie Lee shook her head. "She's emptying her house, so there will be room for all the new stuff she'll bring back with her. That woman loves her things."

Aunt Celeste looked thoughtful. "What about her husband? Her family? Are they all right with her plans?"

I shook my head. "No husband. No family."

She pursed her lips. "Really?" She looked around. "I think I'll browse. Maybe I can find something to read out on that lovely patio of yours."

Carla came in a bit later. She'd talked to several business owners and filled out applications. "Paper applications," she said in a kind of stunned voice. "Not online."

Jennie Lee cackled. "Hills of Andrew is a little behind the times in lots of ways. But that's a good thing. Folks here like to look a person in the eye when they talk about a job."

Carla nodded. "Yeah. I mean, I got asked all sorts of questions about where I lived and who my people were. They all knew I wasn't from around here."

Jennie Lee snorted. "Of course they knew. It's your accent."

Carla frowned. "What accent?" Jennie Lee laughed.

She and Aunt Celeste were waiting for me when I got back from work. I changed quickly, and we drove to Molly's.

"We're doing what again?" Carla asked.

"Helping a friend," I explained. "But she has many really cool things she's been giving away and selling off. You might find some cute stuff for your room."

"Yeah. Maybe," she said slowly.

We ate first, and after meatloaf so flavorful and probably the best macaroni and cheese I'd ever had, Carla was feeling much more generous. We spread ourselves around the attic, which, thankfully, had tall ceilings and lots of light. It also had lots of boxes, furniture pushed into corners and paper shopping bags stuffed with paperback books, old magazines and rolls of cloth.

"That was from my quilting phase," Molly explained. "I was going to make hand pieced quilts as a side hustle. Found fabric at garages sales and spent months collecting the stuff. Once I sat down, though, I went crazy. You ever tried quilting? Lord, that's tedious work."

"Is all of this yours?" Celeste asked, gazing at the furniture heaped in the corners.

Molly shook her head. "No. Home inspections weren't such a big thing when I bought this house. I never even looked up here until about a month after I moved in. Hester left me lots of treasures. I took a bunch of junk out, but just like a goldfish grows into however big his bowl is, my belongings expand to fill up empty floor space. Nature abhors a vacuum. Especially my nature."

It was late when we finally had most of the furniture down and in the front hallway. It was mostly chairs of various styles, and small tables of assorted shapes and sizes. There were two narrow dressers and half a dozen lamps.

"Excellent. Tomorrow Jennie Lee and James can help bring down that bedstead, and all those boxes," Molly said. "Carla, honey, you want anything? I hear you've got an attic of your own."

Carla pointed. "Can I have those little tables? I bet I can paint them up real cute and maybe put them in that little consignment shop in town."

Molly nodded. "Sure thing. Celeste, why don't you come by tomorrow? We'll load them up and you can take them back to Sara's. Carla, you can probably do the work in that garage, right?"

"Excellent," Celeste said. "I have to say, I'm exhausted, but this was fun. I love old stuff."

"Well, no wonder we get along so well. I'm about the best old stuff you'll find around here."

They looked at each other, and I could almost feel something in the air: a recognition, a beginning.

"Then I'll see you tomorrow," Celeste said. She poked Carla in the ribs. 'Let's go, kiddo. I need a drink and a bath."

I watched her walk out the door and turned to Molly.

Molly was watching her too.

. . .

Carla came with me to yoga class. She'd taken classes before, and when I mentioned it, she asked to come with me. I texted Dante, and he had said she'd be welcome.

When the class was over, there was a little more buzz than usual. The other women asked Carla a few questions and welcomed her to the group. She was friendly with them, but she couldn't take her eyes off of Dante.

I could understand why. The man was beautiful. And when the other women had left, and there were only the three of us left in the studio, I remembered that she was beautiful, too.

"How do you like your room?" he asked her.

She looked confused.

"Dante painted it," I explained.

"Oh." She turned back to him. "Thank you. The colors are perfect."

He laughed. "I can't take credit for that. Shelia Birch picked them out. She's fabulous. Sara, have they met?" He focused his attention on Carla. "She's an artist too. A potter. She's crazy talented. You work in charcoal? Sara showed me that sketch you did. It was great."

Carla blushed. "I can't believe she still has that. It's, like, a hundred years old. I was just a kid when I did that." She stopped. "I'm not a kid now," she said. "I'm all grown up."

He nodded slowly. "Maybe."

She was a tall young woman, and she didn't have to look up to meet his eyes. "Not maybe."

There was a long silence.

"I have to get ready for work," I said. "Thanks, Dante. Excellent class as usual."

We got into the car and began the drive back to Bracken Road.

"He seems nice," she said finally.

"He is. He's an unusual man."

"How so?"

I shrugged. "You'll figure things out on your own, Carla,

eventually, but this place differs from what we're used to. I was told to watch out for him because he taught yoga. Like it was some unnatural practice. Most people I've met are great, they really are, but you're going to come up against some very different opinions down here."

"Burning crosses?"

"What? No. Nothing like that. But I have met some folks who are a little narrowminded, that's all."

"Molly isn't like that," she said.

I nodded. "No, she's not."

"Is she a lesbian?"

"What? Why would you ask that?"

She shrugged. "I don't know. She and Aunt Celeste were having a great time together. Wouldn't it be great if they fell in love and Aunt Celeste stayed down here?"

"Are you serious? They just met."

"So. All sorts of things can happen to people who just met."

I pulled into the drive next to Aunt Celeste's car and watched as Carla got out. I thought back to Jack Lockhart, standing on the other side of the counter in the library, tongue-tied and flustered when we first met.

She was right. All sorts of things did happen.

My brother Dominick called me.

"Hey sis," he said when I answered. "What's the word?"

"You tell me."

He sighed. "You know Vincent. "

"Sadly yes. Did you call me about him?"

"No. I called about you. And Carla. She's settling in?"

"She just got a job. She and Aunt Celeste went out for ice cream."

"She got a job? That's good. Good." He paused. "Ice cream, huh? That was a dad thing."

"I know." I stood outside and watched the moonlight on the

bay, waiting for Carla and Celeste to come home with ice cream so I could walk up Bracken Road to Jack, where I would spend the night. "How are the girls?" His daughters were ten and twelve.

"You know. Gymnastics. They're costing me a fortune and I'm running all over the Tri-state going to meets and showcases and competitions. They better both make the friggin' Olympic team."

"I miss them." And I did. As much as I had been driven to leave so much of my old life behind, I had a family that I had loved. Still loved.

"They miss you. Zoe still talks about that time you made the cannoli with them. Remember?"

I laughed. "Of course. God, that was fun." It had been before Dad got sick. They had been so tiny they had to stand on chairs, and I helped them as they got much filling in their hands and faces as they had stuffed into the shells.

"You still make those?" he asked.

"Not lately."

We were quiet. "So, how long is Aunt Celeste going to stay down there?"

"Another week, I think. She seems to like it here."

"Where's here?"

"Hills of Andrew. Virginia."

"Is it far?"

"Far enough."

He cleared his throat. "Did you really have to go all that way?"

"I could have gone even farther. I stopped here because I found a place that spoke to me."

Pause. "What did it say?"

I thought. "Maybe."

"And?"

"And I think I can find some peace here, Dom. I think I can find my way back to who I've always wanted to be."

He sighed. "I always thought you were perfect, you know. You were my big sister. That was enough."

"Not for me."

Another pause. "Love you."

"I love you too. And tell, well, everyone that I'm good. Carla is good. We're together and it's going to work out just fine."

He hung up, and I stared out at the water until I heard laughter. Carla called my name and I went inside to eat ice cream with my family.

On Friday, just before closing, Jennie Lee told me that Rose wanted to see me before I left for the day. I went back to her office.

"Congratulations," she said.

"For what?"

"Your sixty days are up. On Monday you will officially be an employee of the county. I'm having the HR person over there send you a benefits packet. Vacation, sick days, pension, all the good stuff." She smiled. "The board will have a final vote next Wednesday at their monthly meeting, but that's just a formality, and they really have no say in this matter. And I can already tell it will not be unanimous, but you will be hired and all of us here are really pleased."

I was standing in front of her desk, and I looked down at her, puzzled. "Why won't the vote of the board be unanimous?" I asked.

"Because you are a stranger here, and certain board members think you are too liberal for this particular job. I've seen nothing in your behavior to support that thinking, but that will be the excuse." Her hands were folded calmly on the top of her desk, but I saw her fingers tightened, then flex open. "If I were you, I'd celebrate."

I stood. "Thank you. I will."

I went back to the front desk and Jennie Lee looked up.

"You in?" she asked.

I nodded. "Yes. I'm official as of Monday."

She nodded. "Good."

On the way home, I stopped at the grocery store. When I dragged all my shopping bags into the house, Aunt Celeste jumped off the couch and followed me into the kitchen with interest.

"What's all this?" she asked.

"My probation is over and, well, I'm an official employee of the library, and I feel like celebrating."

She watched as I pulled ground beef and pork out of the bag, canned tomatoes, cheese.

"Celebrating how?"

"I think a dinner party. I sent out a few texts and everyone so far has said yes."

Her eyes lit up. "Oh, that's wonderful, Sara. Congratulations. And a dinner party? Those ingredients look like my mother's lasagna."

I nodded. "It is. I'll make the sauce tonight and finish it all off tomorrow. Can you make your cheesecake? I think I remembered all the ingredients."

"Of course." She rearranged a few items on the counter. "Did you ask Molly?"

"Yes, I did. She said absolutely."

Aunt Chelsea beamed. "How nice. Listen, Carla took my car. She's at the mall filling out the paperwork for *her* job and she's bringing home pizza for dinner."

"Good. I'll start now."

I changed and put on my apron. First, I browned the ground beef. Aunt Celeste opened a bottle of wine and she sat on the stool as I cooked.

"She would have ground that herself," Aunt Celeste said.

I nodded. "We ground our own at the restaurant. I just don't have the right tools here. She had that huge monster of a thing, and she'd turn the handle and I'd watch the meat spill out. It was like magic."

"When we were little," she said, watching, "your mother was the only one who was allowed to help. The rest of us were too little, she always said, but now I realize there wasn't room in that kitchen for us all. But Maria never loved it. She never watched my mother like you did when you were little. I remember coming into that hot apartment and you followed her every move."

I chopped onion and garlic and took the cooked beef out with a slotted spoon. I cut the sausage casings open and dumped the pork into the hot pan, smashing it with the spoon. The house smelled like the tiny first-floor apartment I grew up in.

I heard the front door bang open.

"Okay, the job is mine," Carla called. "At the mall. It's an art supply place, so I'll get a discount, and the guy is really nice." She stopped as she turned into the kitchen. "What are you cooking? It smells amazing."

"Lasagna. For tomorrow night. And now we have two things to celebrate. I'm an official library employee and you are an official... what?"

"Minion." She set the pizza box down on the counter. "Is this your Nonna's recipe?" she asked in hushed tones.

"Yes."

"Are you going to make your own pasta?" she asked.

I nodded.

"And your own mozzarella? Like you did at the restaurant?"

I looked over at her. "Not this time."

She nodded, her eyes on the deep pot of seasoned pork cooking in the hot oil. "When you do, will you teach me?"

"Of course." I added the beef, then the onion and garlic, and smashed the meat even further with my spoon. I took the stalks of dried oregano in between my palms and rubbed. The bits of dried herb drifted down into the pot and filled the air with its scent. I nodded toward the pizza. "Hand me a slice."

She and I ate standing at the stove, Aunt Celeste perched on her stool. I added tomato paste to the meat, scraping it along the bottom of the pot so that it sizzled in the oil and fat. Carla helped me drain the tomatoes from the can and scoop out the seeds, then squeezed the flesh into the pot. Next went in went the tomato puree, and a few shakes of red pepper flakes.

"Now, it cooks," I said.

I'd gotten a television now we sat together on the couch and watched The Great British Baking Show. I got up every half hour to stir the sauce, and finally pulled it off the heat to cool. Jack was at the theater until late and didn't knock on the door until after ten. By then, Aunt Celeste and Carla had gone to their rooms.

"Is that something Italian I smell?" he asked as he came in.

I nodded my head. "Yep. And it's all good. Nothing in the garbage this time. All I have to do tomorrow is make the pasta, prep the cheese and put it all together." I nuzzled his neck. "Piece of cake. How are things? Will you be ready?"

Guys and Dolls was scheduled to open Memorial Day weekend, and he'd been worried about inconsistent rehearsals and low ticket sales.

"We have to be ready. It will be fine. My God, this smells delicious. I'm coming to dinner tomorrow?"

"I'm having a party. Probation is over and I'm now officially a library employee. Carla also got a job. I'm cooking. Lasagna."

His arms were around me as we stood in the living room, and they tightened as he smiled. "Did I hear that correctly?"

"Yes, you did. I. Am. Cooking."

He put his forehead against mine. "A party?"

"Yes. But you know everyone. Shelia and Dev, Molly, Bess, Dante and us. You'll come?"

He nodded. "Of course. How can I miss your lasagna? And I'd love to stay longer tonight, but I'm exhausted."

I kissed him. "Go home. Rest up. No excuses tomorrow."

He kissed me back. "Be ready baby, 'cause I sure will."

In the morning, while I walked with Jack and Rags on the beach, Aunt Celeste baked her lemon ricotta cheesecake. I had been begging her for years for the recipe, but she always refused.

"I have to have at least one thing I can cook better than you," she always said.

As I came through the door, she came out of the kitchen, brushing her fingers through her hair. "Did you have a nice walk? Yes? Good. I like Jack. He's a little, I don't know, too in love with you for his own good, but..." she shrugged. "Turn off the oven in exactly one hour and fifteen minutes. Open the door just a crack and let it sit for another hour, then take it out and cool it on a cooling rack. Do you have a rack? I noticed your kitchen isn't quite up to snuff."

"Yes, I have a rack. And he is not in love with me."

"If you say so. I have a few errands. And I'll run up to that little bakery off the highway and being back bread." She gave me a quick kiss on the cheek. "Later."

In the afternoon, with the cheesecake sitting high on top of the refrigerator, away from any cat-paw-print possibilities, I made the pasta, pulling together the eggs and flour, rolling it thin with marble rolling pin that had been Nonna's.

Carla sat on the stool, pad and charcoal pencil in hand, sketching. I cut the pasta into long strips.

"Don't you have to boil it first?" she asked.

I shook my head. "Not fresh pasta. It cooks in the sauce." I shredded the mozzarella between my fingers. I could feel the difference in the texture from the homemade, but it would be fine

I took out the two ceramic pans I had bought weeks before and began to layer the pasta, the meat sauce and the cheese until the pans were full and there were only a few sheets of pasta and a spoonful of sauce left.

"You made just enough," Carla said.

"I always did," I said.

The lasagna baked. I set the long pine table with my Blue Willow china. One of the things Aunt Celeste rescued from the house before it was sold was my mother's sterling flatware. It had been used every day in my childhood. It was too beautiful to hide away, my mother had said. We used it at every meal, and after she died, I made sure we still did. But after I went to Italy, it had been pushed to the back of a cabinet and was all but forgotten. It was heavy, ornate stuff, each piece engraved with the letter 'C'.

"I've never seen this before," Carla said, arranging the pieces on the pale blue linen tablecloth.

"Buried treasure," I said. "This was my mother's wedding silver."

"Tell me about your mom," Carla said. "Dad never talked about her. At all."

I stared down at the sterling silver forks in my hand. My mother had put these forks down on her table every night. "She was so happy when she lived in the apartment," I said slowly. "She never got used to life away from her mother. She never became friendly with the other women in the neighborhood. They wore jeans and listened to folk music. She was in her own bubble. She was very lonely, but for me which was great because I became almost like her best friend."

"Grandpa never talked about her either."

I sighed. "She was his everything. He had no family. Literally. He grew up in an orphanage. He never talked about his childhood. He always said his life began when he met mom. He never got over her death."

"Neither did Daddy," she said quietly. "I think that's why he's so closed up and angry. Why didn't you become like him?"

"Because I didn't have time. I was too busy cooking and cleaning and running the house. He and Dom just sat around feeling sorry for themselves."

"But it must have been just as awful for you," she said.

I nodded and felt years of buried grief churn in my heart. "It was." I closed my eyes tightly, refusing to let any tears fall. "It was also a long time ago," I said. "Let's get the wine."

I opened the wine to let it breathe. I washed the greens for the salad and then dried them carefully with a towel. The kitchen was getting hot from the long bake, and I opened all the windows. The air was warm and full of the scent of spring and the brine of the bay.

I felt my mother standing beside me. She had never left, but for years, I had chosen to ignore her. To turn around and face the memories of her long and painful death had always been too much for me, but she'd been with me all along. Now, the gift of time and new-found courage let me recognize all that I had lost, and that made her all the more real in my memory. There were no tears, just a smile of quiet joy.

I took the lasagna pans out of the oven and set them on the counter. The tops were bubbling, and cheese oozed from the edges.

"We're ready," I said.

Jack arrived first, daisies in one hand and more wine in the other. I had a vase now, a simple white column, and I arranged the flowers carefully.

"So, this really is a party," he said, looking at the table.

I came up beside him and put my arm around his waist. His arm went over my shoulder in a warm hug. "Yep," I said. "Going all out."

"Can I do anything?"

"Nope. I just took out the lasagna. I have to toss the salad. Aunt Celeste is bringing bread, but no, you can't slice it."

He laughed and kissed the top of my head. "I saw her earlier. Celeste."

I looked up. "Oh? Where?"

"Molly's place."

Really.

Shelia and Dev arrived next, Dev giving Jack a friendly hug before going off in search of Shoes and Socks. Shelia looked at the table, grinning. "I remember when this room was so empty. Everything looks so lovely, Sara. Really."

Carla came down and handed me the sketch she'd been working on while I'd been cooking. It was simple, sure lines and smudges of shadow. It was of me, rolling out pasta on the floured countertop. My hair curled in wisps around my forehead, the muscles of my arms strained from pushing down on the rolling pin. The light coming from the window caught the lines around my eyes as I squinted in concentration, my jaw clenched. A woman at her work.

"Oh, Carla." I felt a catch in my throat. "This is amazing."

"I figured this meal was an occasion that needed commemorating," she said.

I nodded. "Yes. And this is the perfect way to do it. Thank you."

Then Celeste came through the door, Molly behind her. Celeste had an armful of long, thin loaves of bread, and sputtered apologies. "I didn't mean to make dinner late," she gushed. "We just got carried away."

"It's fine," I told her. "Bess isn't here yet. Everyone, outside for a glass of wine."

Dev came down the hallway, Shoes wrapped around his neck. "They seem happy," he said with a grin.

I grinned back. "So do you. Go. Outside. And no comments about my garden. Oh, Bess, here you are. Just in time. I'm so glad you could come. We're having a bit of wine before dinner."

The patio was crowded, but not really. Behind it was a brilliant blue sky and the line of darker blue that was the Chesapeake. I poured everyone a glass of wine.

"We're celebrating two special occasions," I said. Jack put his arm around my shoulder and I leaned into him. "I am now officially an employee of the Northumberland County Library System, and Carla here is also officially employed."

"As third cook and bottle washer at Trident Art and Supply, down at the mall."

"That's wonderful," Shelia said. "For both of you." There was a murmuring of congratulations as everyone drank wine. The sun dipped farther in the west, and the patio fell into shadow.

"I just don't know how we're going to do this, Aunt Sara," Carla said. "There's no bus or anything, and I don't have a car. How am I supposed to get there?"

"We can work something out," Shelia said. "I mean, I don't need my car."

"Or," Aunt Celeste said, "she can use mine."

I stopped, my wine glass halfway to my lips. "And how would that work from New Jersey?" I asked.

She shrugged and looked very pleased with herself. "I'm not going back to New Jersey. Not right away, that is. I'm going to go with Molly. It's perfectly fine for a woman to drive across the country by herself, but it makes more sense for her to have company. I'll be that company."

There was a moment of stunned silence. Carla broke the moment by bursting into giggles. "See Aunt Sara," she sputtered. "I *told* you."

Yes. She certainly had.

Chapter Eighteen

W hen summer came, it was a wave of heat and traffic, the quiet streets full of sun-burnt tourists, the beaches noisy and crowded. The library was busy, and by July Fourth weekend, I couldn't wait for the fall to settle in, the summer people to go home, and for life to sink back into its quiet, peaceful rhythm.

On an early Sunday, Molly and Aunt Celeste pulled into the driveway. They looked happy and relaxed, and we talked and laughed our way to dinner. Carla, when asking about their travels, cut right to the chase.

"So, are you two going to live happily ever after or what?"

Aunt Celeste laughed. Her hair was longer, and I could see where the ash blond was growing out of her hair. She had on no makeup, but her skin was clear and glowing.

"Let me tell you about traveling across country with someone you barely know for eight weeks," she said. We were on the patio, and she reached to grab Molly's hand. "Every morning for the first few weeks I woke up wondering if she had taken off without me."

Molly nodded. "And every morning *I* woke up wondering if

she had crept out in the middle of the night and found a fast bus back here."

Celeste laughed again, her eyes bright. "It took us almost a month to realize neither of us were going anywhere, and things got a lot better after that."

"So," Carla said with a grin, "that's a yes?"

Molly let out an exaggerated sigh. "Well, I know that I'm only in it for the sex, but if she wants to stay for any other reason, I'm okay with that."

Celeste actually blushed. "I'm going to sell my place in Jersey. We'll drive up together in a few weeks, I think. Luckily Molly's house is almost empty, so there will be plenty of room for all my things."

Molly pulled back her hand. "You have things?" she asked in mock horror.

Carla burst into giggles. "Oh, boy. Does she have *things*."

And we all laughed.

I had forgotten what happy felt like. I'd spent so many years on guard, waiting for the next blow, then trying to fight my way back to the top, that I'd forgotten how simple life could really be. Getting up in the morning and going to work. Talking to people who were no longer strangers about books and food and town politics and a little gossip, even if I knew that, behind my back, I was much of that gossip.

And then one morning, right after Celeste and Molly's return, Jack came to me at the library, his face pale and serious.

"Owen was in an accident," he told me. "A tire blew out and his car went off the road."

I looked over the counter. "Is he okay?"

Jack shook his head. "He's in the hospital. I just left Katie there. He's going into surgery, but he should be okay. Here's the thing." He looked at me steadily. "If the café has to close down for any length of time, he and Katie both will be hurting. They count on summer dollars to get them through the winter."

I felt my heart begin to thrum.

"Oh?"

"If they don't keep the café open, they could lose everything. You know better than most how narrow the margins are when you own your own restaurant."

Yes, I knew. I counted every day that La Cucina had been closed, counted the lost income, the drain on my own money trying to keep my ex-employees from finding other jobs. I cancelled food orders, knowing I might lose a trusted vendor. I paid my rent on an empty building in hopes I could reclaim my space, only to have it all just disappear in a puff.

"They need to find a way to keep the café open," Jack said. "Harry already said he can do all the baking, all the bread and muffins. And Louisa does all the pies. She's on your library board." I remembered the lady with white hair who baked the lemon pie. "Harry can't do more, because his own place is so busy during the summer."

Rose, who had been discharging books, came up behind me. "You can probably ask Greg and his wife. They own the pizza place. They probably don't know too much about anything other than making pizza, but they might be able to help."

Jack was still looking at me. "Katie runs the place. And she knows everything there is to know. But she can't cook. They really need somebody in the kitchen."

My mouth felt dry. "I have a job, Jack. Here. And we're busy too. I just can't leave."

"But Molly is back," Rose said. "I bet we could get her to step in. It's only temporary, right Jack? A few weeks?"

"A month," Jack said. "Maybe two. The doctors aren't sure. He'll be home in a week, maybe, but there will be therapy and lots of recovery time. So that means the café would be closed for at least the rest of the summer."

Rose was talking again, but her words were just noise, drowned out by the sound of the blood pounding in my ears.

"Why are you doing this?" I whispered. "You know how hard..."

Rose suddenly stopped and took a step back, realizing that the shift in conversation was more than she understood. Jack dropped his eyes and placed his hands, palms down, on the counter. "I've known them both a really long time," he said quietly. "They are both my friends. And the café means a lot to this town. They need help. I know how you feel, but I also know that you're part of Hills now. And you are one of the few people who can do anything for them. Otherwise, I'd never ask."

I closed my eyes and took a long, slow breath.

I heard Rose's voice in my ear. "Why don't you take a few minutes, Sara? You and Jack obviously need to talk."

I opened my eyes, nodded, and stepped away from the counter. I hurried to the front door of the library and pushed it open and stepped out into the blazing summer heat.

I felt Jack behind me, his hand on the small of my back. "If you say no, I'll understand. You know I will. I know better than anyone how hard this would be for you. And I know that cooking for me and your friends is much different than stepping back into a restaurant kitchen."

"Especially a kitchen like theirs. I make pasta. What do I know about anything else?"

I heard the humor in his voice. "How many different ways are there to fry an egg? Or flip a burger?"

I closed my eyes, shook my head, opened them and gave him a long look. "You really don't know a damn thing about cooking, do you?"

He grimaced. "I just said something really stupid, didn't I?"

"Yes. You did. I've been cooking my whole life, but I've never been a short order cook. That's a skill set that had always terrified me, to be honest. Everything happens on the fly, and you have to be fast. That's the whole difference between someplace like the café and La Cucina. Folks aren't willing to wait for the perfect scrambled egg. They want food good and hot and right away."

He nodded. "I get that. But *could* you do it?"

I thought back to the dinner at Shelia's. Owen and I had talked shop, briefly. He told me he and Katie had only been in Hills of Andrew for five years, and they finally felt they had reached a level of financial security where he wasn't losing sleep at night.

I knew that feeling. I had lived it, and I wouldn't wish my result on a total stranger, let alone two people as lovely as Katie and Owen.

I could see the café, its small counter, the tidy booths. My brain opened up into a space that had been shuttered for a long time. How many plates did they turn in a day? They opened at seven for breakfast, and most days closed by three. Dinner was only served on Thursday and Friday nights. The place closed on Mondays. "It's not just the kitchen. Somebody has to step in for Katie. She'll have Owen to take care of."

Jack must have heard the change in my voice, because his own was even and reassuring. "I'm sure we can find an ex-waitress around here somewhere."

"Carla can do those few nights" I said. "She's only working part-time at the mall. Mostly days. She's free after four."

"There you go," Jack said.

I looked down at my hands and was pleased to find them steady. I turned them over. My palms were dry. The panic I'd felt rising in my throat was gone "I need to talk to Katie. And Molly. I won't leave the library in a lurch. That's my job now."

"Of course," Jack said.

"And it's only for a month?"

"Maybe more. but Owen is tough, and both he and Katie will want to get back as soon as they can."

I smiled at him. "I like them too, Katie and Owen. And you're right. The café being closed will hurt everyone, not just them. Call her and tell her I'll look around. I can't promise anything. I may step into the kitchen and freeze up. Or throw up."

"Well, that would certainly decide things," He was smiling

now. "I'll call her. And I can go with you. I've always wanted to see behind the scenes."

Behind the scenes, in this case, was small and spotlessly clean, all gleaming stainless-steel counters. Aluminum pots, dented and dark from constant use, hung from hooks. Katie looked exhausted, dark circles under her eyes.

"He's going to be fine," she told us. "He's just broken bones and torn things. It's going to be a slow recovery. Sara, are you sure you can do this? Harry has helped us out before, but you barely know us, and you already have a job." her voice trailed off, exhausted.

I ran my palm along the gas cooktop, six burners and a huge, flat griddle. A bank of ovens was against the wall, and there was a large walk-in refrigerator.

I looked around. There was enough room for three, maybe four people to work comfortably. Owen had kept his menu small and basic, making up for lack of variety by cooking everything perfectly. The kitchen was just right for that sort of workflow. No need for multiple stations. No crowding for space. Everything and everyone in place and doing their job.

"Harry will do all the baking," Katie explained. "He'll come here first, before his place opens. He can only stay a few hours, but we'll have fresh bread and muffins. And we have Ramon. He's helped Owen for years.

"Ramon? He knows the menu?"

She nodded. "Yes. Does all the prep work. He helps bus the tables and run the dishwasher. He scrubs pots and sweeps floors." She sighed tiredly. "He does everything, really, except cook. And it's funny, he's never wanted to do more."

I nodded at that. I'd had people in my kitchen who knew their jobs and did them well, but never wanted to learn anything new.

Katie went on. "We're running at full speed right now. Every table filled."

I opened the walk-in. "What about supplies?"

"We have standing orders. I handle all of that. Always have. Besides, we're not the kind of place that hand-picks fish at the docks or squeezes every tomato at the market." She made a face. "I bet you did that."

I nodded. "Yes. I did. But this will be much easier to manage." No delicate organic mushrooms here. No freshly made ricotta. No hand-ground sausage.

Jack had been right. There were only so many ways to fry an egg. And if I couldn't figure out how to make corned beef hash, I had never belonged in a kitchen in the first place.

Katie went on. "Owen's sister is coming from Atlanta. She's a retired nurse, and she can help with Owen, so I can still be here every morning, take care of the day-to-day stuff. Like I said, he stayed in the kitchen. So, all we really need is someone to cook. And we can cut the dinner hours. The specials were always all over the place, and much harder to buy and plan for."

I shook my head. "No. I bet you're packed those nights. I can manage all that. My niece, Carla, can be here part of the time. She works days at the mall, so she can cover your two nights open and maybe the weekends. She already asked her boss." I smiled. "He's a regular, and when he heard why she needed to change, he agreed. She's waited tables before. She'll do a good job. Your dinners are covered. Would you mind a few variations?"

She smiled for the first time. "You mean, something other than meatloaf with mashed potatoes and greens? Go for it."

I shook my head. "We'll keep the meatloaf. I'm not sure your regulars will be willing to let their favorites go. But I'll come up with a few surprises."

Jack, leaning against the swinging door leading back to the dining room, grinned. "I'm requesting that pasta dish with the olives and breadcrumbs."

I grinned back at him. "Noted." I looked at Katie. "Have Ramon meet me here tomorrow. I need to see how things work.

We can reopen the day after that. Molly is on board to step in for me at the library. We've got you covered."

Her eyes filled with tears, and she nodded rapidly, then stepped forward and threw her arms around me. "Thank you," she whispered. "Thank you so much. From both of us."

I hugged her. "I'm happy to help. It will be good."

She stepped back, wiped her eyes and sniffed. "Yes. It will. I can't wait to tell Owen. He's been so worried."

Jack came up behind her and rubbed her shoulders, and she leaned back against him. "Thank you too, Jack. For thinking about Sara. I never would have, well, you know."

She reached up and patted his hand, and he kissed the side of her head.

"We're lucky to have her here," he said, looking over her shoulder to meet my eyes and smile gratefully.

Katie nodded. "Yes. Yes, we are lucky." Then, she made a bit of a crooked smile, and walked out of the kitchen.

I stood, looking around. I felt a little nervous. There was a flutter in my stomach, but a good kind of flutter. More excitement than fear.

"Are you sure about this?" Jack asked. He wasn't just asking for me, I knew. I had just committed myself to help two of his friends, and my failure would be his as well.

I nodded. "I think I'm going to be just fine."

I had spent the next morning with Ramon, tall and broad with grizzled hair under a blue and white bandana. We went over everything; the recipes, the weekly specials, when the rush usually hit, when we could relax and take a breath. Here was a person who spoke my language, and by the end of the morning I felt so good about opening the cafe the next day, I found myself wondering what I had been so afraid of in the first place. This was my safe space. Surrounded by pots and knives and stainless-steel whisks, I felt like I had returned home.

Carla was at work when I got home. She was saving money wherever and however she could. She scavenged furniture off the side of the road whenever she found it, repainted or refinished it, and kept up a steady stream to the consignment shop on Main Street. She spent the rest of her time off drawing everything in and around Hills of Andrew.

As I came in that night, I saw her sketchbook lying on the couch. My first thought was that she was lucky the kittens hadn't gotten to it. Lately, they had been going after scraps of paper like they were bits of tuna. I picked it up, turning the pages, admiring a seagull perched on a light post, a small boat half in half out of the water, Shoes and Socks curled around each other. Then a sketch of Dante. He was leaning back in a bed, shirtless, a sheet halfway up his chest, one arm draped across his eyes. I looked at it for a long time, then closed the notebook.

"I wouldn't worry," Jack murmured when I told him what I'd found. "They're young."

"She's young. Him, not so much."

We were in his bedroom; the moonlight coming through the open window. We lay on top of the sheets, me on my side, with his body curled behind mine, one hand trailing lazily down my arm.

"I'm sure they're fine," he said.

"Then why hasn't she told me about him?"

He didn't answer, just pulled me back and tighter into his body. "She needs to find her own way," he said softly. "Just like you did."

"I screwed up so much."

"Did you really? What would you do differently?"

I thought. Every missed step had been a lesson. Every moment of despair had eventually passed. There had been nothing I didn't somehow emerge from, if not better, at least stronger. Even grief hadn't kept me down.

"Are you happy here?" he asked unexpectedly.

I turned to face him, his expression hidden in shadows. "Why do you ask me that?"

"Do you love me?"

"Yes." The answer came without thought. Of course, I loved him. There was still so much about him I wanted to learn, to know better, and maybe Maribeth was right. Maybe I would find some fatal flaw. But now, at least, I knew I would survive that too.

"Good," he whispered. "Because I love you too."

"Ah, Jack?"

"Yeah."

"I kinda figured that out already."

"I thought as much. But I wanted you to know for sure."

Radagast suddenly jumped on the bed, wriggling his way between Jack and me. I felt his cold nose against the nape of my neck as I turned to sleep.

Yes. I knew. For sure.

At six o'clock I parked in the alley behind the café. I walked to the open back door and saw Harry standing in the light of the kitchen, the screen door blurring his movements.

I went in slowly, and he turned and looked at me, smiling.

"Right on time," he said. He rubbed his hands together, and the flour drifted off them in a puff. The kitchen smelled of baking: yeast, sugar and spice.

"I just started the bacon," Ramon said, standing at the counter. "We bake it off, then reheat on the griddle. Potatoes are cooked also. Just fry them up."

I hung my bag on a hook inside the door and reached into my bag to draw out my knives. I pulled a clean apron off the shelf and pulled it over my head, tying the ends around my waist. Then I unrolled my knives on the stainless-steel counter.

Ramon glanced over. "Nice," he said. "Onions are behind you."

I grinned at him. "Really? My first day and you're making me dice the onions?"

He shook his head and chuckled. "I hate that job. Worst job in the kitchen."

"Hey," a voice called. Linda, who worked the counter, came through the door. She nodded at me, gave Ramon a quick grin, hung her bag and grabbed an apron. "I'll start the coffee," she said, and went past me to the front.

I peeled onions, my eyes smarting like they had when I first worked in kitchens, tears streaming down my cheeks until I wiped them with the edge of the apron. The stiff cloth across my eyelids felt as familiar as the warm wood of the knife handle in my hand, the smooth cool surface of the stainless-steel counter.

Harry pulled cooled loaves of bread off the rack by the walk-in, and ran them through the slicer, lining them up on a tray. Ramon stacked up cartons of eggs and began to mix batter in a large stainless bowl. I moved to dice the green peppers, then the tomatoes, lining the ingredients up before me like soldiers in a row. We worked soundlessly, seamlessly, three people who knew what needed to be done. A team.

I heard music in the front and smelled coffee. I could not feel Nonna looking over my shoulder. My mother was far back in the recesses of my memory. This was new, all of it. The sausage here was mild links from the walk-in, not imported pork ground with garlic, oregano and red pepper flakes. The bread was white, whole grain and sourdough, not the slim crusty loaves that were made all day in the back of a crowded kitchen. Desserts were lemon meringue pie and red velvet cake, not hand-crafted tarts and cannoli.

"You want coffee?" Linda called.

I stepped away from the counter and walked out front. The lights were on, the cutlery rolled in large paper napkins and sitting on the end of the counter, next to the menus.

Linda handed me a steaming cup. I sipped. No, not espresso,

just strong, rich coffee that went straight to my belly and warmed me.

"We're going to be fine," Linda said.

I looked out the front window and saw Katie driving by. Orange juice sat behind the counter in glass pitchers. Harry came in and stacked fresh-baked muffins under gleaming glass domes. "I can stay a bit longer if you think you need help," he said.

I shook my head. "No, you go ahead. You've got your own kitchen to look after. We're good."

I heard the back screen door open, and Katie appeared, tying her apron. "If I hadn't just left Owen grumbling at home, I'd swear he was right where he belonged. Everything looks just as it should." She took a breath. "So, I guess we're doing this?"

I walked across the empty café and unlocked the door. I opened it and felt the hot summer air wash over me. There were already cars on Main Street, and I saw a family of four crossing the street, looking in the direction of the café.

My first customers.

I smiled and nodded. "Yes," I said softly. "We're doing this."

The End